For Paul, always x

BLACK
HEART

ALSO BY ANNA-LOU WEATHERLEY

Chelsea Wives
Wicked Wives
Pleasure Island

BLACK HEART

ANNA-LOU WEATHERLEY

bookouture

Published by Bookouture in 2018

An imprint of StoryFire Ltd.
Carmelite House
50 Victoria Embankment
London EC4Y 0DZ

www.bookouture.com

ISBN: 978-1-78681-345-9
eBook ISBN: 978-1-78681-344-2

'There is no WHY, since the moment simply is, and since all of us are simply trapped in the moment, like bugs in Amber.'

Kurt Vonnegut

CHAPTER ONE

She pushed through the revolving doors, the sound of her stiletto heels clacking against the ornate marble flooring as she walked into the plush hotel lobby. It was busy. This was good. Her eyes flicked towards the concierge behind the shiny, curved reception desk and the groups of well-dressed Japanese tourists, businessmen and wealthy guests buzzing around it, designer luggage piled high behind them. Her timing was perfect – and deliberate. La Reymond, one of the most prestigious five-star hotels in Knightsbridge, operated a late check-out policy, at a premium of course, and its exclusive clientele thought little of paying for such advantages. She would go relatively unnoticed in the bustle of human traffic.

It had been raining heavily outside too; another bonus, people were always preoccupied in wet weather, too concerned with ruining their expensive blow-drys and suits. She brushed a few droplets of rain from the shoulders of her Burberry trench coat, which she'd worn with the collar turned upwards, and concentrated on walking straight ahead towards the lifts, careful not to slip on the wet marble floor, her patent stilettos proving even more treacherous in such conditions.

She entered the lift, smiling briefly at the occupants before turning her back on them, then slipped out on the third floor and walked two flights of stairs up to the fifth. Penthouse suite 106. She rang the bell and heard his hefty bulk shift as he got up to answer it.

'Hello Daddy Bear.' She entered the suite, throwing her bag onto the huge round bed and opening her coat. Immediately she spied the magnum of Krug on ice and a small duck-egg blue Tiffany box with a white ribbon on one of the plump pillows. Muted pornography was playing on the 60 inch flat-screen TV. She took her coat and thin black strappy dress off almost simultaneously, discarding them onto the silk upholstered chaise longue, one of an exquisite pair, she noted.

'Well, helloooo Goldilocks,' his eyes widened as he drank in her expensive lingerie, lingerie he'd hand selected for her from Agent Provocateur just for today's occasion, 'you look… sensational.'

She adjusted one of her stockings.

'Excellent choice, I must say,' she admired herself in the large floor mirror, 'I particularly like the way the basque cinches my waist, and the *ouvert* panties…' She gave him a sideways glance, 'Dirty, filthy, bad Daddy Bear…' She watched as he lay grinning on the bed, his heavy form leaving an imprint on the delicate sheets. He was half naked; his stomach protruding over his tight briefs. 'Take them off.'

He instantly obeyed, glad to be rid of them.

'Champagne?' he went for the bottle. 'I have a gift for you.'

'Afterwards.' She pushed him back onto the bed and straddled him.

'Mmmm, Daddy Bear, so hard already,' she closed her eyes and began to moan a little as she slid down onto him.

'Only for you my angel, all just for you…'

She laughed, throwing her head back as she began to ride him hard. He felt like a bouncy castle.

'Baby… baby, slow down… I'm going… I'm going to…'

Too late.

She looked down at his round face, where traces of ecstasy were gradually dissipating, along with his almost instant orgasm; beads of unhealthy sweat glistened on his forehead.

'I'm sorry,' she shrugged, 'I just wanted you so bad.'

He almost purred with delight, his ego engorging almost as rapidly as his erection was dwindling.

'You… you're something else, do you know that Goldilocks?'

She smiled; she did.

'Shall we have champagne in the bath?'

She got off him and padded through to the en suite. Impressive, she thought, surveying the large sunken tub and gold taps. She ran the hot tap, perusing the selection of high-end pampering products, undecided between the Jo Malone Lime Basil & Mandarin bath oil or the L'Occitane Fig, eventually opting for the former. Humming a tune, she began pouring the sweet, fragrant liquid into the running water.

'Come on Daddy Bear, where's that champagne?' she called out to him in the bedroom, catching sight of herself in the mirrored tiles. She was still wearing the basque and suspenders and began to take them off, teasing herself in the mirror until she was naked. 'It's the perfect temperature,' she said as he trundled, cumbersome, into the bathroom, naked but for the ice bucket and champagne magnum.

He poured them both a chilled flute.

'Mmm, divine,' she purred, champagne in the bath, so… decadent.' She piled her platinum blonde hair up high onto her head with a bulldog clip as she stepped into the bath, careful not to get it wet. 'Well, are you getting in Daddy Bear?'

His meaty bulk caused the water to rise considerably as he ungainly sank into the bath.

She relaxed back, placing her feet on his bulging stomach like a cushion, and wiggled her manicured toes, giggling a little as she sipped on her drink.

'I know, I know, I need to get *this* down the gym,' he grabbed at his excess flesh awkwardly. 'I've been meaning to,' he apologised, reaching for a Charbonnel et Walker truffle from the complementary box that had accompanied the magnum. *The ones she'd had sent up.* He popped one in his mouth and held another out to feed to her.

'Not for me, sweetie,' she wrinkled her nose, 'I have to watch my figure.'

'You're kidding aren't you?' he said, 'you're absolutely perfect.'

'Perfect for you, Daddy Bear.'

He laughed, besotted, unable to take his eyes from her. The tips of her dark nipples poked in and out of the water, tantalising him.

She allowed her toes to move further down his stomach.

'Did you write the note?' her voice was saccharine.

He swallowed another chocolate.

'The note?' He looked momentarily perplexed. 'Oh, yes… that… yes, it's in my briefcase.'

She smiled lasciviously, her toes massaging him intimately as she seduced him with her eyes.

'My good, darling Daddy Bear.' She watched as his head began to roll back on his shoulders slightly, his eyes beginning to look a little heavy.

'Gosh, I feel tired,' he suddenly exhaled loudly, 'and a little nauseous.' He shifted his bulk, water sloshing over the sides as he attempted to shake off the uncomfortable feeling he was experiencing.

'Must be all the exertion. You should have a little nap,' she suggested, 'get all refreshed in time for the big finale.'

'Finale?'

She picked up the flannel; it was wet.

'Let me wash your face,' she said, 'you're covered in chocolate crumbs.' She tutted at him like a child. Kneeling up she moved her body onto his and placed the flannel over his mouth. His eyes widened for a split second but the nausea he was experiencing had significantly muted his reactions and he was slow to raise his arm. He was attempting to speak, his voice muffled.

'What was that, Daddy Bear?' she said, 'I'm afraid I can't make out what you're saying.'

He grabbed her arm, continuing to try to say something, but his voice was slowing down, it became a little slurred around the edges and incoherent.

She blinked at him, smiling into his eyes.

'Night night, Daddy Bear,' she said, 'sweet dreams.'

His head made a small thud against the ceramic tub as it fell back onto his shoulders.

He was out cold. Finally.

She sighed, removing the champagne flute from his hand. His arm flopped over the edge of the bath almost comically and she had to stop herself from laughing. But the urge soon faded when he began to gradually slide down into the water. She had banked on his sheer size preventing this from happening and suddenly felt cross. It was the slippery bath oil.

'Oh no you don't. Big fat, fucking Bear.' Jumping from the bath she got behind him and attempted to pull him upright by the armpits. It wasn't easy; he was a dead weight on top of all the extra he was carrying and he kept slipping back down into the tub. Cursing under her breath she grabbed one of the fluffy white towels from the rail and shoved it behind his back. It provided the resistance she needed to keep him upright but she knew she must act quickly.

'Now you stay there, Daddy Bear, I'll be right back.'

Naked and still wet, she hurriedly went into the bedroom to get what she needed, her adrenal glands working overtime as she rifled through the large tote. Back in the bathroom, she took hold of one of his wrists and slit it open vertically with one deep cut. A fountain of bright red arterial blood immediately spurted from the wound. She stepped back but not quickly enough, and a mist of spraying blood hit her face and chest. *God damn it!* Watching almost mesmerised as blood pumped from his main artery, forming an impressive pool on the shiny white marble flooring, she quickly took hold of his other wrist and repeated the process. The initial spurt was less impressive than the first, but this was only to be expected as he'd already begun to bleed out. She stood back to observe her handiwork, watching the life drain from him. The bath water turned from pink to bright red, like paint.

Some moments later, a second flurry of adrenaline brought her out of her trance state and she looked down at herself and tutted. What a mess she was! Snatching a flannel from the side of the bath she ran it under the tap, observing his toes as they bobbed just above the water. Once she was sure there was no visible trace of blood left on her, she flushed the flannel down the toilet, wrapping the razor blade inside it. Stepping around the pool of blood, she made to leave the bathroom, but not before taking one last look at the scene she'd created. The view from the doorway was somehow even more spectacular, almost cinematic, she thought. His blood had travelled, squirting up the mirrored tiles, and it was now making a slow descent towards the edge of the bath and trickling back into the water. She was struck by how pale his skin looked contrasted against his vivid ruby-coloured blood. His bloated stomach was protruding above the waterline, his genitals, just visible, gently swaying with the natural momentum of water. His head was titled backwards at an awkward angle, making it look almost as if his neck had been broken, and his eyes were wide open, a look of despair in them, like he somehow had known. He was dead, of course. It really was quite a beautiful picture, sublime even, and she tilted her own head at the same angle as his, savouring the moment a little longer.

Padding back into the bedroom she considered ordering room service but decided against it. She could do without any more

DNA traces to cover. She'd grab a burger on the way home; one of those gourmet ones she liked from that new place near her apartment.

She poured herself another glass of Krug and took the clothes from her tote bag. A pair of casual black slouchy pants, an Adidas T-shirt, a beanie hat, some biker-style boots and a khaki bomber jacket. She dressed herself carefully, folding her dress and coat and placing them with her stilettos inside the tote, then she reapplied her make-up: smoky eyes and bright red lips, kind of punky she thought. Her lipstick matched the bath water. Then she tied her hair up into a top knot, placing the dark shoulder-length wig onto her head and straightening it out in the mirror before placing the beanie on top.

'Not bad,' she congratulated her reflection as she admired her complete transformation. Taking a slug of the Krug, she took a dry cloth from the fancy kitchen area, put on some rubber gloves, and began the process of wiping down all surfaces she'd touched, using the can of Mr Sheen she'd brought with her, humming an old Oasis track whose title she couldn't remember as she polished. The smell reminded her of her mother's house.

Once the careful clean-up was complete she opened the gift he'd bought her. 'Hmmm,' she said, taking the Tiffany earrings from the box and holding one up to the light. She watched appreciatively as it glinted between her thumb and forefinger. 'Very nice, thank you Daddy Bear,' she said, removing her small gold hoops and replacing them with the diamond studs. She smiled in the mirror, pulling her hair back from her ears to inspect them. She finished her glass and after pouring herself another half glass, carefully using the accompanying napkin to hold the bottle, she did a walk-through of the penthouse, checking that she'd left no visible traces of Goldilocks. She'd been meticulously careful not to touch too much but it would pay to be thorough. She didn't want to give anyone anything to work with. Once the main suite had been assessed, she checked the bathroom. She hadn't used the toilet or dried herself with a towel, and she'd flushed the flannel and razor blade down the cistern. As a precautionary measure however, she wiped down the surface areas, paying particular care to the sink where she'd washed herself. She inspected the floor for any visible hairs, nail polish chips, lint and the like, and was satisfied she'd left no trace of herself.

Perching on the bottom of the bath, she looked at him once more; he'd stopped bleeding now, his chubby left arm hung lifelessly over the edge of the tub, his other arm was submerged in the red liquid water. Blood was already congealing on his wrist and hand, and his exposed wound had darkened to aubergine. His eyes were still open and for a split second she thought of closing them, a final act of kindness, a thank you for the gift he'd bought her, but rational sense told her not to. Still, she was glad he'd not suffered. His organs would've shut down pretty rapidly with the arsenic he'd ingested from the chocolates. Ah yes, the chocolates! She picked up the small heart-shaped box. There was only a couple of the six left. *Gluttonous, greedy Daddy Bear.* She took the remaining two from the box, wrapped them in toilet tissue and flushed them away, returning the box to the floor where she'd found it.

Swallowing the last of the champagne, she took her glass into the kitchen and began washing it thoroughly in soapy hot water, drying it with a dishcloth before placing it back into the ice bucket alongside the half-full bottle. Such a waste, she sighed. Perhaps she'd pick some more up herself to accompany that gourmet burger on the way home. That reminded her; she began to look for his wallet and found it on the bedside table, beside his Rolex. She opened it and found almost £500 cash. She took £230 and left the rest. That's what they'd agreed on and she certainly wasn't a thief. Next, the briefcase. It immediately opened with a satisfying click. In that moment she actually felt a little love for him; she had accounted for time spent cracking the lock-code, but there was no need. *Thoughtful Daddy Bear.* She rifled through his papers for a few seconds until she found the note.

It had been handwritten on bonded paper, just as she'd requested, and she took it from the briefcase along with a fancy ballpoint silver pen. Walking barefoot back into the bathroom she casually took his arm and placed the pen between his fingers, pressing down hard. Then she placed the note next to the bath and randomly dropped the ballpoint on top. She looked at the mantle clock, just visible from the doorway: it was 3.45 p.m. She'd been in the suite for just three quarters of the hour she had set herself to complete the task, and she was pleased she'd managed everything in such good time. But had she forgotten something? A nag in her solar plexus told her she had. She stood for a moment, mentally going through the list. The razor blade! *Jesus*, she berated herself silently as she retrieved a fresh one from her make-up bag and returned to the bathroom. She dipped it in some of the congealing blood on the floor before attempting to place it between his thumb and forefinger. Clearly however, he no longer possessed the ability to grip. On the third attempt she cursed him and gave up, watching as it remained in his fingers for a split second before falling into the pool of blood next to the bath. That could figure, she surmised.

Returning to the main suite, she removed the rubber gloves and placed them into her tote before taking a final look around her, running through her mental checklist. Once she was satisfied she had not overlooked anything, she took the small soft toy bear from her tote and threw it onto the bed, picked up her bag, slid into her boots and opened the door with the sleeve of her jacket.

'Adios, Daddy Bear,' she said quietly as she shut the door behind her, removing the 'Do Not Disturb' notice on the handle.

CHAPTER TWO

Suicides. They're a hazard of the job. One of many you encounter as a copper, you're probably thinking, but suicides especially bum me out. I have empathy for suicides, for the people that top themselves and those they leave behind. Believe me, not so long ago I wasn't too far from that kind of despair myself. Still, my heart sank when I got the call from my governor, Ken Woods.

'We've got a body down at that fancy hotel on Knightsbridge, La Reymond. Some banker in the penthouse suite. He's been ID'd as a Nigel Baxter, forty-seven. It looks like possible suicide.'

'Why a suicide?'

'His wrists were slit,' Woods says dispassionately.

'The chambermaid has just found him in a bath full of blood.'

I hang up, sigh, make a U-turn and head over there.

The maid's crying when I reach the hotel. She looks shaken up, understandably so. She's not getting paid enough to have to deal with this kind of shit. Come to mention it, neither am I.

'I… I find him this morning.'

She's Eastern European, I can tell by the accent. 'What's your name?'

'Irena,' she sniffs, wiping her nose with her sleeve.

'Irena, can you tell me, was there a 'Do Not Disturb' sign on the door of the suite?' I keep my tone as gentle as possible, poor girl looks like she's about to collapse.

'No… No sir, it was not there… I check… and is why I go in.'

I nod, make some notes. The manager's standing next to her – looks full of his own importance, but perhaps I'm being too quick to judge, another hazard of the job. His name is Martin Spencer, a pretty un-fancy name for a pretty fancy hotel.

'A standard double room in this establishment costs around the £600 mark,' he tells me, as if this of any relevance.

'A night?'

He casts me a look.

'Yes, *a night*, and the penthouse suite costs around £3,000.'

I raise an eyebrow. For that sort of money, I'd expect Angelina Jolie to change my sheets.

'Was Mr Baxter a regular client?'

'No,' he says sharply, 'not that I'm aware of, but we have a lot of clientele, Detective and I don't get to know them all personally. I can double-check on the system to see if he's been here before though.'

Helpful.

'Do you know if Mr Baxter arrived alone?'

'Yes, according to the concierge, and no one checked in as his guest either.'

The maid looks like she's going to throw up, so I quickly ask her what time she entered the suite this morning and she looks at her manager as though asking permission to speak.

'I think… maybe 11 a.m.,' she says nervously.

It's now 11.38. Apparently there are already two PCs in the penthouse with the body, so I nod and immediately head up in the lift. I hope to God they haven't disturbed anything.

As I step out of the lift, my phone beeps. I have a good idea who it might be and I'm right: Shirley, the online date I met for the first time a couple of days ago, after a week of sending pleasantries through cyberspace. For the most part, the few women I've actually met since I began my online quest to find happiness again after Rachel – if that could ever be possible – have seemed intrigued by the fact I'm a copper, a detective copper no less. Maybe a couple have even been impressed. But one or two have clearly been put off by my career; no doubt by the thought of long hours, shift work and the potential emotional residue that can come with dealing with murders, rapists, paedos and life's ne'er-do-wells.

Rachel never minded my work. She was the woman I knew I was going to spend the rest of my life with. She was also going to be the mother of my child, maybe even children. But then she was taken from me. One day she was here, and we shared a life together, and then it was all over. Finished. Done. The piece of shit who ploughed into her motorbike got two years. Death by dangerous driving. Me and her family got a life sentence instead. A life without Rachel. Oh, and a life without our ten-week-old baby who was growing inside her.

I don't read the message and it's already left my mind as I enter suite 106. The stench of death and of perfume are the first things I notice when I walk in. My sense of smell is acute; Rachel used to say I could smell a sparrow's fart from ten paces.

'Hello Sir,' two PCs greet me respectfully with a nod, 'we've ID'd the body, there was a wallet on the bedside table,' the male PC says.

'Good,' I say, giving the room an initial once over. 'Has anything else been touched?'

'No Sir,' the female PC responds, 'forensics are on their way now.'

I nod. 'Nice job.'

The suite is huge, a massive studio-type room with white leather couches and glass bowls filled with green apples. There's a large zebra-print rug on the floor and a low glass table with an open briefcase on it, plus a posh kitchen area with one of those huge American-style fridges that dispense ice, and plenty of other high-end gadgetry. It looks like nothing's been touched. One of the PCs shows me Nigel Baxter's ID – his driver's licence – and I note it's registered to a Chelsea address. The shutters are drawn so I open them to let some light in and get a better perspective, before putting on a pair of blue latex gloves. I see a Rolex watch on the bedside table and a small teddy bear on the bed. The bed is round and large – big enough for an orgy – and it looks as though it's been occupied, or at least laid on, as the pillows are a little out of place and there are slight indentations on the sheets. There's a pair of men's Calvin Klein briefs on the floor next to the bed. They appear to have been discarded in haste, gusset side up.

I nod to one of the PCs and he shows me into the bathroom. Baxter is lying in the bath, his head tilted back onto one side with his eyes and mouth open. His left arm is flopped over the side of the large tub, covered in blood from the wrist down. The wound looks deep and I note that it's vertical. He's naked. There's a considerable amount of blood on the tiles next to the bath – drips, splashes and spray, no doubt from the artery explosion when he, or someone else, cut his wrists open. His toes, which have taken on a touch of blue, are sticking ghoulishly out of the red water.

'It smells of perfume in here,' I say to the PCs.

I hear forensics arriving and leave the bathroom for a moment to brief them.

'Seal off the room, bag up his belongings and the bear after you've done the scene pics. Okay? There will be a standard inquest.' I hesitate. I haven't decided what's what yet, but my subconscious is nagging at me. 'Oh, and dust for prints, yeah?'

One of the forensics looks up at me. She knows that's not standard procedure in a suicide.

Paramedics arrive and I let the PCs deal with them. I need to get a handle on things first, make an assessment. There's a letter on the floor beside the blood, a silver pen and a razor blade – standard men's single edge. It's almost completely covered in blood and I tell forensics to bag it up. The note says: '*My beautiful darling, I'm sorry, please forgive me*' and it's signed with a kiss. There's a heart-shaped empty box of chocolates. They bag that up too.

I scan the bathroom and notice that there's only one bath towel on the rail. There's a flannel missing too. I get a whiff of perfume again and I have a weird feeling I know what it is. It's a familiar smell and I wonder if it might be a scent that Rach used to use? She wasn't a particularly girlie woman, not high-maintenance at all, but she was still feminine somehow, even in her biker leathers. And she liked perfume. I wish I'd bought her more.

I look at the products and make a note to ask the hotel about them, to check and see if any are missing. There's nothing in the waste bin.

The coroner, Vic Leyton, is on the body now. I like Vic; she's eccentric but warm, witty and very good at her job.

'What's the estimated TOD, Vic?' I ask.

She shrugs a little by way of greeting me. A gesture that suggests we shouldn't keep meeting like this.

'I'd say anywhere between 2 and 5 p.m. yesterday afternoon.'

I nod.

'And what do you reckon?'

'Difficult to tell… obviously he, or whoever, meant business though. The cuts were vertical.'

'Vertical?'

'Yes, verticals open a larger amount of the vein, therefore he would have bled out faster, plus it's more difficult to stop the flow by applying pressure. He hit an artery both times by the look of him, but as the song goes, the first cut was the deepest.'

I smile. Good old Vic. She could still crack a funny joke even when faced with such a miserable scene.

*

The paramedics begin lifting the body from the tub. Poor bastards. Then I notice the towel wedged behind his back, almost like some kind of support. This is odd. *Why would you place a towel behind your back while you were in the bath about to commit hari-kari?*

I let the paras do their job and go back into the main suite. As I walk through the room I get a whiff of furniture polish, like the place has already been cleaned. I spy an ice bucket and a bottle of champagne, one of those magnums, the big ones all those Formula One drivers empty over themselves when they win – I've always found that quite vulgar, a gross display of excessive wealth. There's a solitary glass on the marble kitchen worktop with a drop still in it, and a second glass that appears unused still in the ice bucket with the bottle.

I start summing up: there's a rudimentary suicide note that gives nothing by way of explanation as to why Nigel Baxter opened himself up in the bath; he'd ordered a magnum of champagne and eaten chocolates – a final meal? The teddy bear on the bed and the bath towel behind him, the perfumed smell of the bathwater and the polish, like the place had been given a once over. On the surface, it appears as though Mr Baxter had been alone and had decided to kill himself in in the most brutal way. But the post-mortem might shed more light. And I need to speak to the maid and hotel staff in more detail, check the CCTV. But there is something… my intuition mainly, that makes me think that Baxter wasn't, or hadn't been, alone in this room. Over the years I've come to trust that feeling. Like Rach used to say, 'I'm a professional cynic'.

My phone rings. It's Woods.

'I've got Janet Baxter down in one of the interview rooms,' he said. 'She came in to report her husband – Nigel Baxter – missing. Can you get back here now?'

I inwardly sigh, feeling my lungs deflating as I reply, 'Yes Sir, on my way.'

Suicides: I really fucking hate them.

CHAPTER THREE

Janet Baxter looks as you might imagine someone who has just discovered that their husband of nigh-on twenty years has just done himself in would look. Her round face is puffy and red from crying and she's hovering precariously somewhere between shock and full-blown hysteria. I feel for Janet: I've been there too, and it ain't a nice place to be. 'Can I get you some coffee, or a tea perhaps? She shakes her head. 'Is there anyone I can call for you, Janet? Anyone you'd like to be here with you?' She continues to shake her head.

'There is no way my Nigel would have done this,' she hiccups, pulling her coat around her solid frame in an obvious bid to comfort herself. 'We've got two beautiful children, our youngest has only just started secondary school, and Lara, Lara's halfway through her GCSEs... Those kids were his life; *we* were his life. He was happy... no, no I won't have this... my Nige would never have taken his own life!'

I try not to say too much at this point, I just let Janet speak, or shriek; let her vent, release some of the anguish, frustration and pain that's visibly tearing through her like a tornado. I can see she's in denial, the early stage of disbelief when she's heard the words but they've yet to sink in. I know that stage: it's fucking painful. But worse, I know the real anguish is yet to come.

'When did you last see your husband, Janet?'

'Before he left for work yesterday morning. He kissed me goodbye.'

'Did you notice anything unusual, any cause for concern?

'No. Nothing, nothing at all. He seemed in a good mood, normal… just Nigel… but when he didn't come home that evening… well, naturally I panicked. Nigel often travels for work, mainly to Japan and the US, but those trips are planned in advance and he always, always makes me aware of them,' she splutters. 'We've been together over two decades,' she says, pain evident in her voice, 'and Nige has never, ever not once come home without telling me first… without calling.'

I nod, understanding as she goes on to tell me, through mucusy sobs, that they would've celebrated their twentieth anniversary next week and that they were planning a big family gathering at their Chelsea home.

'Instead', she says, 'I'll be planning his burial now,' and finally breaks down.

The female PC with me, Jill Murray, who looks young enough to be Janet's daughter, attempts to comfort her, but it seems futile – and all three of us know it. Still, Janet seems like a nice, unremarkable kind of woman: your average middle-aged, stay-at-home wife and mother, devoted to her husband and kids, putting herself last in the process. I feel for the woman because we both know – though it's of course unspoken – that after today her life will never be the same again and that everything she has known is going to irrevocably change. And she never asked for any of it.

I broach my questions with gentle consideration, wishing I didn't have to ask. 'Janet, can you offer any explanation as to why Nigel might have been occupying the penthouse suite at La Reymond hotel? Did he tell you he was going to be there? Was there any indication that he was suffering from depression, you know, lack of appetite, unusual behaviour, loss of libido? Was he under pressure at work? Did he have any financial issues, family or health problems? Had he lost a loved one recently?'

Each question is met with a resounding 'no'.

'My Nige loved his food and he loved his job, even if it was a little stressful at times, but then whose isn't?' she asks.

I like her for that. Even now she's considering others. But now I have to ask the question I really don't want to ask, the one that always sends the wives into an even darker abyss. 'Janet, could Nigel have been having an affair?'

She breaks down again, crumples like paper in front of me, almost shrinks before my eyes.

Hazard of the job.

'No! No… I don't think so…' Her face reddens. 'We were happily married Detective, in *every sense*, even though… well… the honeymoon phase had long since passed.'

I nod, manage a small smile.

'We got on well, rarely argued. We were happy.'

I tell her about the note and she cries harder; I don't tell her about the champagne, the teddy bear, the smell of perfume or the towel. I'm judging this one on a need-to-know basis.

'I don't know how I'm going to tell the kids,' she says, as much to herself as to me. And I nod again and give her the spiel about family liaison and victim support, and ask Jill to provide her with whatever she needs. Only, what Janet Baxter really needs is for Nigel Baxter not to have topped himself.

'I want his computer checked by forensics, his phone records gone through, his schedule scrutinised,' I tell the team back in the incident room. 'I want to dig deep into Baxter's life, find out his movements, find out what, or whom he's been hiding. We need to wait for the inquest outcome, but in the meantime I want CCTV from the hotel, and the staff questioned.' There are nods and murmurs from the team as they gear themselves up for business. Suicides usually leave an open verdict, but there's something, besides his adamant wife, about Nigel Baxter that tells me that something is not quite right, that things are not as they seem in this case.

And I do like to be right.

CHAPTER FOUR

She took the communal stairs up to her apartment on the fourth floor carrying the purchases from a day's West End shopping trip. Spending money had felt good; she'd earned it. High on adrenaline, she took the stairs two at a time, an abundance of energy coursing through her and making her feel powerful as the array of designer shopping bags she was carrying in both hands scraped against the walls. She'd spent around three and a half grand in as many hours today in Gucci, Victoria's Secret, Selfridges, All Saints… But it was the thrill of what had taken place at La Reymond in penthouse suite 106 that had really given her a sense of omnipotence. She marvelled at how easy it had been to take another life and the unadulterated pleasure rush she had derived from it, and she wondered why she hadn't done it sooner. Getting away with it felt like a reason to celebrate. She knew the first forty-eight hours were critical and they had passed by with no cause for concern. At least not for her. Clearly she'd covered her tracks efficiently enough and she felt a touch silly at fleetingly having doubted herself. She'd purposefully made the scene look like a grisly suicide on first sight, but she was aware that with further investigation the real motive would become apparent. Subconsciously she wanted it to be, really throw those fuckers into a spin questioning themselves. She'd been careful to cover any DNA trail but the idea that the police would eventually discover that Daddy Bear had been murdered excited her.

She imagined the moment someone, probably the house-keeper, had walked into suite 106 and discovered the gruesome scene. Witnessing something like that scarred a person and it only added to her pleasure to know she had affected a total stranger's life in such a manner. Daddy Bear's wife though, she'd be having *real* problems right about now. That she could count on. He'd confessed to being married with two kids pretty much instantly when they'd connected online; she was sure he'd given their names and ages too, but she'd only feigned interest and couldn't recall them. Now she wished she could, because it would have allowed her to visualise their grief with much more clarity. On a conscious level, she knew she was supposed to feel some type of remorse, pity or guilt for the family he'd left behind. Because that's what human beings are supposed to feel. But her subconscious was blank, void and empty like a dark abyss. She had no access to such emotions and could only picture what they might look and feel like. Her emotions consisted only of visual fantasies, as she imagined his wife, hunched and crying at his graveside, the tragedy taking its toll on her face as she silently blamed herself, and his children, bereft, propping her up as they sobbed and grieved for their fat, useless fuck of a cheating father. She caught herself smiling at the thought of this scenario. It was the first time she'd considered his family since the slaying. *Slaying.* She liked that word; it was somehow more befitting than 'murder'. Daddy Bear had been a sacrifice and his demise had left her feeling a height of euphoria she'd never reached before, not even during her past repertoire of deviant and perverted behaviour. It was sustenance to her psyche, filling up a measurable void inside her to the extent that she almost felt human, real, *alive*.

She wondered if this was how other people felt in their everyday lives? Her morbid jealousy of other people's 'ordinary' lives and their ability to self-generate happiness was part of the disorder that drove her to secure, entrap, then devalue and discard people. But not before sucking the very life from them first; draining them of every good, joyful human feeling and experience and leaving them a broken, empty husk of their former glorious selves.

Taking things one step further towards physical murder however had been a long time coming. It had been a dark, insidious, gradual fantasy until it had manifested itself as a progressively logical reality in her twisted mind. It was a story she needed to tell – one in which she got to write the ending and set herself free.

Thoughts of Daddy Bear's family evaporated quickly as a pang in her belly alerted her to her hunger. All that shopping had given her an appetite. Maybe she'd treat herself to a takeaway tonight before getting back online again. She didn't want to waste time, not when she was riding such a high wave. However, she suspected that procuring Mummy Bear was going to be a trickier process than entrapping Daddy Bear had been.

Lost in her thoughts, she almost didn't see the woman from the apartment opposite her at the top of the stairs. She was red-faced and looked agitated; a pile of grocery shopping bags was clustered around her feet. The woman smiled almost apologetically when she saw her coming up the stairs.

'Hi,' she said in response to her neighbour's smile. She was in a good, no, *great* mood and felt like she wanted someone to witness it. 'You okay? You look a little stressed out.'

She didn't recognise this woman. She must be new.

The neighbour sighed heavily. 'I've only gone and locked myself out,' she said, shaking her head in disbelief at her own stupidity. 'I'm such… such an idiot. Don't know where my head's at at the moment… All over the place…' she berated herself, embarrassed.

'Oh shit, really?' She smiled, in an attempt to appear sympathetic. 'You not got a spare set of keys?'

The neighbour opened out her palms and looked to the ceiling. 'Well, you'd think, wouldn't you, but no. The spare set's…' she pointed to the locked door, eyes rolling, 'in there.'

'Oops… you poor thing.'

'Dozy arse you mean… honestly, the week I've had…' She shook her head, her unruly curly ginger hair looking almost as angry as she was with herself. 'I'm going to have to call a locksmith now, more bloody expense.'

She nodded.

'Yeah… those guys aren't cheap. You can't call your landlord? He'll have a set, won't he?' She was being helpful, making suggestions. Sometimes it was fun playing human.

'I own it,' the red-haired woman said, apologetically again.

She realised she was the type of person whose foot you could stamp on and they would end up being the one apologising to you for having a foot in the first place. A *nice* person. Now she had her interest.

'Oh, you bought the place… lucky you. Wish I could afford to buy. The rent's extortionate on my place.'

'Part of my divorce settlement; he got to keep the house, but he didn't get to keep me… It's okay though,' she quickly added, clearly not wanting to overshare.

Her mind began to rev with possibilities as she mentally assessed the woman.

'Look, why don't you come inside, bring your shopping in and wait while you call a locksmith?'

The woman's shoulders visibly relaxed.

'Really? Oh, that's so kind of you.' Her neighbour's head fell to the side, reminding her of Daddy Bear and how he'd looked in the bath with his head titled, like it was trying to escape from his neck. 'Only if you're sure… I'm not putting you out am I? It's Saturday, I'm sure you've got plans…'

She smiled. 'Yeah, planning on sorting through this lot,' she held her purchases up proudly, 'getting a takeaway and watching crap telly… it's no bother at all.'

The woman was picking up her bags now. 'I'm so grateful, thank you…'

'… Danni-Jo,' she said. She'd been Danni-Jo for a while now.

'I'm Karen, but everyone calls me Kizzy… my friends call me Kizzy.'

'Nice to meet you, Kizzy,' Danni-Jo reached for her keys, 'come on in.'

CHAPTER FIVE

Kizzy hung up the call.

'They'll be here within the hour,' she said with that apologetic look on her face again, nervously chewing her bottom lip with her protruding front teeth.

'No worries,' Danni-Jo assured her, 'really... I'm not doing much, like I said. Besides, it's nice to meet a neighbour, a friendly one anyway. You know, I've lived here for two years and no one's ever said so much as hello to me!'

Kizzy looked genuinely surprised.

'Really? But you're so nice and friendly yourself.'

She feigned modesty, lowering her eyes slightly.

'That's nice of you to say, but I don't spend an awful lot of time here, I'm always at work. Work, work, work...' she sang the words in the style of the Rihanna song.

Kizzy nodded sympathetically.

'So what do you do Danni-Jo, for work, work, work?'

She thought on her feet. Bought a few seconds by laughing. 'I work in a hotel, up near Mayfair, it's really not very exciting at all... but I'm studying to be an actor. I go to drama school.'

Yeah, that sounded good: an actor. It made her sound interesting at least. She saw Kizzy's eyes wander to the pile of designer bags she'd dumped on the armchair and guessed what she might be thinking.

'My dad died recently, he was an actor too. Starred in a few films, did pretty well for himself really. Enough to see me right when he passed anyway.' The first, and last part, incidentally, were true. Her cunt of a father had recently died. And once news had reached her through the solicitor that she'd been bequeathed his entire estate, she'd celebrated his passing with a bottle of Dom Pérignon and a Domino's pizza. He hadn't been an actor, although he'd done a pretty good job at *acting* like a loving, caring father when he'd needed to. That monster had owed her every penny of her inheritance, and the moment it had been signed over to her she'd promptly sold off the family home in Surbiton and bought her Mayfair pad. That house held nothing but terrible memories; sick, deviant, dark and twisted memories, and she'd been happy to get shot of it. Her mother had died in that house, and had she not been taken away when she had, she felt sure she would've died there too.

'I'm sorry,' Kizzy said mournfully, 'I understand what it's like to lose a loved one. My sister passed away some years ago. Breast cancer, she was only thirty-four.'

Danni-Jo shook her head. 'That's so sad. Was she older or younger than you?'

'Six years younger than me, she was my baby sister. I can remember her being born.' Kizzy looked visibly upset. 'When she went, it made me re-evaluate my life completely.'

'Things like that do,' she replied, guessing. *She was in her late forties. Around the right age.* 'Hence the divorce?'

Kizzy looked down into her lap and sipped on the hot herbal tea she'd been offered.

'I'm sorry, I didn't mean to pry.'

'No, no, not at all… Yes, it was really. It was,' she shifted uncomfortably on the soft couch, 'a pretty toxic relationship. Took me seventeen long years to finally build up the courage and self-esteem to leave him. After Megan died something in me just said "no more". That man took the best years of my life.'

Abuse victim. It figured. Kizzy had clearly been conditioned into feeling invisible. Years of never having her own needs met had whittled away her personality to a subservient shell, apologetic just for being alive. She was skittish, her movements jerky and nervous. She'd reached for a biscuit on the coffee table almost like a child who'd already had too many and was waiting for it to be slapped away.

'Did you have children together?' Danni-Jo knew she was asking personal questions but she figured she had the right to, being as Kizzy was in her apartment sitting on her sofa, drinking her herbal tea and eating her Hobnobs.

'No kids,' she said, quietly. 'I wanted them but I'm glad I didn't have them with him… now.'

'Well, it's never too late,' she said breezily, sensing her guest had begun to feel a little melancholy.

Kizzy laughed but it sounded hollow. 'Oh, I'm way too old for all that now, and besides, I'd have to find a man first!'

Danni-Jo scoffed. 'Well, there's plenty of those fuckers around let me tell you.'

Kizzy's face reddened a bit – at the use of her bad language she presumed, or perhaps it was simply the thought of getting some prospective dick? She couldn't imagine her engaging in such a pursuit.

'Maybe for an attractive young woman like yourself,' she said. 'But me…?'

'Don't do yourself down,' Danni-Jo said, almost wanting to like her for a moment. 'You certainly don't look old.' That was a lie; Kizzy looked every day of her forty-something years and then some, though she suspected with a decent makeover she'd scrub up alright. The teeth were a problem though: she had a large overbite and one of her front teeth slightly overlapped the other, adding insult to injury. They were really quite offensive. Suddenly she had a vision of grabbing Kizzy by the back of her ginger hair and slamming her face into the glass coffee table, smashing her bad teeth to pieces.

'You should get yourself online you know, plenty of divorced men on the hunt out there, plenty of married ones too.'

'Oh nooo.' She shook her head. 'I'm not brave enough for that. All that… rejection.' Kizzy smiled awkwardly.

'Well, you never know, this locksmith might be "the one".'

'I admire your positivity,' she replied.

Positivity. Now that was a first. She was actually beginning to rather enjoy her odd neighbour's company now. Kizzy clearly saw Danni-Jo as superior; prettier, more talented, wittier, younger and more confident. She basked in such an image of herself being reflected back to her.

Poor woman literally reeked of *eau de* low self-esteem and with her almost childlike gestures, she suspected she may be mentally challenged in some way, bipolar or borderline perhaps. Not that it mattered, so much the better. This would make her tracks easier to cover. Suddenly she thought of the bottle of arsenic, the tiny vial hidden in her kitchen cupboard along with the condiments. But no, she couldn't, could she? She hadn't thought it through properly, hadn't had enough time to plan thoroughly, and she hadn't established a genuine relationship with her: not yet at least. But the situation had somehow seemed to present itself to her and she decided this must be a sign. A *positive* sign.

'Listen,' Danni-Jo said, resting on the arm of her sofa and meeting Kizzy's watery green eyes, framed by crow's feet, 'once the locksmith has done his job and you're all sorted out, if you fancy it, give me a knock. I've got a night off and I'm getting a Chinese takeaway and opening a bottle of Prosecco if you want to join me? We can watch *The X Factor* together if you like? I've got a guilty crush on Simon Cowell, but don't tell anyone,' she giggled conspiratorially and Kizzy joined in, placing her hand over her mouth as though it were the most outrageous confession she'd ever heard. Perhaps it was.

'Really?' she said, clearly taken aback at the unexpected invitation. 'Well, you know, that's so lovely of you but I couldn't possibly intrude on your Saturday evening.'

'Don't be daft,' Danni-Jo lightly dug her in the forearm, 'I'd love it if you could join me. Better than sitting here all on my tod.'

Kizzy looked elated. 'Well, if you're sure, then that would be great. I love Prosecco and I could murder some sweet-and-sour pork balls.' She laughed at the irony of her statement.

'Pork balls it is then.'

CHAPTER SIX

I'm driving down the M25, doing around 75 mph and listening to Kasabian. They're a hybrid mix of Oasis and Muse in my opinion: all driving guitar riffs and catchy choruses with a lot of swagger, even though they're from Leicester, which isn't a particularly rock-and-roll place all told. I imagine they're right jumped-up little dickheads, you can just tell, but they've got a few tunes so fair play. I'm contemplating messaging back 'Keen Shirl' – as I've decided to call her – and agreeing to a second date, but I've come to the conclusion that it wouldn't be fair, because I just don't think I fancy her. I reckon she'd have sex with me though, Keen Shirl. In fact, I'm sure she would, and I don't mean that in an arrogant way. I just know, you know, but really I'm not that kind of bloke. I've never been one of them fuck 'em and forget 'em types, just out for the score. And I'm too old for one-night stands now.

Rach had never had a one-night stand in her life, so she told me, and I believed her. 'They all just kept coming back for more,' she laughed, throwing her head back like she did whenever she laughed. She had an infectious laugh, you had to join in. Often the laugh itself became the joke. *God help me, I miss that girl.*

My mind wanders back to Janet Baxter, even above the din from the stereo. I'd rather it didn't, and I turn Kasabian up a few notches, but it doesn't drown out my thoughts, so I go with them.

'My Nigel would *never* kill himself.' I see her shaking her head vehemently, grief and conviction in her watery, red-rimmed eyes.

She says this is as an absolute unwavering fact. Cynicism in this job is par for the course. You could sum it up with, 'you think you know someone…' Being a copper has taught me that, hey, you might *think* you know someone, but one day you wake up and find you're married to a serial killer. That shit really happens. What I find interesting in those situations is the doubt that's often directed towards the wives. 'She must've known, surely? She must've suspected her husband was a rapist/paedophile/cross-dresser/whatever, they've been married for twenty-five years!' It's pretty unfair, because I think in some cases the wife genuinely *doesn't* know the person she's married to. You've got to remember who you might be dealing with; psychopaths are absolute masters of disguise, able to shape-shift and operate on a level that would make a chameleon look like an amateur. They are incredibly skilful at pulling the wool over people's eyes; their ability to manipulate and con makes them utterly convincing, consummate liars of the highest degree, devious beyond the realms of human comprehension and devoid of a conscience and empathy. The absence of empathy: that's the crux of their disorder, the heart of the matter. Empathy prevents most of us from murdering, pillaging and raping each other. Conscience and the ability to empathise with fellow humans stops us from butchering a child, cutting its body into pieces and inviting its mother round for tea and biscuits. But it *does* happen. I've seen it.

The teddy bear, among other things, is troubling me. Martin Delaney, my number two on the case, did some research and tells me it's one of those Steiff Bears, quite expensive apparently, collectable. It still had the label attached to its little bear ear when we picked it up. There's no indication that Nigel Baxter bought it himself, no receipt in his paperwork or in his wallet. I told Delaney to check out the shops where they sell them and it turns out the little bastards are everywhere, mainly in shopping centres and department stores. Apparently you can even build your own, and kids have in-store parties where they get to stuff their own bear and choose its clothes before putting it in a box with a birth certificate and taking it home. They go mad for it apparently, and I wonder if our kid, mine and Rach's, would've loved these bears too. I guess we'd have found out about this kind of thing if he or she had been given the chance to live. Anyway, I tell Delaney to start digging, ask if anyone recalls this particular bear being made. He's wearing a suit. He's a business bear. Alan Sugar, but furry.

The other thing that's bothering me, aside from Kasabian who have started to grate a little now, is the perfume. The housekeeper at La Reymond gave me a list of the complimentary toiletries allocated to each room. The penthouse list reads like a Space NK till receipt. High-end stuff. Rachel was into her smellies, well, what woman isn't? I liked buying her perfume and candles – she loved a scented candle. Jesus, maybe we were a pair of clichés after all? So, the list. The L'Occitane stuff was still there: tick. The Tigi hair shampoo and conditioner: unused, tick. The Cowshed body butter: all good, tick. Shower cap, pumice stone and one of those squeegee body puffs that you wash yourself with: all in place. Tick, tick, tick. The Jo Malone Lime Basil & Mandarin bath oil: gone. *So where was it?* Wasn't in with the rubbish. There was no rubbish save for the champagne cork and wrapper. So the Jo Malone stuff is missing. Vanished. But it was used. It was in the bath water, the bloody bath water. I could smell it. And something tells me that Nigel Baxter didn't put it there. You've got to ask why a man like Nigel Baxter would add a few slugs of sweet smelling oil to his bathwater just for luck? I'm not saying it's not possible. I mean, who knows what's going through the mind of a man about to take his own life with a razor blade? But I'm pretty sure it doesn't have much to do with smelling good. Janet Baxter told me her husband never used 'cologne' – an old-fashioned word for an old-fashioned kind of lady.

'I don't remember him using cologne, or ever smelling it on him,' she'd said, sadly, as if she'd long since given up on trying to spice things up between them. So the bear and the bath oil are bugging me. And the towel that was wedged behind his back. Come to think of it, so is the 'suicide' note – not much in the way of explanation from a man seemingly of former sound mind and character. In my experience, which is sadly greater than most people's, suicide is a symptom of deep depression. Victims usually have a history of self-harm or addiction; it could be a second or even third attempt; and there's nearly always an event that triggers it – a job loss, financial problems, an affair discovered, a loved one lost, drug or alcohol abuse and all that ugliness. It's pretty rare that a man with Nigel Baxter's background just wakes up one day and says, 'enough's enough' and opens his veins up in the bath.

Cyber have got his PC and his phone and I'm waiting to see what that throws up. I'm not a betting man – though I did once win a hundred quid on the Grand National – but if I was, I'd put a tidy lump on them coming back with some revelations. A double life perhaps? A mistress at the least. I'd stake our flat on it. 'Our'. I keep thinking that like she's still here. I suppose she is really, living on in my thoughts. *When do you let go? Do you ever?*

Whenever there was an unsolved case, usually involving a man – a case that I couldn't quite get my head around or that was causing me consternation – Rach would always say, 'there's a woman involved.' Don't get this wrong, Rachel was essentially a feminist; she loved her own sex, appreciated what it was to be, feel, love and exist as a woman. But she was a realist as well. Rach was nobody's fool. She knew what was what and how people felt and operated. She understood humanity and life, and people's idiosyncrasies – in fact, they fascinated her. I remember this one case I worked on: some bloke, a window cleaner, fell from his ladder to his death. It happened in some little suburban town just outside of London, a pretty unremarkable place. Anyway, when we turned up it looked like an accident, you know, a hazard of a window cleaner's job, ladders and all of that. There was no reason to suspect any foul play. But then a nosy neighbour made a comment about him cleaning that particular house's windows once a week. And when I told her, Rach said, 'He's shagging the wife, it's pretty obvious…' She turned out to be right. Said wife's husband took umbrage to this, as one might, and decided to give him a friendly shove. Sadly, to his death, but you take your chances. Anyway, what I'm saying is that Rach wasn't one of those women who thinks men are to blame for the world. I loved her for that. Among other things.

I'm thinking about Nigel Baxter, poor old tormented Nigel Baxter, and that bear and the perfumed bath water and all I can hear in my head is Rach's voice, soft but raspy saying, 'mark my words, Danny, there's a woman involved.'

CHAPTER SEVEN

It's dark by the time I reach my apartment – *our* apartment – and I'm emotionally exhausted by the nagging suspicions in my mind about the scene that I witnessed today. I am also bloody starving. I go straight to the kitchen and open the fridge, still in my coat. Sighing as I view the contents, or lack of, I hear the words of that bloke, the nasal American one off the telly who has his own range in overpriced pasta sauces – *fuck, what is his name?* Anyway, his catchphrase is 'who lives in a house like this?' I take a ready-made chicken jalfrezi from the 'selection', puncture it with a fork and throw it in the microwave. Rach would've hated the way I eat now, she was a chef after all. *Fuck, what is that American guy's name?*

The two coppers that came to me the night she died, Bob Jenkins and Dave Smart, now I will *never* forget their names. I didn't know them personally, but I do now. That kind of encounter bonds people together. Bob was a big bear of a man, Welsh with a beard and a soft lilt, and Dave was indicative of his surname, in a decent suit with slick hair. I felt sorry for them, because there's nothing remotely redeeming about telling a person that their loved one is dead. It's a no-good situation all round and believe me, no one, not even some of the hardest men I've met on the force, can say that they don't feel anything when they draw that particular short straw. So, I kind of knew, when they turned up on our doorstep, and Bob was holding her helmet, the Triumph one, and some stuff in a sealed bag. Rach's things. I remember just looking at them and feeling pity. That was my overriding emotion in that moment, pity. For them. For having the shitty task of telling me the woman I loved and adored was dead.

I boot up my computer and log on to the sad singles website I joined in a mad moment of despair, and I think about having a beer. Instead, I take the last clean glass from the cupboard and pour myself a generous slug of Jack. It was Rachel's tipple of choice so I still keep a bottle stashed away in her memory. She could drink me under the table when the JD came out, which wasn't that often. Neither of us were big boozers, but she had a good constitution for Jack Daniels, considering she was half my size.

I silently toast her, take a slug and check my messages. I have five new ones. Promising.

Linda, forty-eight… nice enough face but too old, sorry Linda. There's Elaine, forty-four, funny nose but big smile… again maybe too old, for kids anyway. And Sarah, thirty-six, age about right and— oh hang on now, I like the look of Florence. She's a blonde, thirty-two, from North London. Local, which is handy. The picture quality is bad though, dark and grainy, and I can't really make out her features all that clearly. Shame. In the age of the selfie, you'd think that she could manage a half-decent profile shot. Anyway, I read her blurb. It's witty and warm, not too long. She says she's got a thing about London parks, and loves to eat al fresco; she watches documentaries and hates soap operas; one of her favourite things is walking barefoot on beaches; and apparently the best thing you can wear in life is a smile, (or failing that Louboutins!). Something about her captures my interest. I think it's the paradox of walking barefoot on beaches and wearing towering stilettoes. It reminds me of Rach.

I send Florence a wink anyway. Nothing to lose.

My phone rings. I swallow the rest of the Jack and answer it.

It's Chris Baylis, a particularly tenacious DS who doesn't mind getting his hands dirty.

'Baylis. What's happening?'

'Hello Gov. Well, quite a lot it seems. Vic's been on the phone. She wants you to go down there. Says she's found "something of interest".'

Baylis is talking fast, excited, and he's tripping over his words like his mouth can't keep up with his brain. I like this about him.

'I think we're looking at a homicide, boss.'

'I'm on my way,' I reply.

'And there's something else.'

'Go on.'

'Cyber have thrown some stuff up on Baxter's phone…'

'And…' I pause '… a woman, right?'

'Looks that way, Gov.'

I smile. Rach was right. Damn it, she always was.

'Okay Baylis, thanks. I'm leaving now. Oh, and Baylis…'

'Yes Gov?'

'What's the name of that American plank who snoops round people's houses, he did a TV show and his catchphrase was "who lives in a house like this?"'

There's a second's pause.

'Loyd Grossman, Gov.'

'That's it!' I say. 'That's the bloke!' And I grab my coat just as the microwave pings.

CHAPTER EIGHT

'Wow, this really is a beautiful apartment.'

Kizzy, clutching a chilled bottle of Prosecco, looks around properly, inspecting the apartment like a prospective buyer might. 'There's so much to do in mine… a new bathroom, the kitchen needs ripping out… all of it.' She sighs heavily as if she knows that none of it will ever happen.

'Well, I've been here almost two years… These things take time.' Danni-Jo places the fish-shaped dish down onto the glass coffee table along with a selection of Chinese starters, sesame prawn toast and some ribs. 'The pork balls are on their way.'

Kizzy beams, handing her the Prosecco.

'So they got you in okay, the locksmiths?'

'Yeah, £125 later.' She rolls her eyes.

'I'm in the wrong business,' Danni-Jo replies, 'but at least your shopping didn't spoil – you manage to save the milk?'

'Thankfully… Still, it was my own fault. Shouldn't have been so careless.'

'Don't beat yourself up about it,' Danni-Jo reassures her, 'we've all done it, locked ourselves out. Speaking of which, was he fit?'

Kizzy looks at her blankly.

'The locksmith guy… Was he hot?'

She blushes. 'Fraid not… well, not my type anyway,' she looks like she's not entirely sure what her type is. Maybe anyone who isn't an abuser. 'I'd say he was pushing sixty, looked like he needed a good wash.'

Danni-Jo laughs.

'Ah well, you win some…'

Kizzy flashes Danni-Jo that apologetic look again, the one that says, 'thanks for being so kind to me, even though I'm such a loser.' Shaking out her unruly ginger hair as she looks down at the platter of starters, she says, 'This is so lovely, I really can't thank you enough. Please let me pay for the food at least.'

Danni-Jo dismisses her with a wave.

'I wouldn't hear of it. This is more than enough,' she holds the bottle of Prosecco up like a trophy. 'It's the least I can do after the day you've had. And anyway, it's just so nice to meet a neighbour… a friendly one anyway. So let's crack this baby open, eh? I'm sure you could do with a glass.'

She watches as Kizzy admires Danni-Jo's apartment with wide eyes, the squishy, white L-shaped couch and pony-skin animal rug beneath it. The huge eight-armed white chandelier, similar to ones you might see in trendy bars and restaurants in London, and the Moroccan-style leather poof.

'I'd love my apartment to look like this,' she gushes, 'it's so… stylish.'

Danni-Jo smiles, coming back in from the kitchen with the rest of the Chinese – including the pork balls – on a large serving tray. She notices her guest has taken her shoes off and has put her feet up on the couch. Usually such familiarity might irk her, but Kizzy clearly feels relaxed in her company and this pleases her.

'Well, I can always help you do yours up if you like. If you let me know your budget, I can source some things for you.'

'Wow, that would be amazing. Although buying the place practically cleared me out,' she adds. 'I had a nice home once… with him… I kept it nice because well, he'd freak out if he saw a speck of dust anywhere. He had terrible OCD, among other things.'

'Sounds like a keeper,' Danni-Jo remarks wryly, wondering if she too might end up knocking ten bales of shite out of Kizzy if she was forced to be in her company for more than a few hours. She was just so… insipid, so simpering and eager to please.

Danni-Jo had doubts she'd even be missed, not like Daddy Bear. She thought of his family again, imagining their grief in that moment, the reality of his ugly death crashing through their denial like an out-of-control train.

She had dismissed the earlier thought of poisoning her neighbour on a whim. Killing her now would be the equivalent of masturbating before sex. She was also debating whether Kizzy might not be a little 'too close to home', quite literally.

'Cheers' she says, chinking Kizzy's glass, 'here's to making new friends.'

'New friends,' Kizzy repeats.

CHAPTER NINE

Vic Leyton is leaning over Nigel Baxter's bloated body, her face close to the corpse's mouth. She inhales deeply, like she's sniffing a particularly delicious pot of stew bubbling on a stove. It's not a sight you see every day.

'Can you smell it?'

I don't fancy taking a whiff of dead man's breath but I move in closer.

Vic nods her encouragement.

'Well…?'

I look down at Nigel Baxter's bluish corpse and reluctantly lean over him. He's been opened up already, the ugly black blanket stiches form a Y-shape from his arms down to his pelvis, making him look cartoonish, like something from a Tim Burton movie, ghoulish and unreal. I try not to think about how the same thing must have been done to my Rachel, that she'd been cut open and her organs inspected and dissected before being stuffed back inside of her and sewn together. It had been bad enough witnessing her head injuries when I'd gone to identify her body. My once-perfect Rach broken and battered on a slab, like a piece of meat. I hadn't wanted the pathologist to touch her, to pull her guts out with scissors or slice her skull open with a scalpel to reveal her damaged brain. I didn't want them to stick needles in her to determine if there was alcohol in her blood (there wasn't, of course) or to check her urine and the bile from her gallbladder, and everything else they do as a matter of course. And I *really* didn't want them to open up her pelvis and expose her uterus, which was cushioning a small embryo that would've been our child. But it was their job to, it was a necessary evil. Just as this is. I don't suppose Janet Baxter is over the moon about it either.

It's a funny old calling, cutting up dead bodies and looking inside them for a living. I imagine it must take a degree of emotional detachment. But it's got to have some psychological impact, especially when it comes to opening up kids or horrific abuse victims, people who've been brutally raped and the like. To see the horror inflicted upon the human form day in, day out, that would take its toll on a person wouldn't it? I know it would affect me. Maybe it's why 'paths', as we call them in the business, have got a bit of a rep for being oddballs. Though Vic Leyton comes across pretty normal – comparatively at least. She's methodical, meticulous, highly professional and even has a sense of humour. Hell, you'd need one in her game I should imagine. She's not bad with a needle and thread either.

'Almonds,' I say, 'marzipany.'

She looks like she's about to give me a gold star.

'Ten out of ten, Riley,' she says. 'It's one of the first things I noticed.'

'And?'

'You tell me, Detective.'

I don't know Vic particularly well, not on a personal level anyway, but well enough to know that she likes to ask you the questions before she presents you with the answer, a bit like a teacher. She loves her job, you can tell, and she wants you to be as enthusiastic about it as she is, to play a little forensic pathology game in a bid to educate you. I go along with the game because it's to my benefit in the long run. Bombard her with too many straightforward questions too quickly and she turns into one of her subjects. She's quid pro quo is Vic.

I pause and she sighs. I'm not a model student I realise, and she senses my urgency.

'Mr Baxter here was in fact in rather good health, considering he was overweight,' she informs me, 'no visible signs of heart disease; lungs, liver, kidneys all functioning pretty well, no indication of decay. He wasn't a smoker, or a drinker really.'

I nod, not wanting to interrupt her flow.

'There were no other visible marks on his body, other than the incisions of course, no bruising, no contusions, no signs of struggle, defence marks or broken capillaries, no damage to the neck or head.'

I stare at Baxter's face and imagine how his voice might have sounded. He is, of course, expressionless; his mouth just a grim, thin line, yet somehow I see him as having been a rather jovial sort of chap. Janet certainly described him as such. She told me, among other things, that he was the regular Father Christmas at the local children's hospice each year for almost a decade and that the children adored him. And I can visualise him with a white beard and a red hat making all those sick kids happy with his jolly 'ho ho hos.' Depressing.

'We found minimal alcohol in his body. 0.01ml trace in his blood, urine and tissues – he'd had a glass or two but he certainly wasn't drunk when he died.'

Vic pulls back the paper blanket that's covering Baxter's body, exposing his right wrist. There's no longer any blood visible, just a thick black line that widens in the middle, a tear.

'This was the first incision made. Ventrical,' Vic explains, 'a little over 5cm in length and deep enough to completely sever the radial artery. It resulted in fatal exsanguination; the invagination process of the artery stumps is controlled by the elastic structure of the vessel walls and consequently the spontaneous arterial haemostasis is obstructed.'

I look at her, my eyebrows raised, and she smiles at me pitifully. Such a philistine, I know.

'He bled out, basically,' she says.

'How fast?'

'Not as fast as you might think, it might have taken up to an hour, though the depth of the cut suggests it may have been sooner, mercifully.'

I inwardly wince.

'And the same on the left side?'

She places his arm back underneath the paper blanket, gently I note.

'Identical, almost. Again, ventral cut, perhaps even deeper than the right, severing that all-important radial artery. The wounds are in keeping with the razor blade used.'

My own wrists begin to buzz a little.

'What's interesting however, is that our Mr Baxter here was right-handed.'

I know what she's going to say, but I don't say it for her. Like I said, Vic likes to show and tell.

'Seems slightly curious to me that he would slit his right wrist first, don't you think?'

I nod. She's building up to something, I can sense it.

'So, cause of death was blood loss then?'

I get a vague whiff of that scent again, almonds and perfume, a sweet mix, and suddenly I remember the smell of furniture polish in the penthouse, like someone had given it a spring clean even though the housekeeper had said no one had been in for twenty-four hours.

Vic Leyton stands back from the body and looks me in the eyes. She's got nice eyes has Vic. Big and brown. Lord only knows the horrors they've seen.

'Well, you would think that, but actually, no,' she says, pausing for dramatic effect, 'I don't think the blood loss killed him.'

I stay silent for a second or two, let her have her crescendo moment. I can hear my heart beating inside my chest, fuelled by the influx of adrenaline that's just dropped in my guts.

'Oh?'

She nods conspiratorially.

'There's something else,' she says slowly, accentuating the words. 'That smell, that almondy, marzipany scent you detected?'

'Yeah...'

'... Arsenic.'

I literally take a step backwards away from the table. The adrenaline has risen up through my diaphragm now and is attacking my galloping heart. I feel a little lighter.

'There was a little over 400mg in his urine, an exceedingly large amount, enough to shut his organs down pretty rapidly...'

'But I thought you said his organs were in good shape?'

'I did, and they were... but that was before he ingested a substantial amount of poison, Riley.'

My mind races.

'From the chocolates?'

Vic looks like she's about to give me a round of applause.

'Uh-huh. Arsenic poisoning tends to be a slow affair. Like I say, a substantial amount was needed to kill him, not least for his sheer size.'

'But I thought with arsenic... you're sick, you vomit the stuff up, the body tries to get rid and you can't breathe...?' Hey, I've seen a few Agatha Christies in my time you know. 'Indeed,' she nods, seemingly pleased with my knowledge on such a matter, 'which is why I wasn't all that surprised to find traces of chloroform in his blood too, around 21mg...'

'Jesus fucking Christ.' I realise I've said this aloud and hold my hand up in apology.

She dismisses my blasphemy with a faint smile.

'So basically, to sum up, Nigel Baxter was given chloroform to render him incapacitated, he'd already ingested arsenic, which was shutting him down, and *then* his wrists were slit open?'

Vic sighs at my reductive statement. 'I'd say, in my experience,' she flashes me a look that translates as 'which is extensive', 'the arsenic in his system caused his vital organs to shut down internally while he simultaneously bled out. One perhaps happened before the other, my guess is his organs. You're right about the vomiting though; had he been conscious he would've been violently sick, short of breath, heavily perspiring, but he wasn't… conscious, that is.'

I'm speechless for a moment as I stare at Baxter's body, his poisoned, incapacitated, slit-open, murdered body, and I envisage Janet Baxter's reaction as I inform her, duty-bound, of Vic's findings.

So, the good news, Mrs Baxter, is that your husband didn't take his own life after all! The bad news however, is that someone else did. Every cloud, eh?

I look at Vic and she shrugs.

'I'm sorry', she apologises in her clipped Home Counties accent, 'looks like I've made quite a lot more work for you, Dan.'

Her use of my Christian name, a first in all the years I've worked with her, jolts me out of the thousand-yard stare I'm fixed in, breaking through the plethora of questions that have begun marching through my brain like a platoon of Marines as I stare at Baxter's corpse.

'Yeah,' I flash her a sarcastic smile as I look up, 'Thanks, I appreciate that… *Vic.*'

There's a hint of a smile on her face as she begins the process of washing up, scrubbing the scent of death from her skin. I wonder, given her daily exposure to it, if she ever manages to get it off completely.

'Well, whoever killed him,' she says with her back to me at the sink, 'they certainly wanted to make sure there was absolutely no room for error. They clearly made sure they finished the job.'

I turn to leave then, taking one last look at the greying face of Nigel Baxter, aka Father Christmas.

'Didn't they just,' I say.

CHAPTER TEN

'Murdered!' Janet Baxter is thankfully sitting down on the couch in her home when I break the news to her, because I'm guessing if she wasn't, then she'd collapse right about now.

'No... no, that's not possible...' She says this with the conviction of a woman in deep denial, like I'm playing some perverse practical joke on her. She's shaking her head, like it's on a spring. Her face is pallid, almost translucent it's so white, and she has serious bags underneath her watery red eyes. Her skin looks angry from all the crying she's been doing and her short curly brown hair is unkempt, probably more so than usual judging by the family photos dotted about all over the large living room; she even looks quite attractive in some, in a mumsy sort of way.

I realise it's little consolation for her knowing that her husband didn't actually commit suicide, but was murdered instead. Talk about the lesser of two evils. I think she'd been hoping for an 'accidental death' verdict from the outcome of the post-mortem, though let's face it, opening up one's own wrists could hardly be described as accidental. But I sense that somehow it would have been easier to deal with if she'd heard her husband's demise was just one great big misadventure. Less of a stigma to live with, I suppose. And now muggins here has to go and ruin it all.

She's crying again but I don't think she even realises anymore. I sit down next to her on her expensive-looking leather couch. It's one of those 1920s style ones that you see in those gaudy overpriced shops on Edgware Road; the shops that have those life-sized porcelain tigers that all the rich Arabs seem to love in the window. It doesn't fit with the rest of the room somehow, which is understated and even quite tasteful.

'Can you think of anyone, anyone at all, who might want to harm your husband in any way, Janet? A disgruntled neighbour, a feud with someone at work that he may have mentioned, a builder he didn't pay on time? Anyone he mixed with you didn't like the look of? Any altercation, however small or insignificant it seemed… anyone at all?'

Janet looks at me with her round, tear-stained face and brings her stubby hands up to it. Her fingernails have been bitten to the quick and look bulbous and sore. That gets to me a bit. She shakes her head again, her lank curls wobbling – even her hair looks sad.

'Nigel was loved by everyone. I mean, in the all the years I've known him he's never really had a bad word for anyone, not one cross word, not an enemy anywhere… Well, not that's ever been brought to my attention.'

That's just it though, not 'brought to her attention'. I don't want to tell her about what cyber found on his mobile phone. She looks fragile as it is and I figure that kind of bombshell might just be enough to push her over the edge. But I have to. No choice.

'So, my Nige didn't take his own life after all… but… someone else did?'

This is more of a statement than a question, like she's having to say it aloud to process the reality. I think she's gone into shock again.

'Yes, I'm afraid so Janet.'

She gets up suddenly then, shuffles over to the sideboard and pulls out a bottle of Grouse. 'You don't mind if I…?'

I shake my head and hold my palm up. Frankly I wouldn't blame her if she downed the bottle in one hit. I'm glad she's fixing herself a drink because she's probably going to need it when I say what I've got to say. DS Willis, the family liaison officer who's here with me, is in the kitchen talking to the Baxters' children and at this moment I'm not sure which one of us has drawn the shorter straw.

Her bitten fingers are shaking around the glass as she throws some of the scotch back. You can tell she's not a drinker because she pulls her teeth over her lips and gasps. Her eyes are wide like an owl's. In fact, Janet Baxter is quite owl-like to look at. I imagine that's what she'd be if she was to be reincarnated as an animal.

'It was made to look like a suicide,' I explain, 'but actually Janet, he was… poisoned.'

'Poisoned?' she takes another sip of the scotch, repeating the word as if it were somehow perfectly normal.

It's a sad reality that the words 'poisoned' and 'murder' will now become part of Janet Baxter's repertoire.

'Yes… then he was incapacitated with chloroform and… and his wrists were slit open.'

She is staring past me, remarkably calm as my words hang in the air above her like poisonous gas. This is not a good sign in my experience. I'm expecting her to shout, or scream, throw the glass, collapse in hysterics. But she's statue-still, there's no emotion on her chubby face and it's worrying me. Like the calm before the storm. I shift a little closer towards her on the sofa.

'Janet,' my voice is so soft it's almost a whisper, 'Janet were you aware that your husband was having an affair?'

Her head spins round to face me and she widens her eyes. And it's funny, not funny *ha ha funny*, but funny *peculiar*, that you can tell a person their loved one has been brutally destroyed in the ugliest way imaginable and they'll somehow accept it, yet break the more common news that they've been getting their 'jollies next door', as my old man used to call it, and they act like you're speaking Greek.

'An affair! What are you talking about? Nigel wasn't having an affair!' Her features have changed: her brow is furrowed and her eyes have narrowed into dark slits. I am now officially the enemy.

'Janet, I'm so sorry, but we've reason to believe he was involved with another woman. There were messages on his phone, text messages to a pay-as-you-go number. We've yet to trace the owner of the phone but the messages are…' I pause. I've tried to say too much in one breath, the verbal equivalent of ripping a plaster off quickly. 'Well, they suggest he may have been sexually involved with another woman.'

Janet almost folds herself in half, her head falling into her lap. It's always the straw and the camel, this one.

I shuffle closer to her again, a little awkwardly. I want to comfort the poor woman but my judgement tells me not to touch her, that I'd likely be given short shrift.

'Janet, I'm really so sorry, I know this is not what you want to hear. I understand, believe me… I know how it feels to lose someone you love in tragic circumstances.'

She turns to me then and I see the pain in her eyes, the disbelief as she's faced with the realisation that she might not have known her beloved Nige quite as well as she thought. *Do we ever really know anyone?* I try not to think like this myself, because it's the sort of rhetorical question that can drive a person mad, that can make them very suspicious and miserable. And frankly, I'm more than enough of the former thanks to the job, and I don't want it to make me the latter. Otherwise it's a psychological mindfuck. You can overanalyse to paralysis and still get nowhere. Futile.

'You understand… oh YOU understand do you?' She stands up, her shapeless dress that's creased like a map falling mid-calf. 'You… you come here, to *my* house… with *my* children in the next room and tell me that *my* husband's been murdered, *murdered* and as if that's not enough, that he's been… behind my back…

you understand do you?' She turns away from me in disgust, unable to repeat the accusation for fear of it becoming her reality.

I dip my head but don't take it personally. It's difficult, but I've learned not to. I know Janet doesn't hate me, Dan Riley, she just hates what I'm having to tell her, what she's having to hear. She's wrong though: I *do* understand.

'I lost my wife two years ago,' I suddenly blurt out, 'she was killed in a motorbike accident.'

Janet looks back up at me. I don't know why I've said it, I never have before and I know it's unprofessional, but somehow this case has already got to me; *she's* got to me. Owl-like Janet Baxter, a nice, decent, unassuming woman whose world has been shattered. It's not my fault, I know this: it's the killer's. But I still feel a sense of responsibility towards her.

'She was ten weeks pregnant with our child. I didn't know at the time…'

Janet blinks at me. She looks apologetic almost instantly and I wish I'd kept my trap shut. It was a deliberate pity play and I hate myself for it.

'I'm sorry,' Janet says. Her voice has returned to normal now and I feel like a shitbag for using my own tragedy to stop her from hating me. I like to think Rach would've understood though. And I hope she'd be happy for me to call her my wife, because she was really. My soul-wife. We never needed a piece of paper though now, of course, I wish I had married her.

'It's okay, Janet,' I say quickly. 'I'm sorry I've had to tell you all of this, believe me. But I need to know what you know, so that we can catch whoever has done this to your husband. If Nigel was seeing another woman it makes things more… complicated, there's more likelihood for a motive you see, a disgruntled husband or boyfriend perhaps.'

I'm choosing my words carefully, consciously, I really don't want to explain to Janet that this also puts her firmly on the

suspects-with-possible-motives-for-murder list. I don't think I
need to. Janet Baxter seems harmless enough, but she's not stupid.
She looks like the type of woman who makes a nice casserole and
is happy sitting in front of the telly every night watching *Strictly*,
but that doesn't mean she isn't capable of murder. I've seen the
destruction affairs cause. Money and passion are the two greatest
motives for taking someone out.

'I was here, at home the night he died, the night of the mu—'
she can't finish the sentence, it sticks in her throat, almost visibly.
'You can ask the kids, oh, and our housekeeper, Chi, they will
tell you.'

I nod.

'We may need to see your phone records, Janet. Please understand this is purely for elimination purposes. The sooner we sort
that out, the sooner we can work out who did this to Nigel.'

She nods, her eyes closing in resignation.

'Of course, yes.'

I smile gently, gratefully.

There's a moment's pause.

'So, this other woman… do you know who she is?'

'We don't know yet Janet,' I say, 'it seems they made contact
over a singles' website; that's all we know at present.'

Her mouth forms a grim line.

'So he went looking for it then,' her words sound weighty,
almost as if she's suddenly realised that her life has been too good
to be true and everything she's ever thought and believed in has
been a lie. It's shitty to witness.

I don't answer. I don't need to.

I lightly touch Janet's arm as I stand to leave. She doesn't flinch,
that's something at least.

'If you can think of anything, Janet, anything unusual, anything about your husband's behaviour, something he may have
said… something he—'

'Wait!' Her short, stout frame bolts upright. She's remembered something. 'Hold on.'

She leaves the room and is gone for a minute or so before returning.

'This…' she says, 'Nige gave it to me a couple of weeks ago. He said a client gave it to him. I thought it was odd, you know, an odd thing for a client to have given him – a male one anyway, or at least that's what he said…' Her voice trails off sadly, like she's suddenly realised her whole marriage has been a sham. 'I don't know why he gave it to me… he knows, he *knew* I don't really like teddy bears.'

CHAPTER ELEVEN

She made an appreciative noise as his picture enlarged on her computer screen. Not bad, not bad at all. Definitely a contender. She smiled as she lit a cigarette, putting her feet up onto the desk and leaning back in the swivel chair. Florence's profile was proving popular. But then that was only to be expected. This guy was quite attractive though: thick, dark hair with the lightest first smatterings of salt-and-pepper grey around his hairline, good teeth, neat and straight – a must for boyfriend/potential baby-father material – and icy marine eyes, neither blue nor green but somewhere in-between. He was smiling, looking relaxed in a V-neck white T-shirt which showed off a light tan; it was probably a holiday snap, she decided. The ease of his smile and the hint of sexuality behind his eyes suggested that a woman had taken it…

His profile said he was forty-one, slightly older. She was looking for someone with a bit of experience, someone who knew his way round a relationship with a woman, someone with marriage and fatherhood credentials. The various dating and hook-up sites that she'd been using were the perfect hunting ground – such fun getting to be whoever you decided, so… liberating. She had procured Daddy Bear on Sugarpop.com, a site solely dedicated to older men looking for younger women to fuck and spoil – no harm in that, at least not for her. It was mutually beneficial as far as she could see. It had been fun phishing for victims, creating a new and different persona for each one of them. It had proved quite lucrative too, both sexually and fiscally. The men she'd come into contact with had been carefully selected for their usability, whether for sex, dining out, receiving gifts and trips, or in Daddy Bear's case – committing murder. She marvelled at how easy it was to have her every desire and whim fulfilled simply by using a few choice words and a decent profile shot. These internet dating sites were a veritable smorgasbord, a chocolate-box selection in which she'd taken her pick. She was careful not to stay on any of them for too long however; as soon as she'd ensnared her chosen victim, rinsed them of whatever particular need she required at that time, she would delete her profile and join another, careful not to leave a trail. But now she wanted an actual boyfriend, a much more discerning task. He had to be loyal, clean-cut, a nine-to-fiver; the type of guy who was as happy with a pizza on the couch on a Saturday night as he was in a crowded trendy bar... someone to go on weekend breaks with, date nights to the cinema and trips to the supermarket with. A *regular* guy, the perfect ruse. And this dude, forty-one, from London, certainly seemed to fit the bill. She composed a short message:

'Hi there, thanks for the wink, I'm flattered to receive attention from such a good-looking guy – few and far between on this site, that's for sure, lol! I'm Florence, I'm thirty-two and single, obviously (!) and I'm training to be an actress (Theatre Studies, mainly) for my sins, though I assure you I'm no drama queen. I don't get much free time but what little I do have, I'd like to spend getting to know someone. Could that be you? If you'd like to meet for coffee sometime then message me back. Flo x'

She re-read it quickly and feeling that it struck the balance between friendly, funny and complimentary, she fired it off.

'Florence' lit another cigarette. She was bored and restless and decided to knock Kizzy up. Their relationship had been developing rapidly. Kizzy had even given her a key to her apartment, entrusting her with it should she ever lock herself out again. Poor old damaged, downtrodden Kizzy, so trusting. Her caring, nurturing nature made her so gullible, she was looking forward to killing her and putting her out of her misery. She rang the bell. There was no answer and she felt a little deflated – she must be at work. She heard Kizzy's cat, Esmerelda, meowing behind the door. It was a whiny, mangy old thing with sticky eyes and bad breath, but Kizzy adored it. 'He got the house, I got the cat!' she'd laughed as she'd said it, like she was somehow resigned to having been so royally fucked over. *Loser*. She decided to let herself in anyway. It was cold inside Kizzy's flat and there was a warm biscuity smell of cat's piss lingering in the air. Esmerelda seemed pleased to see her, winding herself around her legs and purring. She roughly pushed the hapless animal away with her foot. She hated cats, this one in particular. It was just like its owner: needy and overly affectionate. Wretched thing was probably hungry.

She padded into the kitchen and opened the fridge, helping herself to a glass of rosé from an open bottle. She turned the radio on. It was playing The Verve's 'Bitter Sweet Symphony' and she cranked up the volume – she liked this tune and began to sing along 'it's a bitter sweet symphony this *liiiife*…'. She rifled through Kizzy's mail; it was boring, nothing but bills, oh but hang on, there was a letter from her GP. It was an appointment to see her therapist. There was a prescription slip next to it for Diazepam.

Sipping on her wine she walked into Kizzy's bedroom, all pink floral curtains, a matching duvet and valance, stupid wooden signs that spelt out pathetic affirmations like 'sweet dreams' and 'home sweet home' – as 'girlie' as it gets. It looked like the bedroom of a love-struck teenager. But then she knew Kizzy believed in love, *really* believed in it. They'd discussed it a few times.

'I've always only ever wanted that kind of love where, you know, you meet that one special person and they just *know*, you know? They know that it's just you and them against the world… together… A soulmate, unconditional love, where you don't know where you end and they begin… invisible threads that bind you… two minds and hearts intertwined… Love that knows no boundaries… the kind of love where that other person walks into a room and your heart skips a beat, even thirty years after you first met, one heart, one mind… Do you know what I mean, Danni-Jo?'

She'd nodded as she inwardly sneered. Poor, deluded old Kizzy. No wonder she'd been abused all her life; she had co-dependency written through her like a stick of rock. She had no idea this 'kind of love' did not and never would exist in hers or anyone else's lifetime and that her beliefs belonged only to the abused, the used and the hoodwinked. Such beliefs were pathetic, futile and idealistic. People lied about love; society lied, your parents lied, the films and songs and poems in birthday cards… lies, lies, lies. Love was simply a concept to hurt and manipulate people with. But the heart will swallow anything when it's hungry, will tolerate such treachery and pain just for this so-called emotion. But why should it? Love is not supposed to hurt. Real love doesn't, or so Kizzy thinks.

This was simply not a truth that Danni-Jo believed in. For some people 'love' manifested itself through pain and murder and hate. She hated Kizzy for having all these honest, positive, clean beliefs. Even after the atrocities this woman had endured at the hands of 'love', she still believed in it. *How could she?* Kizzy was insane. She was ill. She must be if she believed anyone would ever love her in that way. She was nothing more than a fantasist; eternally let down by her unrealistic beliefs. She *needed* to be put out of her misery, she really did. It had been and it would always be a lifetime of disappointment for Kizzy, despite her eternal optimism. Optimism. It could only lead to no good. Kizzy had not yet reached her own depths of despair; of that she was sure. And she didn't want Kizzy to: she would die with the idea of a forever love. A beautiful love that lasts forever. She deserved that. It was better that way for Mummy Bear.

But first, Esmerelda.

There was nothing of note in the bedroom, so she left it with a bad taste in her mouth. Taking the arsenic from the vial, she walked through to the living room, where the small kitchen area was, and opened the fridge. There was a tin of Whiskas cat food in the inside draw, half-full. She screwed her nose up as she took it out, the fishy stench turning her stomach as she sliced a quarter of it into the cat bowl, adding the arsenic and mixing it up with her own hands before replacing it. Esmerelda purred gratefully around her calves as she went to work on the cat bowl. She really was hungry, poor thing.

'*Bon appétit*, Esmerelda,' she said, as the cat's wet nose poked through her legs.

CHAPTER TWELVE

So, I'm looking at the CCTV, standing over DS Davis' shoulder. The overriding smell inside the incident room is of testosterone and the overheating plastic of computers, with overtones of stale coffee and sweat. It's a unique scent; the smell of hard work and dedication, not altogether pleasant, but I still can't say I don't like it.

However, as I lean over Davis I get a waft of her perfume. She's been going through CCTV from the hotel lobby on the day of Baxter's death, and from the twenty-four hours before and afterwards. This girl has been on it for almost three days now. I want and need these kinds of people on the force, the job, or whatever you want to call it, because her tenacity has paid off: she's found something.

'Talk me through it, Davis,' I say, though my causal tone belies the flurry of adrenaline that's clawing its way through my veins liked barbed wire. I've been in this game long enough to know how it often works; once you get that first break in the case the rest starts to roll. It's like a chain reaction, one lead leads to another and then another, and then… gotcha! But it's getting that first break that can be a real pisser. And you need it quick on homicide. It's human to have momentum at the start of a murder case, and it's also human to gradually grow despondent and weary when you don't catch a break. I've worked on cases that have gone cold, though admittedly, luckily, only a few, and while momentum wanes, the team doesn't want to give up. Giving up is the worst feeling in the world. It's failure. You failed to do your job, you failed to catch the bad guy, but most of all you failed the victim, their family and their need for justice. And I'm not about to fail poor old Nigel Baxter, or Janet and her kids for that matter. I'm not in the habit of failing.

'Well, boss,' Davis says, starting to run the video, and I can hear the triumph in her voice already, which sends my adrenaline further into overdrive. I have to grip the back of her seat, my face almost touching her hair. It smells nice, kind of herbal. 'I'm cross-eyed with this after going through it over and over again… At first look, I saw nothing of note, like twenty-four hours of nothing of note…' She clears her throat in preparation, 'The lobby was busy that day… really busy… but I couldn't put my finger on something—'

She's dragging it out and I let her because she's earned it. It's only fair. To deny her her build-up to the moment would be like sex without foreplay, and I'm not a one-way street kind of bloke, at least I hope not. Rach never complained anyhow and I'm sure she would have. She wasn't the type to hold back.

'Go on,' I say coaxing her gently.

'There were so many people coming and going…' she sounds retrospectively weary. 'But I've studied them all… every single person who entered that lobby that day and the following day… I know who came into that building and who left… and given the time line…'

Her hair is reacting to the static from the computer and the cheap plod carpet, and it's beginning to fly up a little in my face. I want to brush it away, but it seems too personal so I let it stick to my chin. I miss being personal with a woman… Maybe I will reply to that woman, Florence, on SadSingles.com when I get home and agree to coffee. Nothing to lose when you've already lost it all.

I swallow back the desire to spin Davis around in her chair so that she quickly gets to the point but like I said, she deserves this moment: she's worked for it.

'So, I think there's no one of note... at first,' she says, briefly looking back at me, her tired eyes shining. 'Baxter arrives,' she continues, 'there he is...'

She plays the video and I'm glued to it, the image burning through my retinas. I see his large bulk enter the lobby and I feel a pang in my chest because he looks happy, you know, it's in his step and demeanour, silly, fat sod. And that poor man, he has no idea he's about to meet his end.

'So,' Davis says, efficiently, 'he checks in around oneish... all good.'

The CCTV captures him heading to the lifts on the left-hand side. Then he disappears out of view.

'We lose him here.'

'Okay... ' I say with an intake of breath. I'm about to combust. Davis runs the tape forwards.

'And then this...'

I'm up closer to the screen now, nose almost touching it, like I don't trust my own eyes.

'It's 3.36 p.m. The blonde there, see her? She doesn't check in... goes straight into the lift... look... she's seen again on CCTV going up to room 106... the camera gets her, Gov.' Davis looks me fully in the eye then, grinning. This is ambrosia and we both know it.

'She knocks on the door and goes into the room...'

My heart is galloping like a bunch of wild horses and I'm pretty convinced Davis can hear it, even above her own heartbeat.

'And there's no CCTV of her leaving...?'

'Nope...'

I implode. 'Fuck me...' I swear. I actually swear.

'Or so I thought at first...' She's teasing me now; the performance isn't over yet, there's more. 'But then I kept running and re-running the tape because I figured, what goes in must come out.'

Logical thinking. I like it.

She rolls the CCTV forward and the whirring sound of the machine grinds on me. 'It's almost 4 pm… three quarters of an hour later. Look…' She points to the screen '… see the girl here…?'

I stare at the image: a dark brunette with a beanie hat on, dressed in dark jeans and a bomber jacket. She's wearing glasses.

'An accomplice?' I'm speculating now, because I don't know what she's getting at.

'No boss,' Davis says with an air of confidence that suggests she already knows something I don't. 'It's the same girl. It's the blonde.'

I stoop down and she freezes the frame, but I'm still not seeing it; she's nothing like Blondie, the hair, the get-up, it's all different.

'A disguise you think?'

Davis nods profusely.

'Exactly.'

I feel a bit deflated because, well, it's an assumption rather than fact, and in all honesty it's not even a very clear assumption if my eyes are anything to go by.

Davis senses this and says, 'It's her, boss, I'm telling you. This is the blonde who went up to Baxter's suite an hour earlier… and this is her leaving.'

I nod. I don't want to discredit what she's saying, rain on her parade, but I'm not entirely convinced. 'I suppose it's conceivable,' I say, 'she could've gone incognito.'

'She did,' Davis says quickly with a conviction I admire, even if I don't actually share it. 'We might have to get the experts in on this one; the facial recognition people. And

that means more time and money spent.

'What makes you sure it's the same woman? Am I missing something?' I keep the disappointment from my voice, or at least I try to.

Davis beams at me triumphantly, infectiously. I find myself smiling back at her. 'Yes Gov, you are.'

I shrug my shoulders and open up my palms.

'Enlighten me.'

'See that?' she says, rolling the tape on a bit and freezing it on a full frontal of the brunette as she exits the lift.

'See what?'

She places a neat short fingernail on the screen. 'The handbag,' she says. 'The tote she's carrying… it's exactly the same one as the blonde's.'

CHAPTER THIRTEEN

There's a knock at the door and Danni-Jo gives a small smile as she wraps the towel around her damp hair. She's been expecting it.

'Coming…' she sings, pausing for a few seconds before opening the door. 'Hey Kizzy, I was just wash—' She stops mid-sentence, 'Jesus, what's up… are you okay?'

Kizzy's swollen red eyes meet her own. She's whimpering slightly, emitting a primeval kind of mewing, much like her dead cat once used to, and her unruly ginger hair is even more dishevelled than usual. She's wearing a T-shirt with a photograph of Esmerelda on it, one of those cheap, nasty repro jobs you get done on the high street.

'What on earth's happened?' Danni-Jo ushers her neighbour inside with concern. 'You look terrible.'

Kizzy starts crying.

'Oh God, Danni-Jo, it's just too awful, just… just so awful.' She's inconsolable, almost unable to speak through her anguish.

'Let me make you some tea,' she replies, 'then you can tell me what's happened.'

Kizzy appears to relax a little bit, nodding as she loudly blows her nose into a tissue.

'I haven't caught you at a bad time, have I?' Even now, in her depths of despair, Kizzy is being considerate. 'I thought you might be at school… at your classes.'

'No, I have a few free periods this week,' Danni-Jo calls back, busying herself with the tea. 'We're doing Shakespeare at the moment… *Taming of the Shrew*. Rehearsals don't start until next week.' She marvels at how easily the lies fall from her lips, at how she is able to conjure them up without much effort or thought. She really should've been an actress; she is such an accomplished liar. Maybe after this, after she's completed her mission, she'll put this skill to good use, go into politics perhaps. She looks at Kizzy with pity, such sentimentality over a mangy old moggie. She needs to toughen up. Killing her cat was really an act of kindness towards her friend. A lesson she needed to learn. Kizzy would never have gone far in life because of her wretched sentimentality and her belief in love and inherent goodness. She's been setting herself up for a fall her whole miserable life. It's not the way it works.

'I was colouring my hair… I've got a date later,' Danni-Jo continues, pouring boiling water into the teapot. Tea tasted so much better from a pot. Her father had her make it this way. He would only drink tea made this way. Once she had cheated and used a teabag and he'd known instantly, though how he realised, she still did not know to this day. He'd punished her severely for that, in the worst way imaginable. She still had faint scars – they'd faded with time, but her invisible scars were as raw and fresh as if they had been inflicted yesterday.

'But your hair is beautiful the colour it is,' Kizzy hiccups. She's sitting in the armchair now, hunched up, her face a red mess from crying. Poor Mummy Bear, she's such a wreck. That cat had been the child she'd never had. And now it is gone.

'I fancied a change… "Honey caramel" the box said, but it's more of a dirty blonde I think. Dirty blonde…' she giggled, 'I wish! Still, if this date is as half-decent as he looks…'

'You have a date?' Kizzy's voice sounds low but well meaning, 'that's great. A girl like you shouldn't be on her own.'

Danni-Jo smiles. Kizzy's right – she deserves a nice boyfriend. She comes through to the sitting area with the tea on a tray and some Jaffa Cakes. 'Here,' have some tea and a biscuit… or is it a cake?' She shakes her head, 'hashtag first-world problems eh?' She laughs again, thinking how much she enjoys being around Kizzy. The woman exudes emotional pain, it's coming off her like sonic waves and it nourishes her empty soul. She really is going to miss her.

'I couldn't possibly eat anything,' Kizzy's voice is an anguished rasp, 'I had to call in sick I've been that distraught.'

She sits opposite her, pouring the tea carefully into mugs. It's the perfect colour – not too orange, just how her father liked it.

'Tell me what's happened,' she says gently, 'perhaps I can help?'

Kizzy shakes out her matted curls. 'No one can,' she says, 'she's gone.'

'Who… who's gone?' Danni-Jo is relishing the protracted punchline, waiting for it.

Kizzy's head falls forward into her lap. 'It's evil… just so, so cruel… I know it's him… He must've done it – that wicked, evil man.'

She's increasingly unsure of what her neighbour is talking about, and a light flutter of unease settles upon her intestines. 'Kizzy, you're not making sense… What are you talking about? Who's gone? Who's evil?'

'That bastard ex-husband of mine… I mean, I always knew he was wicked, I lived with him for seventeen years. I knew what he was capable of, but this? He knew how much I loved her, what she meant to me. I knew he could be vicious, but I never had him down as a murderer.'

Her eyes widen. 'A murderer?'

'Yes, that sick bastard… Well, he's not getting away with it – not this time. I've been to the police, they know what he's done…' Kizzy's hands are shaking around the mug of tea.

She's growing impatient with her now and she struggles not to let it show. 'Let me get this straight, you're saying your ex-husband has murdered someone?'

Kizzy nods slowly.

'Yes,' she says, placing the tea back onto the tray lest she spill it, 'he murdered my cat. That sick, twisted bastard poisoned my Esmerelda.'

CHAPTER FOURTEEN

Davis done good. And I'm buzzing so much that I feel like going for a celebratory drink. Only there's no time, got to strike while the iron is hot, while the blood is oxygenating my brain and keeping me focused. Blondie, by all accounts, is the last person to have seen Nigel Baxter alive. We need to find her and talk to her. I congratulate Davis on a job well done and send her home. She doesn't argue and I'm glad because I'm in no mood to pull rank, she's earned a good night's rest.

Her seat is still warm when I sit in it and run the CCTV back from the beginning, watching in slo-mo as the ice-blonde walks through the lobby of the hotel. She appears composed, in control. She carries herself with ease and a sense of purpose as she walks towards the lifts like she's on her way to a business meeting. She's wearing a mac, a neat black dress that falls just above the knee and high stiletto shoes, and she's holding a large bag, which Davis informs me is known as a 'tote' among the female fraternity. It's difficult to tell the exact colour, but it looks tan or brown. I zoom in on it. The gold lettering printed on the front of the bag says something: Kate something… Kate Spade, the designer's name presumably. It means nothing to me; I'm not really up on these things, though perhaps I should be. I make a note of it. The image is pretty sharp, high quality, which is what I'd expect from a prestigious establishment such as La Reymond. You get what you pay for and so I'm guessing that blondie here is somewhere around her mid-twenties to early thirties; she's slim and on the taller side of average, around 5ft 5in. She keeps her head titled down at a slight angle, which makes it difficult to get a full-face profile and makes me wonder if she wasn't fully aware of the fact that she was on camera.

The bag or 'tote' has a tassel on the zipper – it looks like leather – like a keyring-type thing, and there's something behind it that I can't make out. Davis called them 'bag charms' and said that they're trendy, that all the fashion-conscious girls have them. News to me. I wonder if I would've known about bag charms and their vogue moment if Rach was still here? Probably. But then I guess there's a lot more I would've known about if she was. Like how to be a father for one thing. Our kid would've been a little over two years old now if she – *if they* – had both lived. The 'terrible twos'. I hear parents discussing it wearily, the stage in a toddler's life where they're just finding their feet and starting to assert themselves, exploring this strange, mad, bad and wonderful world for the first time, and drawing their own conclusions. I wonder whether I would've been father to a son or daughter; what he or she would've looked like? I imagine the sound of their squeaky little voice as they call me 'Daddy'. Sometimes, my imagination goes into such vivid overdrive that I can actually smell my unborn child: the scent of their soft, fluffy hair, of innocence and unconditional love on their new skin. In my mind, in my fantasies, I see our child, mine and Rach's, doddering towards me ungainly, arms outstretched, a gummy smile containing a couple of tiny teeth as I walk through the front door. Some days it's a little girl: she's wearing navy tights and a cute pinafore dress, wispy blonde curls cradled at the nape of her neck. At other times I see a little boy, wearing soft jeans and a dinosaur T-shirt, his hair sticking up almost like a Mohican as he charges towards me and I scoop his tiny chubby body up into my arms. These imaginary memories that I've been robbed of are bittersweet, sometimes when they come, I find myself crying and smiling simultaneously. I like to think I'd have made a great dad. I know Rachel would've been a fantastic mum. She'd have been strict but fair, a little unconventional maybe but definitely fun. People have told me that I will go on to have a family, like they can somehow predict my future. I realise their words are well meant, but I'm not convinced any more. Just because you want something doesn't mean it will automatically happen. Janet Baxter wants her husband back home, where he belongs, alive and well with his family. And that ain't gonna happen. Ever. You see, I don't or didn't want just *a* family; I wanted *our* family. Mine and Rach's. So you see my problem? My thoughts are turning maudlin again and in a bid to counteract them I decide to do something a little reckless: I message the pretty girl back on that Sad Singles' website.

'Coffee sounds great. How about Saturday, Islington Costa on the high street, midday?'

I don't have time for small talk. I'll save that for when and if we meet. Lucky girl.

It's late now, gone 1.00 a.m. and the team have all left. I work well this time of a morning; my brain is often sharper when I'm tired and alone, no outside distractions, no white noise from computers and half-listened-to conversations. I print out the CCTV images and pin them to the whiteboard before grabbing a latte from the vending machine – we've all the mod cons in Homicide – and actually it's not a bad little cup of caffeine, all told.

I pick up the file on my desk that contains transcripts from Baxter's PC and read through them. The emails date back over five months, give or take, with the initial contact coming from a dating site called Sugarpops.com. I google it. The name kind of gives away the purpose of the site; it's self-explanatory really, a hook-up site for rich older blokes mostly looking for a bit of strange on the side to spoil, though the company's blurb attempts to mask the arrangement as something else entirely. It claims, quite ridiculously if you ask me, that there is no major difference between these arrangements and a traditional relationship, besides the 'agreeing terms upfront' part. I chuckle mirthlessly because as far as I'm aware traditional relationships don't include 'terms upfront', do they? It also claims that agreeing such terms eradicates 'misunderstandings' which have the potential to 'backfire' later. 'Backfire'. I like that. Well, it certainly backfired for Nigel Baxter. I wonder if the poor bastard mentioned 'not being brutally murdered' when he agreed 'terms upfront'?

The site is awash with people looking to engage in these 'traditional' relationships, and by the looks of things there is as much supply as there is demand. Young, beautiful women with handles like 'BabyCrumpet' and 'RampantRinser'; not exactly the type of girl you take home to your mum. There's criteria too, asking you to tick what you're looking for; 'spoiling', gifts/shopping/allowance/travel; whether chemistry is a necessity (yeah, seriously); relationship type, open/exclusive/semi-exclusive; duration of relationship and the terms you wish to agree. Romance eh? I shake my head in disbelief. It's not illegal but it is unsavoury. Just women and girls hunting for sad, lonely, unhappily married, deviant, rich old suckers who seem to get a buzz off lavishing them with presents in return for sexual favours – otherwise known as prostitution, a smokescreen for a knocking shop basically. In fact, I have more respect for brothel workers. At least that's a straightforward exchange between two mutually consenting adults. But the lines are blurred on Sugarpops.com; it reeks of desperation and self-delusion, of inadequate men who are fully aware they'd never get a look in at these girls without their fat wallets, yet at the same time it hints at the possibility of forming meaningful relationships. I'm regretting sending that message to Florence already. Perhaps I should set out some terms upfront myself, like, please don't die on me, yeah?

I scan the transcripts with a bad taste in my mouth. I'm not sure if it's the coffee or not. What I am sure of is that Baxter seems to quickly become besotted with someone who calls themselves 'Goldilocks'.

'*Oh Daddy Bear, last night was so amaaaaaazing! I adore my bracelet, you shouldn't have.*' I laugh out loud because quite clearly he most definitely should have, because that's the whole point as far as I can see. The email exchanges between them are short and un-erotic, though they do hint at sexual encounters having taken place. It seems they saved the filth for texts and in person.

I read through their myriad text exchanges, notably the highlighted ones of obvious interest that we gleaned from Baxter's phone. I search through the respective phone records between Baxter and Goldilocks, cross-referencing numbers; Davis has done most of the legwork on this already but I like to be thorough.

'Same time, same place DB? Then you can spank my naughty little ass before you fuck it hard.'

You get the picture. Speaking of which… I rifle through the file. Interestingly, given the base nature of the 'relationship' between Goldilocks and Daddy Bear, aka Nigel Baxter, there are no pictures of Goldilocks in person. Baxter sends plenty of his appendage with cringe-inducing captions like '*Daddy Bear has been thinking of Goldilocks,*' and '*This is all for you Goldilocks, come and get Daddy Bear's hard dick.*'

Hang on though, there's a number here, on Goldilocks' records, a number that isn't recognisable as Baxter's. It's hidden among them, reams of them: a solitary number. I scribble it down on a piece of paper. How did Davis miss this? I pick up my phone and dial it. It rings out. Damn. I try it again. Same thing. I chew my bottom lip absent-mindedly and begin searching through Baxter's phone records in a bid to see if it also shows up there too. It doesn't. Jesus, how did Davis miss this? It's not like her to be sloppy. I feel frustration rise up through my torso, my neck reddening. This will need to be checked first thing. I slam the papers down onto the desk and think of Janet Baxter; mild-mannered, middle-aged Janet Baxter with her matronly demeanour and visceral integrity, her total obliviousness to her husband's sordid secret life. I hope she never gets to know her husband in this way, so that she can preserve her memory of him as she knew him. Sometimes, I have come to realise, ignorance really is bliss.

So Goldilocks has been smart enough not to send intimate pictures of herself or ever sign off using a Christian name. The images she's sent are mostly of items on her shopping list – expensive lingerie and jewellery, handbags and perfume, dildos and eye masks. Forensics are already on it, but, hang on… *handbags…* I pick up the file again, flick through the reams of paper, pulling out the images of Goldilocks' shopping list and happy days! It's there. The handbag. The one Davis picked up on the CCTV. I put it to one side. Soon we'll have traced the IP address and the name of the phone's user. And now that we have a person of interest on CCTV I'm beginning to feel quite confident. Only I don't want to speak too soon, count those chickens before they've hatched. There's something about this case that's given me a sense of unease from the start, like I've already missed something, like there's a bigger picture and I can't quite see it. I select the clearest image of the blonde woman from the footage and open the blinds while it's loading to print. It's raining outside, highlighted droplets dance in the orange glow of the street lamp below. I can't shake the melancholy feeling that's beginning to soften the edges of my earlier euphoria. It rained the night she died. April showers.

I remember that Bob's big woollen duffle coat was wet and smelt of dogs. In truth I've always felt melancholic watching the rain, even when she was alive.

I hear the printer spew out paper and snatch it up.

Goldilocks. I look at her picture. Her face is obscured by a wide-brimmed hat. Only her lips and chin are visible, and certainly not identifiable on their own. The fact she doesn't want to show her face doesn't make her guilty of murder though. Maybe she's married herself and was trying to keep her identity secret? I can hear the defence already. It bothers me, but not as much as my black and unpleasant thoughts are beginning to – I can't will them back. It's my job to let them in. *Goldilocks* is a children's fairy tale, right? The story of a strange blonde little girl who enters the bears' home in the woods uninvited and eats their porridge while they've gone out for a walk. Maybe there's nothing in it, maybe she just decided to give herself an alias to cover her identity – and she's clearly blonde so that would make sense – and maybe Daddy Bear was a cute pet name that fitted poor old Nigel Baxter and it was just part of the whole sordid fantasy. But what's beginning to trouble my increasingly darkening mind is that there were three bears in the story of *Goldilocks*. Daddy Bear, Mummy Bear and Baby Bear. So I'm asking myself, and bear with me on this (no pun intended), what if this Goldilocks is living out some kind of twisted fairy-tale fantasy? She's already dealt with Daddy Bear, in which case Mummy Bear is next and after that...? An icy shiver suddenly runs down the length of my spine.

And then my phone rings.

CHAPTER FIFTEEN

'Dan?'

I recognise the voice but can't immediately place it. My brain is too muddied with CCTV images, teddy bears and things that don't add up.

'Touchy?'

She laughs. 'You sound disappointed, expecting someone else?'

I was hoping it would be the unknown number returning my call.

'You could say that, but don't take it personally,' I smile down the phone at her.

'It's been a while Dan… look, I'm sorry to call so late.'

Touchy is a journalist for the *Gazette*, a crime reporter. I call her Touchy because her name is Fiona Li, Fi Li, see what I did there? It's a shame we met in the circumstances we did really; she was covering the court case, Rachel's court case. She sent me a condolence card too if I recall, for some reason it stands out in my memory – it had Chinese writing and butterflies on the front. I never knew what the translation was in English. Anyway, I liked her.

'So, to what do I owe the pleasure, Touchy?' I ask, 'is this what the youth of today call a booty call?' I can hear her smiling.

'I only wish it was, Dan,' she says. 'I need to speak to you.'

'Well, I gathered that,' I'm humouring her, a defence mechanism, because something tells me I'm not going to like what she's got to say. 'So, what is it that can't wait till morning?'

There's a crackle on the line and I hear her clear her throat, like there's something lodged in it.

'The Nigel Baxter murder…'

My heart sinks. So the press has got wind of Baxter's suspicious death. Good times. 'How do you know we're looking at murder?'

'C'mon Dan,' she says, like I've insulted her intelligence, which I probably have, but I'm not about to start giving anything away, not yet, not when I'm still so in the dark. 'The boss has put me on it… I've been doing a bit of digging around…'

'I always said you should've been a copper, Touchy. So, should I be worried? Have you found something juicy to print that's going to compromise my investigation?' I scratch my head and get a waft of sourness from my armpit. I need a shower.

'I've been talking to a few of Baxter's colleagues, male colleagues and associates…' She pauses again. 'Seems like Baxter was having a little extra-curricular…'

'You don't say.'

She snorts gently. 'So you know about the blonde?'

My ears prick up. 'What about the blonde?' I'm tentative. You have to watch every word you say with journos. Off-the-cuff remarks are straight-up facts to this lot.

'The blonde Baxter was up to no good with—'

'Care to elaborate?'

'Dogging,' she says, 'Baxter and the blonde… they were identified up at a well-known spot near Hampstead Heath.'

Hampstead Heath, the geographical equivalent of a pretty girl with a slag's reputation. Such a shame the place is synonymous with sexually deviant activity because it's a very beautiful part of London.

'Identified?'

'Yes… a man fitting his description.'

Dogging. I think of Janet Baxter and close my eyes. Perhaps this unknown caller was a one of their associates, letting them know there was a meet-up.

'This had better be legit,' I say in my gravest tone, 'you know Baxter has – *had* – a wife and kids.' But my heart sinks because I know what's coming. The *Gazette* will report his death as suspicious, which is fair enough, and factual. And now that they have a whiff of a potential sex scandal, they'll be digging like JCBs on speed and they'll quickly follow it up with a sensational piece exposing Baxter's dirty secrets like they're dishing out dolly mixtures at a kiddie's party. They'll use words like 'allegedly' and phrases such as 'according to a well-placed source', or maybe even convince someone to go on the record.

The press, or certain members of it, are masters at getting people to cough. Like I said, the job's not too dissimilar. Still, it amazes me how people would rather talk to a journo than a copper, because when it comes to integrity there's no contest really. But it's all about the story to a lot of these editors; words on a page and how many people read them; they don't think about the ripple effect, the broken-hearted family or the shame it could bring upon them. And that's why I don't have too much time for them. If Nigel Baxter's been dogging, I can't see it's of any public interest. But it is of interest to me.

'Who identified Baxter?'

'It's come from a good source, Dan, I wouldn't be calling you otherwise.'

I don't bother to ask again. She'll never tell me. Journos protect their sources like they're their firstborn. 'You get an ID on the blonde he was 'allegedly' with?'

'Sadly not, but I got a description.'

I stay silent. Ironically, it was a journalist who once told me that silence is the best way to get someone to speak. Whenever there is silence, people will always be compelled to fill it.

'Platinum blonde, white, average height – 5ft 5in maybe – slim, verging on skinny, 'striking' is how it was put, late twenties to early thirties or thereabouts.'

Adrenaline, the sequel. Sounds like our girl. 'Go on…'

'My source thinks she may have been a HCB.'

'High-class brass? What makes him think that? Is he prepared to talk – to us I mean?'

She sighs. 'It's a *she* actually and put it this way, it takes one to know one… and you know better than to ask me that Dan.'

I raise an eyebrow. 'And you know the law,' I gently remind her.

She sighs again. 'It's possible she might talk, if it really comes on top, no pun intended.'

'Liar,' I smile.

'So, we're definitely looking at homicide then?'

'*You* should know better than to ask a closed question, Touchy.'

'Ah, c'mon Dan, work with me here. We go to print in a couple of hours.'

It's my turn to sigh. 'Yes, we're looking at homicide. All I can say for now.'

'Made to look like suicide?'

I want to trust Fiona Li but I don't, or rather I can't afford to, not yet anyway.

'Did she slit his wrists and then make it look like he'd done himself in? Any ideas for motive? Unpaid services perhaps?'

I shake my head. Truth is I'm as much in the dark as she is. 'We don't know yet, Touchy.' I'm telling the truth. 'I know as much as you do. But I'd like to talk to the source. Baxter could've been involved in a blackmail plot perhaps, maybe he saw something or someone he shouldn't have?'

'Maybe. The boss wants to go big on this, Dan… senses there's more to come and it's got scandal written all over it: well-to-do, middle-class married banker with a mistress and a double life – plus it's been a slow week.'

'He has a wife and two teenage children,' I say again, not wanting to picture Janet Baxter's face when she reads the newspaper and discovers her husband has been dogging with his mistress, but I can't help it. And I hate to admit it, even to myself, but I suspect Fi's boss is right and there's more to come… much more.

She's silent for a moment and I'm about to say my goodbyes and hang up, when she says, 'There's something else, Dan.'

I don't like the tone of her voice, it's uneasy.

'Okaaaay.'

I hear her draw breath.

'Can we meet?' she asks, 'I think this would be better in person.'

My blood runs a little cold. 'Care to give me a clue, Touchy?'

'The White Hart, tomorrow. I'll be in there at lunchtime.'

'Alright,' I reply tentatively, 'is this to do with Baxter?'

'It's important Dan,' is all she says, and I believe her.

'Okay,' I say, 'I'll be there.'

CHAPTER SIXTEEN

A bloody ancient cat, on its last legs anyway, yet she had still viewed its death as suspicious. That's paranoia for you. Danni-Jo had underestimated both Kizzy's love for the animal and her deep-seated paranoia. Now she had a potential problem. Seems the ex-old man used to threaten to kill the damn thing all the time and so naturally Esmerelda's sudden demise had set off alarms bells. Fuck. That was the thing about spontaneous decisions, you only got to think things through after the event, when it was already too late for regrets. Not that she regretted putting that mangy old moggy out of her misery, but she didn't want the police coming to her door sniffing around, at least not yet, that hadn't been part of the plan. Still, a few days had passed already and, as yet, there had been no knock at the door and Kizzy hadn't mentioned it again, so perhaps now that her initial anger had waned and spilled over into mourning she'd forgotten about it. Kizzy had been over at her apartment more than ever, bringing watery homemade soup and dropping by for cups of tea and sympathy. She had even planned a funeral for her furry friend, which Danni-Jo had agreed to attend, pleasing Kizzy no end.

'You're such a good friend,' she'd said, seizing Danni-Jo's hand as she stood in her kitchen, 'you've been so kind to me about Esmerelda.' Kizzy had put her arms around her and hugged her tightly. She felt warm and had a distinctive scent to her skin, a milky, vanilla smell that was both comforting and repulsive in equal measures. Yet it had felt oddly good, such close human contact. She couldn't remember the last time she had been hugged in a non-sexual way.

'I wish I'd had a daughter like you,' Kizzy told her as they'd snuggled up on the sofa together later that evening. 'Your own mother is lucky to have such a thoughtful daughter. Do you see her often?'

She'd dipped her head, allowing it to fall against Kizzy's shoulder and onto the softness of her old cardigan, a tatty old mustard thing that looked, and smelled, like it needed a hot wash, but was comforting nonetheless. She would tell her. What difference would it make? Kizzy would take her secrets to her grave.

'Mummy is dead,' Danni-Jo had said. 'She died when I was a little girl, when I was eight years old. I can barely remember her... Although sometimes I think I can hear her voice in my mind, but the smell of her skin and hair... her perfume... and the fairy tales she used to read to me at bedtime... I've never forgotten them.'

Kizzy had stiffened. 'Good God, you poor baby, I didn't realise... How awful for you.' She'd looked down at her with sad green eyes, her bushy ginger hair lightly tickling the side of her cheek. She began to stroke her hair gently. It felt soothing. 'What happened to her?'

'My father killed her,' Danni-Jo said and she felt Kizzy flinch beneath her.

'He *murdered* your mother?' her voice had risen a few octaves.

'Yes. But it was never proven. He never went to prison for it. One day, I woke up and she was gone, just like that. Disappeared into thin air. He removed all traces of her from our lives after that day. Burned every item of clothing and everything she owned. It was as if she never existed.' She could tell by Kizzy's tight muscles and body language that she was horrified.

'Oh Danni-Jo, that truly is horrendous, darling I'm so, so sorry. I had no idea you'd suffered such tragedy.'

'I knew he was responsible somehow,' she'd said, oblivious to her neighbour's sentiment, 'Mummy would never have left me. She loved me. I know she did. She told me.'

Kizzy started to cry then. She upset so easily, like turning a tap on. 'Oh, she'd be so proud of the young woman you have become, believe me,' she said, with genuine conviction, continuing to stroke Danni-Jo's hair, a little faster now.

'Yes, I think she would be—'

'And what happened to your father?'

She smiled thinly at the mention of him, although Kizzy would not have seen this. 'I became Mummy after she went, after he'd killed her… all her duties became mine…' Her voice had trailed off.

'All of them?' Kizzy's voice was shaky.

She had sighed in her lap, but largely for effect. 'I took her place in the kitchen, did the shopping, cooking, cleaning… I was my father's carer and when I was old enough to work I paid the bills.' Kizzy's stroking had ceased to be soothing now and had become irritating. She felt like cutting her hand off, imagining the look of shock and surprise on her face as arterial blood pumped relentlessly from the fresh stump.

'And what about in… in the bedroom?' Kizzy's voice had been a low whisper, as though she had not wanted to ask the question but felt compelled to know.

'Yes,' Danni-Jo replied, quite matter of fact, 'I became his wife in every sense.'

Kizzy seized her then, hugging her tightly and whispering, 'No… no… Oh Danni-Jo, I'm so sorry…'

For a short moment she had felt on the verge of tears herself. Aside from the therapists and the hospital doctors, she had never told another soul of the atrocities of her childhood. Lying in her neighbour's lap, it was as if she were discussing someone else. She felt no emotional response, no reaction, nothing. Just a cold emptiness that she couldn't quite understand. All she knew, now more than ever, was that she had to kill Kizzy.

CHAPTER SEVENTEEN

'I'm sorry I'm late,' she says, blustering in and taking her coat off immediately, 'had an issue with my neighbour, had to help her with something.'

It's been raining outside; I can see the droplets on her coat and a few in her hair, and I can smell it. I love the smell of rain; it evokes memories and makes me think of Rachel. But then again, most things make me think of her.

'Horrible weather,' she says, 'shitty in fact... I've just washed my hair as well.' She raises her eyebrows, which are a different colour to her highlighted hair and a bit bushy. I like bushy.

'Job well done,' I say, referring to her hair. I could've said it looks nice but that seems too schmaltzy and might make her think that she sounded like she was fishing for a compliment; which I don't think she was really.

She smiles though and it lights up her whole face.

'Been here long?'

I shake my head. 'Not at all. Can I get you a coffee?'

'Mmmm, please. A latte with almond syrup would be lovely.' She reaches into her handbag, shuffles around for her purse.

'I'm surprised you can find anything in there,' I joke and she laughs.

'I'm a woman,' she shrugs, 'I need things. Just in case—'

'In case of what?'

'In case of anything,' she says, still rifling around. It reminds me of the bag on the CCTV footage, large and bucket-shaped, a 'tote', Davis called it.

'Nice bag,' I remark, 'designer?'

'Thanks,' she beams, 'birthday gift a few years ago. A friend bought it back from Thailand for me. Although I admit I can't be positive of its authenticity. She brought a few back as gifts. I like it, I can get all my shi— all my stuff in it.'

'It's nice,' I say, 'all the rage aren't they – tote bags?' I wince. I sound like my father.

She shoots me a puzzled look.

'That coffee then…'

I make my way to the counter. I imagine she's looking at me from behind and I wonder what she's thinking now that she's seen me in person, aside from the fact that I'm a dickhead who makes small talk about handbags. I didn't think too hard about how to dress for our meeting simply because I couldn't; I wasn't granted the luxury of procrastination, which may be just as well. I've come straight from the nick and I need a distraction from the Baxter case, from teddy bears and forensic reports, CCTV and post-mortems and dead-end leads. I need a distraction full stop, either that or a real break. So, I'm dressed in my work get-up: plain shirt and black fitted trousers, a leather jacket; 'smart casual' I think they call it, whoever *they* are, the fashion police I suppose. I had a little brush-up in the bathroom before I left though, cleaned my teeth and splashed on a little Bleu de Chanel that I keep in a washbag in my desk drawer. It was the best I could do.

My heart's beating a little quicker than usual as I place my order with the overworked and underpaid barista. I'm not entirely sure why. I didn't get palpitations when I met Keen Shirl, or the other two dates, if you can call them that, so I'm wondering if subconsciously I already like her. She's very pretty. I remember the first time I met Rach; she worked in a restaurant around the corner from where I used to live and we joked about how we were so close to each other for all that time before our fates collided. It was a Thai place, Gili's, upmarket fast food really. And, like her, it's no longer there today. She was the head chef. My order had been messed up and she came out from the kitchen to apologise personally. That was Rach – professional, and never afraid to admit when she'd cocked up. I was kind of pissed off at the time because the service had been slow and then the wrong plate arrived… but the moment she came to the table, well, I'm not one to complain in restaurants anyway, unless it's really dire and unavoidable because chefs are a ruthless yet sensitive bunch of bastards and I'm always of the mind that they'll do something horrible to your food if you make a fuss. I suppose it was one of those 'eyes met' moments, the kind that only exist in films and books and songs, the kind of moment that you know doesn't really happen in real life. Only it does: it did. And it happened to me. I can't explain it any better than that and when I try to it sounds saccharine and stomach-turning, and I imagine people groaning and simulating sticking two fingers down their throats. But that's how it happened. I looked at her face and that was that. It's a strange feeling, when you meet a person and you know, somehow, deep inside on a level neither of you can comprehend, that you were supposed to love them. I knew all about strange coincidence and the irony of timing thanks to my job, but I'd never been big on fate, not until April 2003, not until that day. I made love to her that same night; I used to rib her about how quickly I got her knickers off, unfair of me I know, double standards definitely. But it was only playful and she knew it. Rachel wasn't promiscuous, her morals were fierce, her boundaries well established. It had just been the logical conclusion of fate. We met, fell in love on sight, went to bed together that same night and she never left. Neither of us were ever embarrassed about admitting it; we never censored our story. That's how it happened.

The harassed barista slides the coffee in my direction and I make an instinctive decision not to tell my 'date' what I do for a living. Not yet anyway.

She takes a mouthful of coffee, licking the milk foam from her pale lips. Her hair is different to how it looked in her profile photograph; it's darker, shorter perhaps. She glances at me from over her coffee cup with low eyes and says, 'shall we sack coffee off and go and get something stronger?'

CHAPTER EIGHTEEN

Her name is Florence Williams, but her friends call her Florrie or sometimes just Flo if they can't be bothered, because it's a bit of a mouthful, so she says anyway. Her mother named her after the Italian city where she was conceived. She's never been but hopes to go one day soon. She's thirty-two and was born in St George's hospital and grew up in Clapham, although her accent sounds more Home Counties than South London, something I'm glad about I have to say. Not that there's anything wrong with an accent, not least a London one, but I like a woman who speaks well. Rachel had a beautiful speaking voice, almost musical sometimes, and her laugh reminded me of wind chimes, tinkly and infectious. Rach laughed a lot, we both did, together. She was also great at accents. Brummie, Scouse, Manc, Scottish, Geordie, American, Australian, Irish, Welsh – you name it, she could do it. I'm crap at accents, my attempts always end up sounding like a weird hybrid of Indian and Australian.

Florence is good at accents too, particularly Irish and American, which she demonstrates to me perfectly, making me laugh. She's not afraid to make fun of herself either which is good because neither am I, although admittedly often it's by default.

She's training to be an actress, hence the accents I suppose, and I listen as she talks about the course she's taking and why she chose such a profession. She used to work as a legal secretary but got bored of the mundane nine-to-five and, feeling there was more to life, decided to follow her childhood ambitions. I tell her I think this is pretty cool and she seems pleased. Her nose wrinkles a little when she gets animated which I kind of like too. She's dressed well: dark-grey skinny jeans, which are low on the waist, with a slubby white T-shirt and a blazer-style jacket that has leather detailing on the collar. Kind of understated, but at the same time pretty trendy. The biker boots steal it for me though. I'm a sucker for a girl in a pair of biker boots. Rachel lived in hers. I particularly liked it when she wore them with pretty floral summer dresses; feminine with a hard edge. That was Rach.

'And so, what do you do, Daniel?'

Florence calls me Daniel and I smile because no one calls me that, not since Mum died anyway. Even the old man calls me Dan, or Danny when he's been at the whiskey and gets sentimental, which isn't often. Leaning onto her elbows on the table, she takes a swig of her Captain Morgan and coke. She's confident, but not to the degree that it spills into arrogance, and she's incredibly pretty. I reckon she could hold her own with the lads down at the station. Something about her face seems familiar, even though we've never met before. I'm taking this to be a good sign.

'I work in architecture, run my own business, it's not nearly as exciting as acting,' I say. I don't know why I lie but I do – I mean, architecture! Jesus, I can't even build a Lego model. I just don't want to run the risk of ruining anything because once I pull the copper card with a woman the atmosphere nearly always changes. I'm no longer Dan Riley, I'm *DI* Dan Riley, the copper, and then the questions come; cases I've worked on; grizzly details of murders and rapists. I don't want to talk about the job; I want to talk about her and myself a little. I want to be judged on the man I am, not the job I do, at least not yet. Rachel never asked me much about my work, she let me speak when or if I was ready and wanted to. It wasn't that she wasn't interested but she knew there was more to me, *to us*, than my job catching criminals. Even on difficult cases, the ones where you become emotionally involved, she wouldn't push for details, but she always knew when something got to me. She could sense my unease, it would be in her touch, a gentle stroke of the arm or face, she'd make a favourite meal, or put on a favourite CD or movie without saying a word. I loved her for that. For everything really.

'A city slicker eh?'

'Hardly.' I grin and she grins back.

'Are you into films?'

'Do bear's sh— do their business in the woods? My girlfriend used to say I was a walking encyclopaedia on them… bit of a nerd, you know, trivia and—'

'Your *girlfriend*?'

She's still smiling as she says it and I suddenly realise what I've said, how it must've sounded. I hadn't meant to tell her about Rachel. I'd not mentioned it to any of the others, not least on a first date, but I've slipped up now so feel I have to explain myself.

'I'm sorry,' I apologise, taking a sip of my Jack and coke; a single, I'm still officially on duty. 'That's not how it sounded, how it was meant to sound.' I'm digging a bigger hole for myself and she's watching me squirm with a mix of pity and humour. 'I don't have a girlfriend, hence why I'm sitting here talking to you…' I shift in my seat. 'Although obviously I have had girlfriends,' I add, 'you know, before… you're not the first,' I laugh, 'not that I'm saying you're my girlfriend,' I'm blathering. I feel tongue-tied around this girl and it's freaking me out a little. I mean, I ask questions for a living; I know how to talk to people, it's a big part of my job and I'm pretty good at it. I should be – I've had enough practice, yet I'm struggling here and I can feel myself beginning to blush like a complete dickhead.

She starts laughing and I join in, laughing at myself.

'I was engaged… I was with a woman for a long time, seven years, but she died. Two years ago. Motorbike accident.'

Well, that certainly killed the laughter.

'Jesus, I'm sorry,' she touches my hand with her fingers and I feel something. It's not sexual exactly but I'm guessing it's along those lines. 'What was her name?'

'Rachel,' I say.

'How old was she, when she… when she died?'

'Thirty-three, she would've turned thirty-four the month after she was killed.'

'Gosh, that's no age at all… Have you had any relationships since she… since she passed? Sorry,' she apologises, 'tell me to shut up if you think I'm prying, I… I just…'

'It's fine,' I smile at her warmly. People never know what to say when you talk about dead people, lost loved ones. Invariably they always feel they've said the wrong thing. But it's worse when they say nothing at all.

'Actually, you're the first person, the first person I've met on that website anyway, who I've told. It's not exactly a pleasant icebreaker, bringing up your dead girlfriend is it?'

She smiles at me a little sadly and now I feel like I'm fishing for sympathy, which I'm not really. I've had more than my fair share of that. I don't want pity, certainly not from a pretty stranger. She probably thinks I'm after a sympathy shag. Good God, this is going from bad to worse.

'And to answer your question, no… no I haven't. I haven't been looking to meet anyone really.'

She nods.

'So why now?'

It's a direct question yet I can't really give her a direct response because I don't exactly know myself. It should be easy to answer, but it's complicated in my head and I'm not sure I can articulate my feelings so I say, 'I'm lonely, I guess,' which makes me sound like a loser. But at least I've told the truth about one thing. 'I miss her, of course. But I miss company and conversation, listening to music with someone, catching a film, going to dinner, travelling, talking, laughing… you know the simple, everyday stuff…' I glance up at Florence and look down with a smile. She's silent so I look back up at her again.

'Touching,' she says, looking directly into my eyes, 'do you miss that?'

I swallow loudly. I'd not expected that but we're both adults so I suppose it's a fair-enough question.

'Yes,' I say, 'I miss that too.'

She holds my gaze for a few seconds and then my phone rings.

'Shit,' I say and cover my hand with my mouth and we both laugh nervously. 'Sorry.' I answer it. 'Shit,' I repeat. 'Touchy… Jesus,' I glance at my watch, 'it slipped my mind… I'm on my way,' I say, standing to leave.

She looks up at me and disappointment flashes across her face. This makes me feel pleased because I'm guessing it means she doesn't want me to go.

'Florence, I'm really sorry,' I say, 'I totally forgot that I have to meet a colleague… I was supposed to be at… at a business meeting,' I explain, badly. 'It's really important. Please forgive me? Can we do this again? Another time? Perhaps I can take you out for dinner to make up for it?'

She nods her understanding.

'Guess it's busy in the world of architecture.' She smiles and her face lights up again. She has a megawatt smile. 'Dinner would be lovely…' She reaches into her handbag and pulls out a pen before writing her digits down on the back of a receipt and handing it to me. Her fingers lightly touch mine.

'Great,' I say, 'it's a date… well, a date meaning it's… well, you know what I mean…' I wish I had my gun on me because I'd use it on myself right about now. It's safe to say that I'm woefully out of practice around women I'm attracted to.

'I'll be in touch,' I say, which makes me sound like even more of a prat, like she's at an audition or something and so I make to leave before I reach the point of no return. I'm guessing she's thinking the same thing because she says, 'don't call us, we'll call you, eh?' albeit humorously.

'Seriously, I am sorry,' I say, 'I was enjoying our chat. I'd really like to see you again, if you'd like to that is?'

She downs the rest of her rum and coke and meets me with those eyes again.

'Yes Daniel,' she says with a faint smile, 'I would like that very much.'

CHAPTER NINETEEN

'I took the liberty of ordering for you.' Touchy greets me with a wan smile and a Jack and coke. Another one.

'I'm on duty, Fiona,' I say, 'and I've had one already today.'

'Boozing on the job, Dan?' she smiles, 'that's not like you.'

'This has better be good. I cut a date short to meet you.'

She raises her brows. 'A date?'

I shake my head as she stands to greet me.

'Yeah, I am now officially one of those online singles statistics, dipping my toes in the lottery that is internet dating, answers to the name of Sad Sack.' I don't know why I'm being so candid with her; I haven't seen the woman in years and she's a journalist. But it feels oddly cathartic to tell someone.

She laughs wryly. 'Welcome to my world.'

'Ah, you too, eh?'

She shrugs.

'How else is a single mum who works practically 24/7 supposed to meet anyone these days? So, any good? The date I mean?'

'Well, because of you I now owe her dinner, so like I say, this had better be worth it.'

She smiles. 'It's good to see you, Dan.'

'It's good to see you too, Fi.' It is, actually. I give her a hug. She smells good. She looks good too. In fact, I'd forgotten how attractive she is. It's been a little over fifteen months since I saw her last, at the trial. 'And just for the record, there's been no one since Rachel. Not like that anyway.'

She releases herself from my embrace gently.

'You don't need to explain,' she says, almost shyly, 'I under-stand. And hey, I'm pleased for you Dan, you deserve happiness.'

'Well, let's not jump the gun eh? She seems nice, she's local and she could string a sentence together, so I guess there's potential there.'

We stand uncomfortably for a few seconds, it feels like longer and I smile at her awkwardly as we sit.

'So, how's tricks then? Still snouting for the *Gazette*? I thought you'd have been snapped up by the nationals long ago… or *The Sun* at least.' I'm ribbing her, albeit without any real malice because she's a good journo really, a decent crime reporter, and I suppose I saw bigger things for her future than the local gazette. Besides, I only take the piss out of people I like.

'Same shit, different day,' she sighs, sipping her drink.

She's a red wine woman. I can only drink red wine with a meal and even then it never really goes down well. A connois-seur I am not. But thanks to the old man I can order a bottle in a restaurant without looking like a total chump. He's a wine buff, bangs on about the stuff like it genuinely matters. I guess it does to him anyway, or at least it has since Mum went, 'passes the time, Danny Boy,' he says, though frankly I think it's just an excuse for him to get pissed.

'You know what it's like, Dan, you're so busy doing the job there's not much time to look elsewhere. Anyway, it suits me for now, if I went to the nationals then I'd never see Cody; I'd have to hire a proper nanny and then I could kiss goodbye to the extra money I might earn anyway; swings and roundabouts, you know?'

I'd completely forgotten that Fi had a young son but now she's mentioned him it comes back to me. She'd spoken about him during the trial, he must only have been a babe in arms at the time. I think I recall her saying the dad had done the off before he was born, decent bloke. I feel a little ashamed that I'd forgotten this; forgotten that other people were going through difficult times of their own back then.

'How is the little man?' I ask.

'Not so little any more,' she raises a neat arched brow. 'He's at preschool now. A right handful.'

I laugh, imagining his face and wondering if he has his mother's eyes.

'Jesus,' I say, 'time… it stops for no one eh, Touchy?'

She snorts softly. 'Ain't that the truth. And then one day you find ten years have got behind you…'

'… no one told you when to run, you missed the starting gun – Pink Floyd, "Dark Side of the Moon".'

Fi laughs.

'You haven't changed,' she says. But we both know I have.

'So,' I say, 'you wanted to see me… I'm guessing this is about the Nigel Baxter case.'

'Partly.' I hear caution in her voice. Makes me edgy.

'What can I tell you, Fi?' I ask. 'It's like I explained, there's not much so far, though your source might be able to shed some light… You think you can get her to contact me? Give me a name, something…? If Baxter is involved in a dogging ring, he clearly had more going on than a round of golf.' I decide to lay my cards on the table. Seeing Fiona in the flesh again has reminded me that I do actually trust her, or at least that I'm prepared to.

'Truth is Fi, we've got nothing. Look, off the record, all we've got is a platinum-blonde female on CCTV who was seen going into his penthouse suite, a brunette we can't identify leaving the hotel… a teddy-bear calling card, or at least that's what I think it was, a murder made to look like suicide and no motive. I've also got a sad, destroyed, middle-aged woman and two teenage kids without a father, who on top of their trauma are about to find out their dad was into dogging, which I'm sure will go down a treat with their mates at school. What do you reckon?'

She looks down at her lap.

'You know it's my job,' she says.

It's my turn to sigh.

'I hope this source is legit.'

Fi nods. 'She says Baxter and this blonde girl were only up at the site twice, or twice that she recalls anyway, and she's a regular, you know. She recognised his picture from the paper and got in touch. She's a brass, specialises in that kind of kinky stuff, got some very high-profile clients, politicians, celebrities, judges; she's got more shit on people in the spotlight than Armitage Shanks sees in a year. She could bring a lot of people down with her if she wanted to.'

'Hmm, I'll bet, saving it for her pension plan no doubt. Anyway, we're tracing the IP addresses and phone records,' I say, 'so I'm banking on a decent lead from there. If we get a name for this blonde, then the least we can do is rule her out.'

'Did he leave a note, a suicide note?' she asks and I ponder over whether I should answer the question and tell the truth, to a journalist.

I nod, leaning back against the bench.

'This is off the record, Touchy,' I'm using her nickname but my voice is earnest.

'*"My darling, I'm sorry for everything, please forgive me."* It was signed, "Daddy Bear".'

She blinks at me. 'You mentioned teddy bears earlier…'

'Yeah, but the wife never referred to him as Daddy Bear, or anything remotely like it by all accounts; she looked at me blankly when I mentioned the name… I don't think the letter was even written for her, although I think it was supposed to look like it was.' I'm shaking my head as if somehow all the jumbled-up pieces might fall into place with a bit of reshuffling. 'All very rudimentary, a half-arsed job, you know.'

'Why make a murder look like suicide if you wanted it to be discovered as a murder anyway?'

I open my palms. 'That's the six-million-dollar question, Touchy – and also what I'm getting paid for.' I cross my legs and tap my fingers on the table. 'A message maybe, fuck, I don't know. She wanted it to look like suicide for a reason though, staged it well enough to make sure it appeared to be at first, but even the untrained eye would've seen through it with a more thorough glance.' I tell her about the crime scene, the hotel room, the teddy bear, the towel behind Nigel Baxter's fleshy back, the absent flannel *and* the missing bath oil.

She's listening intently, but there's something bothering her, the way her almond-shaped eyes keep darting back and forth and avoiding my own, I can tell. Body language. It's as good as a confession sometimes.

'Blackmail?' she says, 'money?'

'S and M.' I snort. 'Sex and money, the two greatest motives for murder.' I lean forward again, 'Only I don't think it was for either, not in this case.'

Fiona looks at me; she has a little red wine residue around the upper corners of her mouth. Rach used to call it a 'tinto tasch.' I contemplate telling her but decide against it.

'So what then?'

I pause. 'I think we're dealing with a serial killer.' I've gone and done an Ed Sheeran: thinking out loud.

She goes to take a sip of her wine, but my revelation has stopped her in her tracks and she places it back on the table. I have this effect on women.

'*Serial Killer*? What makes you say that?'

I run my hands through my hair, grateful I still have some. 'This is off the record, Fi, you understand me? Print this and I'll come after you personally.'

Her eyes are shining like glass beads. 'Promises, promises.'

'I'm being serious,' I say, which oddly never sounds serious when you say it, but I really mean it. 'The girl, the blonde, who

I'm suspecting is the same blonde your brass pal saw with Baxter up on Hampstead Heath, well, they met on some sugar daddy hook-up site. Called herself Goldilocks.'

'Okay…'

I look at the Jack and coke in front of me. Tempting. Fiona is staring at me blankly.

'C'mon Touchy, surely you know the fairy tale? You must've told it to Cody before?'

'Yeah, course, but I don't understand… Oh, hang on.' I can visibly see the penny dropping by her expression. '*Goldilocks and the Three Bears!*'

'Yup,' I say, refraining from giving her a round of applause. 'The *three* bears.'

She finally takes a slug of wine. 'Oh Jesus, but that means… well, there was Daddy Bear… Mummy Bear and…'

'… Baby bear. Yeah, I know.'

Her face contorts. 'Fuck Dan…'

'Look, it's just a theory right now – something I'm thinking about. But we've got no obvious motive, not yet anyway. I don't think this was about money. There was cash in his wallet, and his Rolex was still there on the bedside table. This was no robbery.'

She audibly exhales. 'Well, I hope to God you're wrong is all I can say.'

'Well, it's been known.' But we both know that it's something I try not to make a habit of. 'I guess there's only one way to be sure,' Fiona says, which is exactly what I'm afraid of.

'I don't know, Fi, I don't like it. Got a bad feeling about this one…'

She slides her hand across the table and touches mine. I'm not expecting this, but I don't pull away. It feels strangely good and reminds me how much I miss human contact. *Touching.* I think of Florence then, her eyes as she'd said that word. Perhaps we'd be in bed right now if it wasn't for Touchy here. I don't know whether I'm grateful or pissed off. 'Dan…' She's looking at me nervously; her pupils are dilating.

'So, out with it then,' I say, sensing her apprehension. 'You said "partly" before, that you were here to talk about the Baxter murder, *partly*.' I glance at her hand on mine. 'Don't tell me you've been harbouring impure thoughts about me all these years?' I'm joking because I don't like the look on her face. Although to be honest if she did tell me that I wouldn't be too upset.

She's looking down at her lap again now, she pulls her hand away and tucks her black shiny hair behind her ears. I get a waft of her perfume. Spicy. Oriental.

'Craig Mathers,' she says.

My blood runs icy. His name does that to me. Instinctively I pull away and fold my arms across my chest.

'What about him?'

'He's been released… good behaviour apparently.'

I nod. I've been expecting it I suppose, knew it was coming. *Good behaviour*. Joke really isn't it? Released after serving half your sentence for 'good behaviour'. I'm sure most people can see the irony in that statement. The words 'murderer' and 'good behaviour' don't really belong together in the same sentence. You commit a crime, get sent down for let's say two years, as in Mathers' case, and because you keep your nose clean behind the door you're let out after serving less than half your sentence. You're actually rewarded for being good while you're serving time for doing something bad. Like I've said before: I believe in the justice system, but hey, I didn't say it isn't flawed.

'So, the bastard's going to get out and get his life back. Lucky him. Shame Rachel can't do the same isn't it?'

She casts me a downward look.

'I know,' she says, softly, 'I thought you should be aware… I got a tip-off from someone at the parole board.'

I don't really know much about Craig Mathers, just the basics, and that's deliberate on my part. I don't *want* to know anything about him: his family background; his friendships or relationships; whether his mates and colleagues thought him to be of good character, which incidentally they seemed to at the trial. And I'll tell you why. I didn't and *I don't* want to humanise him because then I might not hate him as much as I do. Because if I didn't hate him I would have to put that hatred somewhere else, and where would it go? Who was it who said, 'let no man take me so low as to hate him?' Was it Martin Luther King Jr.? One of them great people anyway. I'd like to think I could live by that statement, and I think I used to once, but when you lose the love of your life to a jumped-up little prick who gets behind the wheel of a car after ten pints and kills someone, it changes you. It knocked me sick to hear his family and friends gushing on about what a 'decent' and 'reliable' bloke he was in court, and how he'd never been in any real trouble before and was a 'responsible adult' previously of good character. I remember his father, who he worked with as a painter decorator and seemed like a credible, normal bloke – and he probably is – he had nothing but praises to sing about his 'hardworking' son. And yet I just didn't buy it; there was something in his eyes, it's always in their eyes. Eyes tell you everything you need to know about a person, it's a cliché but it's true. In Mathers' case they were small and black with nothing behind them. Evil little black holes. I wondered if I could love a son with eyes like that? But I never got the chance to find out, and maybe I never will now. So yeah, it pissed me off to hear about what a 'likeable' bloke he was, because he killed my girl. He changed my future.

'I'm sorry, Dan,' Fi says, 'apparently he's going back to live at his mother's address with his girlfriend. I just wanted to warn you, I don't want to upset you, I just thought… well, I just thought you'd want to know… that I'd want to know.'

I hold her glassy-eyed gaze for a moment as I let the words sink in, before picking up the Jack and coke in front of me and downing the glass in one.

'Thanks Touchy,' I say, as thoughts of exacting revenge run like a marathon through my mind, 'you're a pal.'

CHAPTER TWENTY

Florence entered her apartment, throwing her handbag onto the floor and kicking off her boots. She felt a little giddy, awash with endorphins; it reminded her of how she'd felt that afternoon in suite 206.

Daniel. She said the name aloud, allowing it to roll provocatively off her tongue. It even sounded like a boyfriend's name. In her mind, she replayed their brief meeting earlier that day with the eye of an observer looking in. Her body language, covertly sexual; his body language, hmm, more difficult to read, but that's what had excited her. Most men were so transparent, like panes of glass, but he had got up and left! He'd actually left her sitting there in the pub nursing her drink, to head off to some crappy meeting. Perhaps it had been deliberate; treat them mean keep them keen, isn't that what people said? Well, it had certainly worked because immediately she began fantasising about how life might be with Daniel in it. An architect's wife! They would attend posh dinner parties together and she would fraternise with other wives, telling them about how they had first met. That's what people do, isn't it, talk nostalgically about their first encounter? 'He stood me up in a pub – *and now look at us!'* She visualised them selecting soft furnishings together, bickering over curtain fabric and mattress thickness. She imagined Sunday morning walks and movie nights and eating pizza in bed. *Me and Daniel.* Normal, lovely Daniel who had to leave because he had a meeting. A meeting that was more important than their meeting. And the way he had been so candid about his girlfriend, how he had opened up to her, showed his heartbreak. He seemed so lost and lonely when speaking of her that it had actually given Florence a pang of jealousy. She wanted a man to feel that deeply about her too. And she decided that Daniel was going to be the one who did. Lucky for her that girlfriend of his was killed, eh? She wondered what she had looked like, if she was prettier, sexier. Perhaps she would do some investigating, search for Rachel on the internet, after all, her untimely death would've made the news wouldn't it?

There was something in their brief encounter, something she couldn't quite explain that made her want to laugh out loud. What was it? Whatever it was, it was the kind of feeling that made her want to listen to music and to hear herself speak – the kind where she wanted to dress up in front of the mirror and see herself as he would see her. She pressed the play button on her iTunes and began singing along to the Chris Brown track that blasted from the speakers. Then she ran herself a bath.

She had a hook-up tonight, a wealthy older man she occasionally saw whenever he was in London on business. He was taking her to dinner at Nobu, no doubt with a little trip to Christian Louboutin first. He had a foot fetish, this one, and during both of their prior meetings he had purchased her expensive footwear, which he liked her to wear naked while walking over his back. She felt indifferent to the obvious infliction of pain this caused him, but it passed the time.

Usually she would be looking forward to becoming 'Lara' for the evening: the sophisticated, bilingual, postgraduate Psychology student with shiny, black bobbed hair but tonight her heart wasn't really in it; her thoughts were preoccupied with Mummy Bear and, now, Daniel. Undressing, she slipped into her kimono robe and poured some Jo Malone bath oil into the water, a sweet-smelling memento, smiling as she watched it create an oily film on the water's surface.

Then there was a knock at the door.

CHAPTER TWENTY-ONE

The sight of the two uniformed police officers momentarily throws her and she instinctively wraps her robe tightly around her frame.

'Can I help you?'

'Hello, I'm PC Burns and this is PC Choudrhi. Sorry if we've caught you at a bad time. Can we come in for a quick chat?' The policewoman smiles but it doesn't reach her eyes. Her male counterpart remains expressionless.

'Yes, of course, please come in. I just need to turn the bath off, won't be a moment… Has something happened?'

They enter her apartment as she hurries into the bathroom reassuring herself that they're not here to arrest her; she'd be in cuffs by now.

'It's Danni-Jo isn't it?' PC Burns asks.

'Yes, that's right. Daniella, Danni-Jo to my friends, or DJ to the really lazy ones.' She grins. 'Can I get you both coffee, tea?'

'No, no thank you,' Burns says, 'we won't keep you long, Danni-Jo.'

'This is about Kizzy, next door' she says, 'about her cat, Esmerelda?'

'Yes,' Burns replies, taking a notebook from the top pocket of her shirt and beginning to write.

Bloody filth. Haven't they got anything better to do than investigate the death of a fucking mangy old moggy? It was a good job she didn't pay her taxes.

'She told me she'd died. She was so upset, poor Kizzy,' Danni-Jo explains, pouting.

'Poor Esmerelda,' Burns says.

'She loved that cat like a baby,' she says, 'bloody evil thing to do… I mean, what psycho kills a cat for God's sake?'

PC Choudrhi is looking around Danni-Jo's kitchen, just looking, but it's still making her uncomfortable.

'Karen has reason to believe that her cat was poisoned. Have you seen anyone unfamiliar in the building recently, anyone acting suspiciously, hanging around outside maybe?'

Danni-Jo sighs, padding over to the kitchen, allowing her robe to briefly fall open and expose a little thigh as she passes PC Choudrhi. She's not sure if he notices. 'No, can't say I have,' she says. 'But I'm not here that much anyway. I'm a student, I'm studying, and I sometimes work nights.'

Burns writes in her notebook.

'Where do you study, Danni-Jo?'

'ECL… Performing Arts, Theatre Studies, ever since I was a little girl I wanted to be on the stage. It's in the blood, my dad, he was an actor.' *Worthy of an Oscar.* She's oversharing and tells herself to stop.

'Love a good musical myself, went to see *Wicked* recently – absolutely brilliant.'

'Isn't it!' Danni-Jo agrees. Great. Burns is onside: panic over. 'I loved *Wicked* too,' she says. She's never seen it. Never intends to. She despises musicals, all that… *joy.*

'Did you see Esmerelda – the cat, often? I believe it was a house cat and it never left the building?'

Danni-Jo lights a cigarette as she begins to make coffee. It's what she'd normally do. Cigarette with coffee. 'I don't even think you're supposed to have them here,' she says, biting her bottom lip, 'I hardly saw it myself, just a few times when I popped round to Kizzy's for coffee and a quick chat, you know? Lovely little thing it was, very fluffy… We've become quite good friends since she moved in, me and Kizzy I mean, not the cat. It's so nice to have friendly neighbours, rarer than rocking-horse shit in London. I mean, the couple who lived there before her never said more than a hello to me.'

Burns smiles and nods. 'Karen says you have a key to her apartment, is that correct?'

'Yeah, she gave me a spare one when she got locked out once, had to get one of those emergency locksmiths out – cost her a fortune. That's how we first got talking actually, she locked herself out one evening… daft as a brush she is, but she's been so lovely to me, looks out for me, stops by every once in a while for a cup of tea, or a glass of wine.' Danni-Jo tops up her coffee from the freshly brewed pot. 'I don't know her very well, but like I said, it's nice, you know, to have friendly neighbours—'

'Have you ever had cause to use it? The key?'

She takes a sip of coffee, folds her legs up underneath her on the sofa and adopts a thoughtful look. 'No, not yet, thankfully. It's just for emergencies. In case she gets locked out again or something like that. She's a bit, well, scatty you know… in the nicest way.' She smiles affectionately.

Burns continues to scribble in her pad. 'Well, we're going to ask security to check the CCTV in the communal staircase, see if anyone entered the building who shouldn't have last Tuesday.'

Danni-Jo feels a flutter in her lower intestine. *CCTV.* In the staircase?

'Didn't know we had it in the staircase?' she says, genuinely surprised, 'I thought it was just in the entrance downstairs.'

'No, actually there's a small camera, hidden behind the big painting, just on the stairwell outside. It captures both these apartments' entrances. Didn't you know?'

No, she fucking well didn't! 'Really? Well, that's good… good for safety.'

'These are lovely apartments, Danni-Jo, and security is very important. The building's management company had it fitted, only recently in fact, after a suspected burglary was reported.'

She nods. She's still thinking about the CCTV, what it might have captured. How did she not know about the bloody CCTV in the stairwell? She glanced over at the small table by the front door, at the pile of unopened letters and bills. There was probably a notification letter in there somewhere... *stupid, stupid girl...*

Burns returns her notebook to her top pocket.

'I hope Kizzy's okay,' Danni-Jo says, sensing the police officers' imminent departure and standing to see them out, 'she's been through so much and this has been a real blow to her. And she was doing so well since her breakdown as well.' She moves closer to Burns, lowers her voice. 'Kizzy thinks her ex poisoned Esmerelda you know... she told me he was abusive, beat her up and all that, sounds like a right nasty piece of work, apparently he was always threatening to hurt the cat because he knew how much she loved it.'

PC Choudrhi is already by the door. He looks disinterested, like he's keen to leave. *Makes two of us*, Danni-Jo thought. 'I just hope it doesn't push her over the edge because, you know, Kizzy's been really kind to me, motherly you know, but I sense she's pretty fragile underneath it all.'

Burns nods like she's drawn the same conclusion herself.

'Yes, she did mention an ex-husband. We'll be looking into it. Thanks for your time, Danni-Jo, sorry again to have disturbed you.'

She smiles earnestly. 'Not at all... if I can help in any way whatsoever... like I said, Karen... Kizzy... she's been, well, like a mother to me.'

CHAPTER TWENTY-TWO

I don't even have time to begin to process the conversation I've just had with Touchy before my phone rings. I answer and turn the radio off. The self-satisfied tone of Chris Moyles's voice was getting to me anyway.

'Riley.'

It's DS Davis, Lucy Davis. And I suddenly remember I need to haul her up on that phone-record oversight.

'This had better be good news, Davis' I say, which is unfair I know, but my head's wrecked about Mathers' release and I'm not in the mood for surprises, *any more* surprises. Her slight reticence tells me I'm not going to like this.

'Tech have been in touch, boss. That IP address, the ISP says it comes from a coffee shop in West London. The geolocaters tracked it to a Coffee Bean place near Oxford Circus—'

'And…?' I close my eyes for a few seconds. 'Been on to them for CCTV?'

'Yes boss,' she replies and I picture her deflated, hunched shoulders as she speaks, imagining more hours, possibly days, of trawling through endless, mundane images that'll send her cross-eyed and losing the will to live. 'But…'

I don't like the 'but'.

'… But they've only had one camera working for the past few weeks, according to the manager. And I suspect when he said weeks he meant months.'

'Fuck it!' I exhale heavily. 'Okay, well, you know the drill. Any trace on the Bear yet?'

'Nothing yet,' she says, her voice disappearing along with my optimism.

'Keep on it.'

'Yes Sir,' she says.

'And the website – the hook-up site – Sugarpops.com? Please tell me that's thrown something up at least?'

'Fake ID. She used a bogus name, Scarlett O'Hara.'

I snort. 'Inventive.'

'Hmm, IP address traces back to the same coffee shop though, or thereabouts. So it seems we're dealing with the same person at least.'

'No shit on this one, eh?' I say, unable to disguise my irritation. Whoever she is, she's clearly been careful to cover her tracks and is savvy enough not to have used a home computer.

'Seems so.'

'I want Baxter's diary: his schedule, parties he went to, events he attended, all of it. Maybe the bitch bloody well knew him. Get Matthews on it,' I say.

'Okay, Gov. Oh, and the court order came through for the phone provider.'

'That's something at least.'

'We'll have a name and address soon.'

'Yeah, um, get surveillance on the coffee shop, yeah. And make sure those cheap bastards get their cameras in working order. I want to know everyone who goes in and comes out of that place, you understand, whether they have vanilla syrup, five sugars or they like it black, okay? She could still be using it as a base to operate from, so my guess is that she works or lives nearby. Oh, and the handbag, that Kate thingy designer one…'

'Kate Spade,' she informs me. 'Around three hundred bags of that particular design and colour were bought in the UK last year, but more were purchased online. There's also the chance that it's a fake, in which case—'

'Yeah, yeah…' I say, 'in which case we're looking for a hair in a haystack…'

I can almost hear the deflation in her breathing.

'Listen, good work. Go home, Lucy,' I say. Her bollocking can wait until we're in person. I prefer face-to-face when I have to pull rank. 'That husband of yours will place a missing persons' otherwise.'

She laughs softly, 'Thanks Gov. Goodnight.'

'Goodnight.'

I hang up and crank up the stereo. Badly Drawn Boy's 'Once Around the Block' is playing – the dude with the Bennie from *Crossroads* hat who won the Mercury Prize back in the 1990s and never really did anything else of note since. Well, nothing mainstream anyway. What was the name of his album again? I have it somewhere, haven't listened to it in ages. I make a mental note to find it. I sing along with the 'do, do do bahs' and 'bo be dos' in a bid to lift my mood; a desperate attempt to stop the words from penetrating my psyche and taking root there. And then I drive over to Mathers' mother's house.

CHAPTER TWENTY-THREE

'This is delicious,' Kizzy says, tucking into the plate of lasagne, 'such a treat, someone cooking for me for a change. I can't remember, I actually can't remember, the last time someone made me dinner.'

'You're so welcome,' Danni-Jo replies, topping up Kizzy's wine glass with more Prosecco and passing her the salad bowl. 'I thought you could do with cheering up after the week you've had.'

Kizzy pushes her fuzz of ginger hair from her face and takes another forkful of pasta. 'The table looks so nice,' she comments, admiring the silver candelabra. 'So thoughtful of you Danni-Jo, I really appreciate it.'

Danni-Jo takes a sip of her own drink. 'Did you hear anything back from the police? I'm so sorry I couldn't be more helpful… Did they pay your ex a visit or make any enquiries? They said something about checking the CCTV in the stairway.'

Kizzy shakes her head, her halo of hair wobbling into her plate. 'No, nothing… They haven't got back to me. I'm sure they've probably got much more important things to do than investigate the murder of my Esmerelda but…'

You'd think.

'… but you'd think they might just drop me a courtesy call, you know, let me know they're taking it seriously. I mean, I know she was poisoned, and I *know* it was him, that bastard,' her face contorts, 'it had to be.'

'But how would he have got into your apartment?'

She's playing devil's advocate – feeling confident enough to.

Kizzy replaces her knife and fork and sits back in her chair. 'I really don't know… perhaps this is his way of letting me know that he can break in. I was worried something like this might happen. If he has, found me I mean, then who knows what he'll do? Perhaps my Esme was a warning?'

She looks at Kizzy's plate, hardly touched. 'C'mon, you've got to eat,' Danni-Jo's voice is soothing, 'you can't let him get to you like this. This is what he wants, you in a state, not able to eat or sleep… upset and anxious.'

Kizzy guzzles more wine. 'I know you're right.' She tentatively picks up the knife and fork again. She's not hungry any more but she doesn't want to be rude, not when her kind neighbour has gone to such an effort. 'I'm sorry, it's not the food, the food is delicious, it's just me, Esmerelda… I'm frightened that he's back and of what he might do to me. I know what he's capable of.'

Danni-Jo reaches for her hand. 'Don't be frightened,' she says, reassuring her, 'you've got me, I'm here. I won't let anything happen to you.' She squeezes her fingers in her own, watching as Kizzy's eyes begin to fill up. 'You've been really good to me Kizzy, like a surrogate mother, that's what I told the police, that you've been like a mother to me. I'd never let anyone hurt you again.'

Her words seem to undo Kizzy completely and she makes a soft whinnying sound as she brushes away the tears streaking down her cheeks.

'Really? Is that what you said to the police, that I'm like a mother to you?'

'Yes, yes it is… and it's true. Now come on, get that lasagne down you, it took me ages to make – Jamie Olivier makes it all look so easy!'

Kizzy laughs. 'Well, you could give him a run for his money.'

There a moment's pause as they resume eating, the clatter of cutlery amplified by their silence.

'I will never have that now – a daughter – left it far too late.'

'Well, I only wish I had a mum to look after,' Danni-Jo says, 'so let's say from now on that you can be my Mummy Bear – and we'll look after each other.'

'I'd love that,' Kizzy says, giggling, 'Mummy Bear.' She feels a little light-headed, *must be the booze.*

Danni-Jo watches her from across the table, sad, pathetic wretch that she is, drowning painfully in her own lack of self-worth, grateful for the slightest morsel of affection; just so trusting and desperate. How horrible it must be to be Karen Walker, trapped in a world of perpetual fear and disappointment forever preceded by unrealised hope. She looks at her with concealed pity and contempt. *She understands.*

'We'll skip desert and go straight to Irish coffee, if you're not feeling that hungry,' she says, beginning to clear away the plates.

'I'm sorry Danni-Jo,' Kizzy apologises, 'I thought I felt okay, but Esmerelda…' her voice trails off, 'this has really got to me. I'm scared. Losing her like that – with her being murdered and everything… I went to see the doctor and she prescribed me some more anti-depressants. I'm cross with myself really because I thought this… I thought that moving here would be a new beginning for me, that I could start afresh, unafraid… I've spent my whole life being afraid.'

She understands. Danni-Jo goes to the kitchen and, smiling to herself, begins to prepare the Irish coffees. 'We'll have these on the sofa,' she says, 'I'll put a film on. Maybe that will cheer you up. I've got *Dirty Dancing* on DVD, I know it's your favourite.'

'Well, I'll drink this with you and then I must go to bed. I'm feeling so tired, unusually so,' Kizzy rubs her forehead with her hand, fighting with it. 'I'm sorry, Danni-Jo, all this effort you've gone to, as well.'

She dismisses the comment with wave of her hand. 'Don't be daft, what are daughters for?'

Kizzy looks at her then, almost lovingly, her head tilted to the side. 'I feel so lucky you've come into my life,' she says after a moment. 'It's like you were sent by the angels, do you know that?' The wine has really gone to her head.

Danni-Jo is glad now that she cancelled her evening with the foot-fetish freak. He'd not been best pleased about her sudden rain check but *c'est la vie*. She had much more important business to attend to.

'Look, if you're feeling tired then perhaps you should go lie down, get some rest? Tomorrow's a new day.'

She shows Kizzy out of the door. She's stumbling now, her movements jerky and erratic.

'I… I just feel so tired…'

'Nearly there,' Danni-Jo says, helping Kizzy as she struggles with the key to her apartment door, 'it's almost over.'

CHAPTER TWENTY-FOUR

Kizzy collapses on the bed inside her apartment. Her body twitches as Danni-Jo watches and waits. Anvil, plus the anti-depressants, Kizzy had ingested them in the lasagne and the Prosecco. She'd put more in the coffee too though it seems they weren't needed.

She's in a slumber now, the first stages, and Danni-Jo observes the room. Kizzy's apartment is almost identical to her own, only in reverse, left is right and vice versa, like a mirror. Kizzy's frame is lumped to one side on the bed. She still has her shoes on and she's fully clothed. Danni-Jo imagines her slipping into a dark abyss of sleeping pills and prescription drugs, and she listens to the weighty heaviness of her breathing as she disappears inside herself. She begins to undress her, folding her clothes neatly and placing them on the chair next to the bed. She's wearing latex gloves. Kizzy moans lightly as she strips her down to her practical underwear. Her eyes are closed, her limbs like iron bars. She takes a nightdress from her chest of draws and pulls her into an upright position, struggling a little to get the garment over her head as it rolls like a marionette's. *A puppet, that's what Kizzy is really, has been all her rotten life.* She removes her sensible shoes and places them on the floor next to her clothes. Silently, calmly, her own breathing low and measured, she begins to search for Kizzy's journal, the one she had found that afternoon when she'd had a snoop around. Finding it in the living area, she places it on the bedside table, open on today's date. There's no entry. She decides to flick through it and scans the previous day's pages. They're filled with despair over the demise of Kizzy's beloved cat. Words jump out at Danni-Jo, 'feeling so low', 'depressed', 'life's not worth living', 'how could he do this?' 'He's found me, he's after me again... I'm terrified'. She flicks through the pages, 'at least I have my new friend, Danni-Jo... she's been so kind to me. There are kind people in this world... people like Danni-Jo, she's invited me for dinner this week... I'm so happy to have made a new friend, she's restored my faith in humanity, a little at least.'

Danni-Jo smiles, genuinely touched.

She leaves the page open and goes into the living area where she sits on the sofa and lights a cigarette, blowing smoke rings above her, watching as they form perfect O's before gradually curling out of shape to nothing. She plays with the razor blade between her thumb and index finger, flicking it over between them, fascinated at how it catches the light from the window. She doesn't bother to draw the curtains; they're on the top floor, they're not overlooked by anyone, no one can see. Her thoughts are troubled once more by the potential issue of having been caught on CCTV entering Kizzy's apartment on the day she poisoned the cat. She's already told the police a lie: that she wasn't there. First thing in the morning, she would pay the building security bloke a visit and somehow get him to erase the past few weeks of footage. This annoying problem bothers Danni-Jo, but it's not enough of a deterrent to put her off returning to her apartment, leaving Kizzy to reach a deep sleep. She has a purpose now, a divine one. She owes it to Mummy Bear, poor unhappy Mummy Bear, a martyr to her own misery, a slave to her own delusions of goodness and hope. Danni-Jo can no longer bear to see her suffer in such a way, just like her own mother did. She *is* kind; Kizzy recognises this in her, just as her mother did too. And so she must, *must* commit this selfless act of kindness and put an end to her suffering.

Danni-Jo extinguishes her cigarette in the sink, pushing the butt down the plughole and running the tap. Kizzy is asleep now, comatose. She moves closer towards the bed and watches her breathing heavily for a moment, the rhythmic sound is almost hypnotic. Entering the bathroom, she opens the cabinet and takes out the selection of pill bottles inside, before emptying most of their contents into some toilet tissue. She saves a few, putting them to one side before flushing the paper down the toilet. Then she places the bottles haphazardly on the bed, and one on its side on the bedside table with the remaining few tablets spilling out of it. She removes the top from the bottle of vodka she's brought with her and empties half of it down the sink, before taking a few generous swigs herself, pulling her lips over her teeth as the breath leaves her body – she hates vodka, it's a disgusting tramp's drink, tasteless and spiteful on the throat, a means-to-an-end kind of drink, crass. She parts Kizzy's lips and pours a little of the clear liquid into her mouth. She begins to choke, a dry, retching sound emanating from her as she convulses. It's enough to cause an involuntary physical reaction, but not enough to wake her, not quite anyway. She moans and murmurs.

'Shhhh now, Mummy Bear,' Danni-Jo soothes her, 'we don't want a scene, think of the neighbours…'

Kizzy coughs, attempting to expel the foreign liquid that's burning into her oesophagus. Her eyes shoot open for a second, only to close just as quickly. She spasms, sits up for a fleeting moment and collapses onto her back. Her heart is beating rapidly.

Music; Danni-Jo decides she wants music. She replaces the bottle on the bedside table and goes to turn the radio on. Magic FM. It's playing Everything But The Girl's 'Walking Wounded'. She smiles at the appropriateness. This is a sign. She's sure of that. A *fait accompli*. She begins to sing softly underneath her breath, 'what do you want from me, you're trying to punish me, punish me for loving you, punishing me for giving to you…' She knows this song. She's heard it before. Her mother liked it. She picks up the razor blade that she's placed on the side of the sink and marches towards the bed. Kizzy's wrist is limp as she takes it in her hand before slicing it vertically. The blood hits her directly, sprays across her chest and lower face, a warm jet on her lips and chin. She isn't repulsed by it like she was with Daddy Bear. She wants this intimacy with Kizzy, with Mummy Bear. She doesn't flinch or wipe it away, but marvels at the warmth of Kizzy's life force on her skin, before taking her other wrist, holding it in her hand like a trophy.

But suddenly Kizzy buckles, her eyes shoot open and she gasps, a curdled scream comes from her mouth. *Oh no, Mummy Bear! Please don't fight it!* Kizzy's eyes open in horror. She knows something terrible is taking place. Quickly Danni-Jo pushes her onto her back and puts her hand over her mouth. Kizzy is awake, a look of despair and confusion in her eyes as she appears to realise the horror of her situation. But she's too incapacitated to fight – to prevent what is happening to her. She tries to call out but her voice is a paralysed, rasping silence instead. Kizzy slips back into unconsciousness.

'Now you were doing so well, Mummy Bear,' Danni-Jo says, 'I'm very disappointed in you.' She opens up her left wrist, watching as the blood rushes to the surface of Kizzy's thin skin. It drips onto the bed. 'It's okay now, Mummy Bear,' she says, soothing her, watching her body twitch and spasm, until eventually it is still.

CHAPTER TWENTY-FIVE

It's almost twilight as she comes out of her trance-like state. Danni-Jo realises, as the fog in her mind begins to disperse, that she has been laying on the bed for some time – possibly hours if the morning light is an indicator. She must've fallen asleep. Mummy Bear is next to her. She looks as though she too is sleeping; at peace, finally. She smiles gently as she observes her, on her back, wearing her nightgown, her ginger hair a mass of fuzzy curls stuck to her forehead. Her face is pale, or perhaps it's just the light coming from the window. She does not see the blood at first, although it is everywhere, all over the bed sheets, like a paint pot has exploded, random splashes making pretty kaleidoscopic patterns. It reminds her of those weird psychedelic films she's seen on TV, the ones from the 1960s where thin, androgynous-looking models stripped themselves bare and covered themselves in paint before rolling onto huge sheets of paper – all in the name of art, of course.

Danni-Jo stares at the wounds on Kizzy's wrists, open and raw, aubergine in colour, glistening, congealing. There's a bottle of pills next to her. She takes it and places it loosely – *gently* – in Kizzy's left hand, a new razor blade in the other. She feels rejuvenated as she does this, empowered by a sense of accomplishment. She has saved Mummy Bear's life; saved her from her inherent misery, from her disappointment in the human race, her perpetually abused positivity, and her hopefulness that happiness would be available to her if only she just tried harder. She had helped Kizzy achieve her peace this way: to reach her nirvana. No one could hurt her now. Her suffering was over and her work here was done.

Light-footed and headed, she walks to the bathroom and wraps the bloody razor blade in the quilted toilet tissue from the roll. It's imprinted with tiny Labradors, which Danni-Jo studies for a moment before flushing the blade away. She feels hungry and thinks about breakfast. Pancakes and maple syrup perhaps, or a waffle and Nutella, something sweet anyway. The thought makes her mouth watery. Suddenly she catches sight of her reflection in the mirror, her heavily bloodied face and hair, matted in dark clumps around her hairline. She doesn't recognise herself. The sight turns her stomach; she doesn't like blood, not her own, and she doesn't want to look at herself, but she begins to check her face with latex fingers for scratches or abrasions. There are none. *The blood, all that blood, it is not hers.* She must leave, quickly. Go back to her apartment and take a hot shower, begin the process of cleaning herself up – get some food inside her. Her stomach feels like her throat has been cut. She looks down at her blood-splattered slippers and makes a mental note to burn them; she'd treat herself to a new pair, some fluffy ones. Re-entering the bedroom, she picks up the small teddy bear she'd brought with her and places it on the bed next to Kizzy, rearranging it a couple of times until it sits exactly how she wants it to. Once she's happy with the juxtaposition, she stands back to admire the image, a rush of adrenaline almost making her dizzy as she smiles sweetly, her head cocked to the side.

'Goodnight Mummy Bear… I love you,' she says before turning to leave. But as she turns she thinks she sees movement, and she swings back round violently, air involuntarily leaving her body in a sudden gasp. *Kizzy's arm is twitching.*

CHAPTER TWENTY-SIX

She rushes to the bed, seizing Kizzy's offending appendage. Kizzy is gurgling now, small rasping breaths are escaping from her throat as she desperately clings onto life. Panic seizes Danni-Jo; a surge of violent energy causing her to focus. This wasn't supposed to happen. She grabs the pillow from underneath Kizzy's head and brings it down over her face.

'Stupid fucking Mummy Bear... Look what you've done... Look what you've made me do... You've ruined everything you selfish, stupid bitch!'

Kizzy can't struggle, not physically anyway, she's been bleeding out for hours, the life draining slowly from her veins. Fuelled by an influx of cortisol, Danni-Jo pushes the pillow hard onto her face, applying more and more pressure until Kizzy is still again. Her hands are shaking as she tentatively removes the pillow. She's half-expecting her to sit up or to struggle for breath again, but she's motionless. She checks for a pulse in her neck. Nothing. She's dead. *Really* dead this time. Pulling Kizzy roughly by her hair, she places the pillow back underneath her head and throws it down in disgust. Her moment of serenity has been shattered. Mummy Bear has ruined everything. She sits on the edge of the bed for a moment, gathering her composure, waiting for her breathing to regulate. Once her heartbeat begins to steady, she gets up and, without turning round to look at her handiwork this time, leaves the apartment, softly closing the door behind her.

CHAPTER TWENTY-SEVEN

Lime Basil & Mandarin. It's a nice combination: citrusy and earthy, unique and heady on the nose, which is probably why it's always stuck in my memory. The assistant in Jo Malone is all over me like a cheap suit, asking me who it's for, explaining the top notes of the fragrance and all of that business. It's wasted on me. She might as well be talking Lime Basil and 'Mandarin', literally. Clearly she's on commission and I feel a bit sorry for her, it must be a drag having to be so upbeat all the time in the hope of making a sale. Still, I feel pleased with myself because my gut, or more accurately, my nose, hasn't let me down. I checked with housekeeping at La Reymond and they gave me a list of all the complimentary toiletries that should've been in Baxter's suite that afternoon, only they couldn't be specific about the particular bath oil that had been used: the list simply stated 'a selection' of Jo Malone products. But I knew I'd smelt that smell before. Rachel used to have a candle with the same fragrance. She lit it occasionally, generally before we had people over because it made the whole apartment smell good. I remember commenting on it once and she told me its name. It was irrelevant at the time, words said in passing you know, but I must've logged it subconsciously, the name and the smell. Rach liked it for the scent of basil; as a chef she was into her herbs and spices. Cost a fortune these candles, she told me. And, the best part of one hundred quid later, I leave the shop realising she wasn't wrong. I buy the bath oil, and a candle – for Rach and for *our* apartment – and I know that when I light it I'll have to try to think about her and not Nigel Baxter's body in the bath. Now I think of it, I'm pretty sure I smelt it on my fleeting date with Florence too. I guess it's popular, which is great for Jo Malone – and pretty shit for me.

Craig Mathers infiltrates my thoughts as I leave with my purchases. I don't know why I went to his mother's house last night. I'm not entirely sure what I wanted to happen and with hindsight I gave myself a bit of a fright. I could feel the anger and resentment rising inside me like a thermometer as I made the journey, the sense of injustice that he, Mathers, is alive and breathing, that he gets to go home to his mother and father, to his girlfriend; he gets to laugh and eat and smile and sing and to make love, to be *normal* again. He gets to put the past behind him; he has the chance to start again, to forgive himself and move on. I imagine he already has – forgiven himself, I mean – and I imagine the things his family, his girlfriend, say, the reassuring words of love and support they give him: 'you've done your time, son, you've paid for your mistake, now it's time to start over, time to start living, to forgive yourself and move on.'

Well, I'm here to remind him; I'm here to make sure he *never* forgets what he's done, the lives his actions have affected, the ripple effect of my girl's death. I want Mathers to know that while his family may have given him absolution, I absolutely have not and never will. They say you dig two graves when you seek revenge and for the most part of my life I have agreed with this statement. But now, now I get it, the crimes of retribution I have witnessed, the natural human desire to hurt someone who has hurt you, destroyed your family, your life, your future. I understand what drives a person to even the score now. And I don't like it, I don't like the way it makes me feel, but I feel it nonetheless. Murderous thoughts enter my head as I make a sharp right; I imagine Mathers standing in the middle of the road, his rat-like features bleached out by my high beams, his forearm covering his face to protect his eyes as I put my foot down on the accelerator…

Mathers' mother's house was a fairly modest semi situated down a suburban cul-de-sac near Southgate. It was secluded and out of the way. A nice road I suppose, the sort of road a builder who's not done too badly for himself would live – the sort you'd expect. I had parked up by a tree a few houses down, making sure I had a clear view of the Georgian-style front door. There was a light on at the front, people at home. I stared at the house, unable to take my eyes off it for a second in case I missed something, what I don't know. I couldn't say how long I sat there, watching, waiting, but after a while a woman left the house. I didn't recognise her, but I presumed that it was Mathers' mother. Upon seeing her, I now remember her from the court case, a brassy-looking blonde woman who wore garish suits and heavy make-up, a bit 'Peggy Mitchell from *Eastenders*' I had thought at the time. She made eye contact with me once throughout the manslaughter case and I recall thinking how sad she seemed. We never spoke but I got the impression she was a salt-of-the-earth type of woman, a little coarse but kind, and that she was sorry; for me, for her son, for herself. This woman's hair was darker though, shorter maybe, which made me think it might not be the same woman. She had a dog with her, one of those English bulldogs with the eye patches and snub noses. She was across the street and I turned away, grabbed my phone and pretended to look at it until she passed. I checked my watch and realised I'd been sitting outside the Mathers' house for almost two hours. It jolted me back to reality and once she disappeared in the rear-view mirror, I started the engine and drove away.

On the drive home I gave myself a talking to and decided that I never wanted to see that man's face again, and that it was stupid and reckless of me to drive over there but it's a battle of wills between the cognitive dissonance I feel, a cerebral stand-off in my brain, literally, between good and bad. And I'm frightened it will be a battle to the death…

When I arrive back at mine and Rach's empty apartment after my pricey shopping trip, I run myself a hot bath, put one of those delicious ready meals that reminds me I'm alone in the microwave, and light the Jo Malone candle. I feel spooked so I decide to have a drink. I fancy getting drunk, blotting out my feelings, feelings that have led to thoughts – dark, black thoughts that are already taking me to places I don't want to go to. *Craig Mathers is a living breathing free man, alive and well, and Rachel's still dead.*

The apartment is cold and I switch the heating on. It's April, and that's kind of depressing. Rachel always wanted to live in a warm climate; we talked about it a lot. She fancied California; LA would've suited her down to the ground, 'right up my boulevard', as she used to say. Barefoot and bohemian, she was cut out for beach life and she'd have loved riding the open roads on her bike. I'd have struggled a bit more I think. 'I'll bring out the gypsy in you yet Danny Riley,' she'd tell me and I'd say I could be like that Ponchorello from *Chips*, riding up and down the highways. I used to love that TV show as a kid. I wonder if anyone else has noticed how much the actor who played him looks like Bruno Mars, back then anyway. A real pin-up was Poncherello. All the girls from my primary school had a crush on him and I wonder, a little miserably, as I pull the plastic off my processed shepherd's pie and pour myself a far too generous tumbler of neat Jack and ice, what he looks like now. I think about googling him, Poncherello, but then my phone beeps. It's Fiona mentioning how nice it was to see me today, which I translate as her wanting to know if I'm okay after what's she told me. She wishes me luck with the online dating too, which is good of her after spectacularly cock-blocking me today, or whatever it is the kids refer to it as these days. She says it will do me good, getting back out there. It reminds me to message flirty Florence. I suppose I should come good on my offer of dinner, although I have to admit – and this doesn't happen to me very often… I got the distinct impression she would've skipped dinner. I check the time: it's gone midnight. Too late to send a text. According to 'Rachel's Rules', as I used to call them, women would consider messages any time after 11 p.m. to be a booty call. I liked her rules; they made sense. How much I wish I could've lived a lifetime by them. I would have abided by every single rule.

I decide to message Flirty Flo tomorrow instead. I doubt she's waiting up for my call anyway. Still, as I get into the bath and start on my Jack I can't help thinking about the fact I haven't had sex in almost two years. My body is screaming out for it, well, a certain part of it is anyway, not wishing to be crude. But although I joke, I do miss the touch of a woman; skin-to-skin contact, soft hair resting on my chest… it's not just the animal act, I miss the intimacy too. Yet as much as my physical needs are screaming out to be heard, my mind keeps silencing them. Because I know, deep down somewhere inside of me, *I know*, that if I was to touch another woman, even without any deep emotional connection to her, a part of me would be letting Rachel go. And realistically, I wouldn't really want to sleep with a woman I didn't feel a deep connection with; it would be like betraying Rach even more. So I'm fucked – or rather, I'm not fucked – whichever way you look at it. I guess I'm just not ready, and it scares me that I might never be. So I masturbate, I have to relieve the pressure somehow. It's only been in the past few months that my libido has returned, a gradual trickle, a pull I'm unable to ignore but which makes me feel guilty and grim. I don't want to feel turned on without her, I don't want to come alone. I think of her as I go about doing what I do; I imagine her skin against mine, her intimate scent and how I felt inside her. As I close my eyes, I visualise my fingers on her, holding her thighs while she's on top of me, looking down… Her breathing is heavier, her small breasts gently bouncing, her nipples stiff as my lips make contact. I'm close to coming now, I feel the familiar sensation in my stomach as it builds, guiding me towards it, and I look up at her face, at those big wide eyes and thick lashes, the smattering of freckles across the bridge of her nose… 'Mmm, mmm, yeah…' her noises get me there and as I come I imagine looking up at Rachel again, but this time her face has changed slightly, her voice too, 'shall we get a hotel, Daniel? Do you want to fuck me, Daniel?'

It's not Rach anymore, it's Florence… Florence Williams.

I'm still for a moment afterwards, I guiltily wipe the vision from my mind and place the Jo Malone candle on the side of the bath; afterwards I add a little of the oil to the water, not too much; I don't want to smell like a tart's handbag as the boys down the nick say. Nigel Baxter comes into my thoughts now; I don't want to think of him either but I do, I can't help it. Baxter betrayed his wife, poor, unsuspecting, loyal Janet; he gave in to his most base carnal desires and this subsequently led him to his unknowing demise. Murdered in a bath, just like the one I'm in now. Dance with the devil and your feet get burned, as my dad always says.

The Jack's gone to my head already so I take another mouthful as I sink into the warm oily water. Baxter wasn't killed for money; his bank account hasn't been touched and his statements show no unusual or unexplained withdrawals. He wasn't being blackmailed, which would be the obvious motive, given his alleged penchant for deviant behaviour. I think of the bear again, its little black eyes shining like beads. The killer's calling card. *Goldilocks*. She left it there, as many killers do, for a reason. *But what?* If it wasn't for money to blackmail the poor bastard, then why?

I'm relieved when I hear Rachel's voice again: 'Sometimes Danny, there is no why.'

CHAPTER TWENTY-EIGHT

Delaney has already kicked off the briefing as I enter the room and I nod at him to continue. I can't quite put my finger on Martin Delaney. It's not that I don't like the man, or respect him because I do, on both counts. He's a tenacious young copper and thus far has proved to be an efficient number two but there's something about him I don't fully trust, not like Davis, I trust Lucy Davis, yet I'm no more familiar with her than I am Delaney. Davis is a tenacious copper too, yet somehow I feel like she's on my side, like she's working for the good of the team. Something about Delaney makes me think he's working for the good of himself first, like he wants to get noticed, more of a glory seeker. Perhaps I'm being unfair but I feel there is something disingenuous about him. It's subtle, but I sense it, the consideration in his words, making sure even his smallest triumphs are claimed. I can't knock his contribution to the case so far though, credit where it's due. But still, I'm keeping a clandestine eye on Delaney because something tells me I should. Something tells me he's watching me closely too, waiting for me to slip up.

'Keep going with the handbag, yeah, Davis?' He nods at her, his tone authoritative.

'I'm tracing purchases made in the UK in the past year but there are enough fakes out there to keep eBay in business for the next ten.' She addresses me first and call me pedantic, but this gives me a tiny slither of satisfaction.

Delaney goes to speak but I get there first. 'Anything from Baxter's colleagues? Any beef, affairs, bad business deals, anyone with a vendetta?'

Harding shakes her head.

'Nothing boss… but there is something interesting you need to know…'

'I'm all ears, Harding.'

She takes a visible breath, her diaphragm expanding. 'That rogue number you found… the phone records between Baxter and Goldilocks…'

'Yes, the number that was missed.' I shoot Davis a look. 'The once you missed, Lucy,' I say, calling her out. I'm not partial to a public slaying but I need Davis to know she's cocked up and never to do it again, but she stares at me expressionless, like she doesn't know what I'm on about. 'The phone records,' I address her, 'when you checked them you missed a number; one lone number that was on Goldilock's record, buried among the rest.'

Davis looks at Delaney and opens her mouth to speak. I watch the silent exchange between them.

'Well,' Harding continues, 'the number was registered to a Janet Baxter.'

I feel my guts drop into my sphincter. *Janet.*

It's my turn to take an audible breath. 'Right, well, this gives a slight spin on things,' I say, as matter of fact as possible, because I don't want to believe, to even think, that Janet Baxter has anything to do with her husband's death, not just because I like her and I feel empathy for her, but because it would mean that my instincts are wrong. But I suppose it would, could, make sense, the spouse is always the first person you look at. Only Janet has at least three alibis and it certainly wasn't her on the CCTV footage coming out of Baxter's hotel suite the day he was murdered – unless of course she'd had a particularly outstanding week at Slimming World and managed to lose at least 50lbs in a couple of days, and grow a few inches taller. That's not to say she isn't involved though. This could be a collaboration, the blonde a stooge to lure him in. She could've found out about his penchant for prostitutes and paid one of them to knock him off; it's feasible, there's motive, it would make sense, only it doesn't. That was no act she put on when I told her of her husband's death. I'd bet my house on it I'm that sure. But instinct doesn't stand up in court, so all avenues must be thoroughly explored. I need to speak to Janet.

'Maybe she found out he was seeing someone else, boss,' Harding says, 'sent his mistress a warning?'

'Perhaps,' I say tentatively. 'We'll need to see the phone. And who's been onto the website… that hook-up site, Sugarpops or whatever it's called?'

'Bogus ID,' Baylis reminds me. 'They've been pretty helpful though. Trying to trace an IP address. Don't think they want the negative publicity.'

'I'm sure.' I raise an eyebrow. I suspect our Goldilocks, like millions of others out there, has a string of false identities, setting up fake accounts and deleting them as quickly as she's made them up. Literally anyone can make up a fake profile these days and it's patently clear that's what most people do. It's kind of the whole point really: anonymity, a society of nameless, faceless people who exist behind computer screens.

'Please tell me forensics have thrown up something?' I scan the teams' faces but there's not a single sparkle between them.

'Not yet boss,' Davis says, keeping her tone upbeat.

'Nothing?' I say flatly, 'not a fingerprint, a hair, not a trace of foreign DNA?'

She shakes her head and I hope my own face isn't reflecting the ones who're blinking back at me because it's my job to keep the fires burning.

'Let's look at what we have got then', I say. 'The bear, unlike the bag, is unique; someone had the little bastard made specially;

it's one of a kind. I want every shop assistant who works in Steiff Bear shops across the country spoken to; check the records of every franchise and every online outlet. Something will come up with the bear, I feel sure of it. We've got CCTV of a potential suspect; a female with blonde and, later, dark hair – it's the same woman by all accounts. Someone saw her that day in the hotel – we need to find them.'

They're making notes. Delaney is silent.

I pause for a moment. 'I've had a tip off, *legit*, that Baxter was into the dogging scene and there's a witness who claims to have seen him with an unidentified blonde woman up at Hampstead Heath. I want the names and IDs of everyone involved in that particular unsavoury pastime, every high-class brass who might be involved brought in and questioned.'

'Sounds like one for you, Baylis,' Harding gives a wry smile.

'Takes one to know one,' he shoots back.

Chris Baylis and Emma Harding, they make a good duo, always bantering, albeit in good humour. It's a running joke – Baylis and Harding, like the soap brand, you know?

'So do you think Janet Baxter found out about it, the dogging, boss?' Davis says, 'it could've pushed her over the edge.'

'It's possible,' I say, non-committal, 'but it doesn't explain the blonde, or the bear, and Janet's alibis checked out. Listen, this woman, this 'Goldilocks' exists in real life, not just in the fantasy world she's created for herself and therefore she can be found. She's not a ghost, despite everything pointing to the contrary. And she's all we have right now, our prime suspect for a murder made to look like suicide with no apparent motive, our *only* suspect,' I emphasise, perhaps incorrectly because now I'm thinking things about Janet Baxter that I'd rather not consider. She's not telling me everything, and it's time she did. 'I realise what we have isn't much to go on, you don't need to be Sherlock Holmes to work that one out, but it's a bloody good start people, so let's get our backsides in gear and not let a few hurdles stand in our way okay?'

'Yes Boss,' they say, almost in uniform. They seem a little more geed up now but we all know we're struggling.

To add insult to injury and my burgeoning sense of inadequacy and failure, Ken Woods collars me as I make my way past his office. I pretend I haven't seen him, forcing him to get up from his comfy seat and call my name from the door. He's not best pleased.

'I'm sorry, Sir,' I say as I pop my head around the door. 'It'll have to wait until I get back.'

He flashes me an indignant look. 'We need to talk, Dan,' he says in that gravely, serious tone of his, 'I just need five minutes.'

Davis is hovering in the corridor by the coffee machine.

'I can't Sir,' I say, 'I'm late for a funeral… Nigel Baxter's funeral.'

He rolls his eyes skywards, though I'm not sure if it's for my benefit or his own. 'My office. As soon as it's over.'

'Yes, Sir,' I nod.

I pass Davis as she gets her first and by no means last, I'm sure, cup of the day.

'Can I speak to you, Sir?' she asks, her voice tinged with apprehension.

'Can it wait, Davis?' I reply, trying to keep the edge from my tone. I'm still a little pissed off about her oversight, but my initial anger has passed.

'Not really boss… it's about the phone file, the number.'

I sigh. 'Look Lucy, I'm prepared to—'

'It wasn't me Gov, I didn't check the file.'

I blink at her, think about grabbing a coffee myself. I need a hit of something to shift my mood. 'I assigned *you* the task Davis,' I say.

'Yes, you did,' she nods, 'but Delaney pulled me off it, said he wanted to go through the records himself, put me back on CCTV… Delaney checked the phone records.'

I'm still staring at Davis, absorbing her words. So Delaney pulled rank on her, and then let her take the rap for his oversight, didn't speak up, no *mea culpa*, just threw her under the bus.

'I didn't want to oust him during the briefing boss,' she says, solemnly, 'that's why I didn't speak up.'

'So you took the fall for him instead.'

She shrugs.

'Good of you, Davis.' My transference of anger is rapid. So, Delaney is the snake I suspected him to be. That close eye I have on him has now just expanded into a pair. I don't like buck-passers. And now I don't like Delaney.

I nod. 'I'll deal with it, Lucy,' I say, using her Christian name for sincerity. 'And you can drink that coffee in the car,' I gesture towards her plastic cup, my anger dissipating.

'I thought you were going to Baxter's funeral, Sir?' she says.

'Yes,' I reply, 'and so are you.'

CHAPTER TWENTY-NINE

If there's one thing I hate more than suicides that turn out to be murder, it's funerals. I owe it to Janet Baxter and her kids to be here today though; I want her to know that I haven't forgotten her or her husband, and that I acknowledge her suffering, even if she's been hiding stuff from me. Plus, funerals can often be quite telling events business-wise; grief can reveal secrets. In some cases, as I've seen before in my career, killers will even attend the funeral of their victim, giving them some kind of twisted gratification in the process I suppose, a chance to relish the grief they've caused and bask in the glory of pulling the wool over people's eyes. While I'm pretty convinced Baxter's murderer will give today a wide berth, I can't altogether rule it out. And given that we're no further along in the case I can't afford to chance it either, even if it means digging out the suit I wore to Rachael's funeral and bringing back my own painful memories.

Janet Baxter looks almost unrecognisable at Our Lady of the Rosary church in a pretty corner street behind the hub of Chelsea. Her face is pale and gaunt and the pounds have dropped off her. The heartbreak diet. I imagine that Janet Baxter has struggled to shift the extra weight her entire adult life. I noticed a diet-club sheet pinned to the fridge in her kitchen during one of my visits, one of those Slimming World things where you spend your entire day counting the points of everything you put down your neck, causing you to obsess about food constantly – which seems to defeat the whole object to me. A healthy diet, exercise and lots of good sex, that's what Rach used to say. I get the impression that none of these things factored into Janet Baxter's life with Nigel though, at least not in the end. In any other circumstance I imagine she'd be thrilled to have shrunk a couple of dress sizes.

She thanks me for coming and musters up a smile for Davis who, admittedly, I have brought along with me for the gentle touch. Nothing sexist about it, just fact. She's got a nice face has Davis, unassuming to the point of being cute. I figured this would be more palatable than mine and Baylis' old grids. *The Gentle Touch*. It makes me think of Jill Gascoine as Detective Maggie Forbes in the 1980s' TV series. She reminds me a little of Janet actually, Jill Gascoine, all that curly hair and the whiff of '80s nostalgia. Come to think of it, Jill Gascoine's husband dies in the first episode, leaving her to juggle single parenthood and life as a working copper. Funny how life imitates art sometimes.

There's a healthy turn out of people for Baxter's send-off. Family of course, friends and colleagues. He was a well-liked and well-respected man by all accounts.

It's a Catholic ceremony. Long and drawn-out. Janet is practising, though she says her Nigel only ever really 'went along with it' and wasn't especially religious. Catholicism is all about forgiveness and I wonder how she's getting on with that after discovering her husband's many indiscretions. Davis and I sit at the back of the church. No one turns to look at us. I pay attention to the mourners and listen intently to the eulogy that Janet and her children give. It's difficult to hear them talking about their 'beloved daddy', sharing intimate stories and recollections of him throughout their young lives. But it's Janet's words that threaten to undo me, the catch in her clipped voice as she recalls the time she first set eyes on 'the one' all those years ago and her anecdotes, bittersweet memories of intimate moments and life events they'd shared together: the times she told him she was expecting; how he put the greens on backwards at the birth of their son and she'd had to help him out of them between contractions and puffs of gas and air – 'he never could dress himself properly,' she recalls. Private moments in time witnessed only by them as husband and wife, partners, parents, lovers and friends.

I tell Davis that I'll meet her outside and she briefly registers surprise swiftly followed by understanding. This is my first funeral since Rachel's. They bury Baxter in the ground. Rach was cremated. 'Scatter me somewhere beautiful, Danny', she'd once said during one of those conversations you have as a couple about the event of your death. A death you never really, truly consider. 'Somewhere like the ocean, near a beach, out in the elements, sun and sand and sea – so that I can become part of the waves, forever turning in eternal sunshine…' she'd said. So I did. Rach wasn't religious, though she did appreciate elements of Buddhist philosophy. I scattered her ashes in a remote place called Moonstone Beach in a small town named Cambria, California. It's peaceful and tranquil, little visited by tourists but stunning nonetheless with grey sands and melancholy surroundings. We stopped there once, on a road trip from LA to San Fran and she commented on its unspoilt natural beauty – words I would use to describe her too. I know she would be happy with my choice. *I hope she is.* I remember painstakingly debating the exact point at which to sprinkle her remains from, clamouring up craggy rocks and assessing the views. Her remains felt gravelly to touch. The term 'ashes' is misleading because what you receive after cremation isn't soft powder, but a kind of coarse grey material with the texture of fine gravel: the ground remnants of human bones.

It's difficult to watch, from a distance, as Nigel Baxter's shiny black coffin is lowered into the earth, into the hole that's been dug for him: his final resting place. In direct contrast, Rachel went through a curtain in a gleaming white casket decorated with pink and white roses and lilies. She liked pink flowers; in that sense she was a girl. My girl.

I remember watching Rach disappear through the cremato-rium curtain to the sound of John Lennon's 'Imagine'. It was no mistake that the first line of the song says, 'Imagine there's no heaven…' I wanted to run after her, I had to physically stop myself. I didn't want to watch my girl as she slowly descended into the 1,000-degree furnace to be turned to dust, or gravel. But I had no choice. Just like Janet Baxter doesn't now. I have to turn away. And that's when I see her, the woman, standing by the tree.

CHAPTER THIRTY

She's young, early thirties max with brunette – almost black, hair. She's standing back from the mourners and observing the burial from a safe distance behind the tree. She doesn't want to be seen but it's a bit late for that now. I nod at Davis. 'Keep an eye on things,' I say making my way over towards the woman, but she's already clocked me and turned on her heels in the opposite direction. I quicken my pace and catch up to her.

'Excuse me, Miss?'

She gives me a quick sideways glance but keeps up her pace. Seems she's not in a talkative mood. She's younger up close, mid to late twenties I'd say, but hard-faced, like she's seen things she shouldn't have.

'I noticed you hanging back by the tree… Are you here for Nigel Baxter's funeral? You a friend of his?'

She doesn't say anything for a few seconds. 'I wouldn't say friend exactly.'

'What's your name?'

'What's it to you?' she shrugs.

'Detective Riley,' I say, reaching for my ID. 'Would you mind stopping a moment?' She's wearing high heels – noticeably high – and her black dress is low-cut and looks expensive. She's got brass written through her like a stick of Blackpool rock.

She rolls her eyes a little. 'Look, Nigel's just someone I… someone I knew, alright… I wanted to pay my respects, that's all, not a crime is it?'

I shake my head. 'Not at all… Miss…?'

'Leah,' she sighs, 'Leah Carlton.'

'Miss Carlton… I'm taking it you weren't formally invited here today. How do you know the deceased? How *did* you know Nigel?'

She takes a cigarette from her handbag and lights it, there's a smudge of lipstick on her teeth.

'Dunno really, we were just mates…' She starts walking again, slower this time like she's resigned to my presence.

'Come on, Leah,' I say, 'you'll have to do better than that. Was he a client?'

She purses her lips, blowing smoking forcefully from them. 'I liked him – he was nice, Nigel. Friendly, kind… and very generous,' she adds.

'When did you first meet?'

'Two years ago, through a mutual friend.'

'An escort agency?'

'Nah… yoga class.'

'Which agency?'

She looks at me. Her eyes are almost as dark as her hair and I try not to think about the things they may have seen.

'I work for myself. I'm my own boss.'

'So he contacted you through an advert?'

'Look, what is this? Are you going to pinch me for attending a funeral?'

'No,' I say, 'but we can always go down to the station and do this there if that suits you more?'

Leah snorts quietly. 'Yes,' she says reluctantly, 'through an advert in a magazine.'

'Which one?'

'Women's fucking Own.'

'Did you visit him regularly?'

'About once a month.'

'How long for?'

She shrugs. 'I dunno, a little over a year, maybe fourteen months… He was a regular until—'

'Until what?'

'Until he found a new girl, I suppose. I don't ask questions. It's not part of the job description if you know what I mean.'

'So he was a regular until he starting using someone else?'

'Yeah… I was kind of upset he'd found a new favourite actually, I grew quite fond of him in the end. Like I said, he was a nice old bloke – easy to be with, quick, pretty normal really… compared to some of them.' Her voice trails off. 'I was sad when I heard what had happened to him, that he'd died and everything.'

Leah uses the word 'old' to describe Baxter. He was forty-seven.

'Do you know her, this new girl he started seeing? Did you ever meet her?'

'Some blonde,' she shrugs again, 'dunno what she had that I weren't giving him though. He seemed quite happy with my services until she came on the scene, stuck-up bitch.'

My heart's racing. 'You met her?'

'No, not exactly, saw them together in a hotel in Knightsbridge one time. Well, not together exactly. I was there with another cli… a friend.' She flicks her cigarette onto the gravel and doesn't bother to extinguish it.

'How did you know they were together?'

'I saw her go into the suite,' Leah says, 'looked like a right toffee-nosed cow… I was staying in the one opposite that night. Pissed me off a bit because he was my bread and butter you know, Nigel.'

'Would you recognise this girl if you saw her again?'

She looks unsure. 'Probably not, maybe? I dunno… She was just some blonde, white blonde, you know, platinum. Older than me though, or looked it,' she says with a slight smirk, 'bit skinny for his taste, Nige liked a bit of something to hold onto. Must've been like fucking Skeletor.'

I see Davis out of the corner of my eye and wave her over. 'How long ago was this, when you saw them together?'

Leah shrugs again. 'Three, four months ago maybe, dunno. Haven't really had to think about it. Look, I just came here to say my goodbyes. I didn't want to draw any attention to meself, what with his wife and kids and that. Can I go now?'

'In a minute. I'd like my colleague to take a few more details.'

She sighs heavily.

'He was murdered you know, Leah. Good, kind, generous Nigel, had his wrists sliced open, and was poisoned and left to bleed to death. It would really help us if you can give us as much information as you're able to.'

Her eyes change a bit and I see a flicker of sadness in them, something resembling regret.

'Alright,' she says, 'but make it quick because I've got another client at three.'

'Thanks,' I say as Davis reaches us.

'Oh, and Leah, which hotel was this, which hotel were you staying in the night you saw Baxter and the blonde?'

Leah looks Davis up and down as she approaches, before taking another cigarette from her handbag and lighting it. 'That posh one up in Knightsbridge: La Reymond,' she says.

CHAPTER THIRTY-ONE

'I just need to check the CCTV footage from the last few weeks. Some things have gone missing from my apartment and I want to make sure it's not that wayward brother of mine pinching my stuff before I go to the police. He's family, you understand, got a bad cocaine habit… and stupidly, a key to my apartment.' She rolls her eyes. 'He swears he's never set foot inside it, but I don't know how else my stuff might've gone walk about, you know. And, well, I don't want to get him in any trouble – he's not a bad kid – just a bit lost, and he is my brother…'

Danni-Jo is looking at the security manager with big blue eyes; her bottom is perched on his desk. She's wearing a pretty floral summer dress, too summery for this time of year or certainly for the climate. He's staring at her cleavage and glancing at her slim exposed thigh.

'I'm not supposed to,' he says nervously, swallowing dryly. 'It's against regulations, I'm sorry.'

She sighs heavily. 'I understand. Well, perhaps you can look,' she suggests, 'I'll just sit here and watch you while you do.'

He half laughs. 'Going back two weeks you say? That'll take a while.'

'S'alright, I've got a while,' she grins. 'How about I get us a few beers and a pizza while we're looking? Make a date of it.'

The word 'date' stuns him. *This girl is a fucking supermodel and she's offering to buy him beer and pizza and practically flashing her fanny at him*. She must certainly love this brother of hers. He hasn't had a 'date' in years, and he's *never* had a date that looks like this one.

'You pulling my leg?' he asks, suddenly feeling self-conscious. He hasn't had a shower in two days and he ate a cheese-and-onion sandwich for breakfast.

'No,' she replies, 'of course not! Although I could pull something else…' she giggles and whinnies like a little pony as she slides off the desk and grabs her handbag.

'What do you like on your pizza?' Danni-Jo asks before he has a chance to respond.

He's staring at her blankly, like this is some kind of MTV prank and Ashton Kutcher's going to turn up any minute with a camera crew and humiliate him on live TV.

'I'm a ham and pineapple girl myself… Let me guess, you like something hot and spicy, you're a meat-feast kind of guy – pepperoni? Am I right?'

He can all but nod, speechless.

'And you drink Budweiser? I can get us a six-pack. I won't tell anyone you've been drinking on the job, don't worry, this will be our little secret, yeah?'

He's nodding like a dog on a dashboard now, wondering if perhaps he's actually still asleep and this is a dream: a fantasy in his unconscious mind. He'll wake up soon, but hopefully not before the action begins.

'Yeah,' he finally manages to respond, 'I like Budweiser.'

Danni-Jo smiles brightly, exposing her neat white teeth. She looks like one of those Victoria's Secret models he masturbates to sometimes, all bouncy blonde hair, tits and teeth. He wonders if she'll let him take a photo? The lads down the The Crown will never believe him otherwise.

'Great,' she says, 'I'll go grab us some beer from the corner shop on Rupert Street. I'll order the pizza from Dominos. I'll be about half an hour maybe… perhaps you can start looking through the CCTV for me while I'm gone, make a head start, yeah?'

He's still nodding, like his head is stuck. 'Yeah, okay…'

'Perfect.' she says, thinking about the Rohypnol she has in her handbag. She'll slip some in his Budweiser. Just enough to disorientate him and induce memory loss. He'll never know if he's had sex with her or not, let him think he did, let the sad, dirty old sicko have his perverted little fantasy of fucking her over his desk. Everyone's a winner.

'See you soon,' Danni-Jo sings, blowing him a kiss. She's hamming it up, almost enjoying herself. His sheer disbelief is written all over his unshaven face. She closes the door behind her and then reopens it, poking her head around and smiling, 'Oh, and don't go anywhere, will you?'

He shakes his head. *As bloody well if!*

CHAPTER THIRTY-TWO

Janet has spared no expense for her husband's send-off; she's hired caterers in and people are getting stuck into the buffet. I wouldn't eat a thing even if I could. It wouldn't seem right. Besides, I'm not here as a guest, merely as an observer. I shouldn't be happy on an occasion like this but I'm buzzing thanks to Leah Carlton. It's not much, I know, but it's an ID, a potential ID anyway, and she's agreed to come to the station to do an e-fit and look at CCTV. As reluctant as she initially was to help – understandable given her career choice – I sense that Leah's a decent girl and she appeared genuinely fond of Baxter. So the funeral, as I'd hopefully predicted, has thrown something up at least. It's a start.

Janet is busy hostessing – drinks are topped up, plates are full – and seeing her fussing around, I suspect she's been this way her entire life. Some habits are hard to break. I stand at the side of the buffet table, watching her.

She smiles at me, her thirteen-year-old son hovering behind her. His face is bloated, swollen from crying and he looks pale. I feel like hurting someone. Because I know that whoever did this will never see or never feel remorse for the paleness on that young man's face. Whoever it was is only wrapped up in their own concerns. I ask him about football. It's what boys and men do. He says he's an Arsenal supporter because his dad was. Janet smiles at this, but it doesn't reach her puffy eyes. When her son is led away by an auntie, I'm glad and I feel guilty at my relief.

'I'm assuming there's no news, nothing to report back to me…?' Janet asks without personal or malicious overtones.

'I'm sorry, Janet,' I say, meaning it, 'we're following every lead we've got, we're leaving no stone uncovered.' I hear the clichés in my own words and feel like sticking my face into the trifle that's on the table next to me. At least it looks home-made. I think about the dogging revelation and brace myself to share it with her; I don't have a choice.

'Janet,' I repeat her name quietly, almost gravely, and she glances up at me with wide and expectant watery eyes. 'We did find a number; a phone number in the records of your husband's suspected mistress…'

She shifts from one foot to the other, her sensible shoes creaking, but her face remains the same. 'We traced this number from a text message sent to this unknown suspect's number, just once.' I pause, take a silent breath. 'It was registered in your name, Janet.'

Janet pauses for a few seconds, a sad half-smile flickers across her lips before she looks up at me again. 'I know about my husband's little pastime,' she says, 'the times he went to various "beauty spots" for that dog…' A sad irony spills from her lips as she says it. She can't bring herself to fully say the word 'dogging'.

I blink back at her.

'I guessed he was doing it again… I saw a message on his phone, I… I got one of those pay-as-you-go phone things, didn't want Nigel to know that I knew. He would've been upset, ashamed…' Her voice trails off before she composes herself again, 'I sent an anonymous text to her, whoever it was he had been messaging.'

I nod. 'And what did you say, Janet?'

'Hold on,' she replies and then disappears, returning less than a minute later with a small Nokia phone, one of those old ones that definitely isn't smart. 'Here, read it for yourself.'

I take the phone and look through it. There's only one sent message on it. I open it.

'I know what you're both up to. Stop it now.'

I stare at the message; it's short and non-threatening, very much like Janet herself, and I feel a wave of sadness wash over me. 'Did she reply,' I ask, 'did Nigel ever mention it?'

'He never mentioned it,' she replies with a gentle sigh, 'and no, she didn't.'

'I see,' I say. 'How long have you known, Janet, about Nigel's pastime?' I wish I could have a drink. The cold beer and Champagne that's being passed around suddenly appears very appealing.

'All our marriage, practically,' Janet answers, her shoulders visibly sagging. The black cardigan she's wearing seems too big for her now: it's swallowing her up as she wraps it around her like a comfort blanket.

'Right. I see. How did you find out about it?'

She snorts a little then, though not with mirth, and bows her head as though consumed with shame. 'Because,' she says, eventually looking up to meet my gaze with her watery eyes, 'I used to go with him.'

See. I told you. Funerals. They're always so revealing.

CHAPTER THIRTY-THREE

So it transpires that Janet Baxter not only knew that Nigel was into watching strangers have sex in public places, but that she was actually complicit in it, for a short time anyway. She suspected, many years ago, that her husband might be having an affair. There were signs she says: he kept disappearing late at night in his car, coming home exhilarated and often 'amorous' as she'd put it, blushing. *Poor Janet.* I could see how excruciating it was for her to make such a confession to me, and at his funeral as well. So, one night she got in her car and followed him up to a secluded area somewhere on the outskirts of North London. She couldn't remember the location exactly. It horrified her to learn that her clean-cut, hard-working, loving, affectionate and respectful husband was going to watch random strangers get their kit off and get down to business in the back seats of cars. She said that as awful as it was, part of her had actually been relieved, relieved there wasn't someone else, no significant 'other', and that he just had a perversion, a guilty pleasure, albeit a sleazy, seedy one that made her feel sick. She'd thought about divorcing him but when he'd broken down and cried she'd felt sorry for him, pitied him. And of course, she loved him. So Janet, good, kind and slightly prudish Janet, did what she believed any loving, loyal wife would do and joined in.

She told me she'd only ever accompanied him twice in his dogging pursuits and that both times she had felt repulsed, dirty and shameful. The first time she had pretended to get some kind of kick from it just to please Nigel; the second time she had broken down and cried afterwards, prompting her husband to promise her he would never again indulge himself. And she had believed him. 'We never spoke about it ever again after that last time,' she said, although she had suspected, on occasion, that he had fallen off the wagon. Recently, she had concerns that perhaps he was once again 'up to those old tricks' but she denied it to herself and never questioned him about it, instead deciding to send the message in a bid to try and put a stop to it.

I told Janet that it had come to our attention that Nigel had been sighted at a renowned spot up in Hampstead Heath and she didn't look altogether shocked or surprised. I explained that he was seen with a blonde woman, possibly the same woman we have on CCTV going up to his suite on the day he was murdered. A flicker of hope crosses her face when she hears this and I can see that despite her guilt and shame and humiliation, she simply wants her husband's killer caught. Whatever Nigel was – or wasn't – she still loved him and she still does. She repressed her own feelings, as I suspect she had throughout her entire marriage, maybe even her life. I told her not to worry and clarified that this information is not in the public domain: only the team knows about it. Janet looked relieved.

'That's something at least,' she said quietly.

I don't mention Fiona Li.

On my way back to the station I send Florence a very brief text message asking her when she's free for dinner. Then I go back to beating myself up about having sat outside my girl's murderer's mother's house for the best part of an evening. I know I could get in trouble for it if Mathers or his mother saw me and made a complaint. But I'm not and I wasn't breaking any rules.

So, against my better judgement and fuelled by a thousand emotions, I go and do it again.

CHAPTER THIRTY-FOUR

She's eating Jaffa cakes and Doritos simultaneously as she flicks through the job section of the local newspaper, ringing potentials with a pink sharpie she found in the drawer along with other miscellaneous stationery. Her feet are tucked underneath her on the battered old sofa that in the right setting, maybe some gastropub in Shoreditch, could pass for being vintage shabby-chic cool. Only this sofa is in the living room of a tiny one-bed apartment above a fried-chicken shop in Penge and therefore just looks like what it is: a filthy, knackered old couch.

The apartment is a world apart from her own: it's dark and featureless, there's paint peeling on the windowsills, next to black spots of mould on the frames. There's lino on the floor, cheap laminate stuff, really nasty. The walls are an off-white colour, decorated with random damp patches and stains. It smells of cooking fat and fried food. There's a kitchen: small, surprisingly cleaner than the rest of the place, and functional. It's equipped with a kettle, a toaster, a small cheap-branded microwave, a cooker that looks on its last knockings and a fridge with fingermarks on the door. It doesn't quite shut properly on first attempt, but with a good slam on the third it sticks. The bedroom is the worst: it's tiny, just big enough for her essentials, with a shabby bedside table and an MDF wardrobe with a mirror that's cracked on the front. The carpet is old, though it feels okay underfoot, soft even. A light cord hangs in the middle of the room, there is no shade and the tiny window lets in limited natural light.

She imagines it's the kind of place where people might commit suicide, an irony that doesn't fully escape her. But no one knows her here and it's cheap. Plus, its only temporary, she's not planning on staying, and with a little luck, she might have got herself a job by the time the rent's due and then she can do a moonlight flit without paying for it. This idea gives her a little thrill. She's renting out her own place for a small fortune through a posh estate agent. It's on a short-lease loan to some rich Japanese student. The estate agent informed her that his references were immaculate and that her apartment was in very good hands. She wonders if Mummy Bear has started to smell yet…

As she expected, she'd been on the CCTV, and together with Simon, the security manager, she'd watched as she'd entered Kizzy's apartment on the day she'd killed Esmerelda. I was feeding her cat she'd said to him nonchalantly as she'd chewed on a slice of pizza, admiring her own image on the screen. She looked good on camera. He'd nodded, adding that she was a good neighbour for doing so. Drink up, she'd told him, handing him a can of Budweiser which he'd sipped enthusiastically, alongside eating a slice of the hot pepperoni. She'd slid up next to him as they'd watched the screen together in silence apart from their chewing, she'd made sure her thigh was resting against his cheap polyester uniform trousers and she swang her legs back and forth for friction. At one point he'd shot her a sideways glance and she'd flashed him her best slutty smile, one she had perfected over the years, and he'd shaken his head in a mix of delighted disbelief, as though he couldn't quite believe any of what was happening was real. He'd started to ask her questions: how old she was, what she did for a living, did she have a boyfriend? She'd answered him enthusiastically, chatting amiably about herself as she waited for the drugs to kick into his system. Once she had begun to notice his coordination slowing down and his speech starting to slur, she got down off the desk and onto her hands and knees in front of him.

'What are you doing?' he'd laughed, looking a little disorientated, his eyelids heavy.

'Shhh,' she'd said, looking up at him as she unzipped his cheap shiny trousers and pulled his cock out.

'Jesus…' his head had fallen back on his shoulders, 'you're… you're fucking insane.'

She'd giggled a little as she'd begun to pull on him, making him hard almost instantly. She continued with this for a few moments, smiling up at him as he relaxed back into the swivel chair. After a few moments she felt his hard-on soften. He was asleep. Getting off her knees with a small sigh she left his limp dick exposed and swivelled round to the screens in front of her, rewinding the footage back to the beginning and wiping the whole lot from the computer system.

Chucking the empty can into a black plastic bag, she grabbed another slice of pizza and began to chew on it as she set about tidying up. She opened a can of Bud and swallowed half the contents, wincing. She hated beer. Her father drank it day and night, and she loathed the smell, the scent of it – bitter and acidic on his breath. Taking the DVD from her handbag she placed it into the drive of his computer and uploaded it. *High School Huneez* began to play on the screen; the low amorous moans and grunts of pig-tailed schoolgirls emanating from the speaker. Then she had left.

Throwing another Jaffa Cake down her neck, she picks up her phone and scrolls through her messages, smiling when she comes to his. *Dan, Dan, the disappearing man.* He's come good on his word and asked her to dinner. *Such a shame.* There had been something about him, something that had made her feel hopeful and… human, though she wasn't quite sure how these feelings were supposed to feel. But she'd liked it, whatever it was she'd experienced in the brief time they'd been together. It would be a gamble… Lying low and staying out of central London, that was best for now. Once she'd finished the story, then perhaps she could go away somewhere – maybe Daniel would come with her? Maybe they would live together in a remote, sleepy village in a little cobblestone cottage with miniature roses climbing the front; a village with a pond and a pub where everyone knew everyone else, where there was a tiny post office and one of those old-style butchers that sold sausages on strings. An English country rose and her darling family waving to their neighbours as they went for their Sunday walk together. Her fantasy is poignant enough for her to reach for her phone and hit reply.

Yes, Daniel would be her future. But first she needed to rectify her past. She needed to write the ending.

She rubs at the dye on her hair. It's beginning to drip, cold black droplets hit her back, making her uncomfortable. She pulls the towel around her shoulders a little tighter and carries on scanning the job section until she comes across something.

'Experienced nanny needed for Beckenham-based family. Live-in. Taking care of a little boy of eight months, full-time with most weekends free. Some light domestic chores. Must have a clean driving license and references.'

She circles it three times. *Bingo.*

CHAPTER THIRTY-FIVE

She's wearing a pretty floral summer dress with the biker boots I remember from before. This stops me in my tracks because it's almost identical to how Rach used to dress – it was her favourite look, or at least it was mine.

Florence acknowledges my surprised expression because she asks, 'You don't like my outfit?'

I tell her *I do* like her outfit: I like it very much. I don't tell her it reminds me of my dead girlfriend.

'I figured you're not the posh restaurant type, that for you it's more about good food than fanciness, am I right?' she says.

She is. *Spot on in fact.*

Florence looks pleased with herself. 'Good,' she replies, 'because there's a sushi restaurant, a favourite of mine, that I'd like to show you.'

I like a woman in charge and tell her to lead the way. She calls an Uber.

The restaurant is small and dark; we have to take our shoes off and sit cross-legged on a sunken floor.

'I'll order for you if you like,' she says, authoritatively. I smile.

'I'll take your lead then, seeing as though you sound like you know what you're doing'. Rachel was the same, especially when it came to ordering food in restaurants. Some people might consider it bossy, but with Rach it came from a good place, a place of knowledge, and also because she knew I was a complete philistine when it came to food, although I learned a lot from her in the end. *The end…*

She orders some saki and a beer for us both, along with some edamame and sashimi, katsu and ramen, nothing too adventurous. I'm secretly relieved. I'm not a massive sushi fan but I don't tell her this. She sips her saki and smiles at me. She's as pretty as I remembered her being, perhaps even more so, but in a different way to Rachel. Rachel's beauty radiated from the inside as well as the outside, and as yet I don't know Florence Williams well enough to assess if her beauty runs below the surface.

'So, Daniel, how's it going in the world of architecture?'

I nod, guiltily, and think about telling the truth. I know I should really and I vow to – next time. If there is a next time.

'Oh you know, busy.'

Florence uncrosses her legs, affording me a brief flash of underwear. White. Cotton. I like white. 'Tell me about your day, I'm interested.'

I make it up: my day. I lie and say I've been to a potential building site, that 'we're' – the company – thinking of applying for permission to build some social housing. The lies come so easily that I surprise myself. There's a part of me that is actually quite enjoying being someone else – seeing the world through someone else's eyes.

'I don't know much about buildings,' she says, 'perhaps you'll teach me… take me to some of your favourites? What are your favourites?' Luckily she doesn't give me time to answer before she continues, 'The Shard looks like a tampon, don't you think? I wouldn't mind if it had been designed by a woman! But it makes me think that men must be thinking about vaginas constantly…'

The sashimi arrives.

Her use of the word 'vagina' kind of startles me, though it shouldn't. It's just a word. I laugh.

'Well, you're probably right,' I say, uncomfortably.

'Only probably?' she replies, taking a thin sliver of sashimi between two chopsticks and dipping it in soy.

'The sashimi is good,' I say, changing the subject, 'tell me about your day.'

She sighs.

'It was pretty boring and uneventful actually, I couldn't concentrate on anything much because I was too busy thinking about you, about tonight.'

I admire her candour and only wish I could say the same thing. My day has been filled with thoughts of Nigel Baxter and his family, with CCTV footage and teddy bears.

'I'm flattered, ' I say, 'so why have you gone down the online dating route? You're beautiful, young, no children – they're queuing up for you, surely?'

'Oh yeah, out the door,' she says, and I can't tell whether she's joking or not. She props her elbows onto the low table and looks directly at me. 'I don't like bars – or boys,' she does that nose-wrinkle thing again that I remembered liking on our first encounter, 'which incidentally they're all full of. I don't like boys, I don't do hook-ups and I'm not into meaningless sex. Sex, definitely, but not meaningless sex.'

I nod, amused. Candour is clearly Florence's 'thing'.

'Sashimi?' She offers me some from her chopsticks, feeds it to me a little provocatively.

'Tell me about Rachel,' she says, 'What was she like? What did she do? What did you love most about her? How did she die?'

I exhale.

'That's a lot of questions,' I say, bracing myself to answer her. Rachel's my favourite subject, but I'm acutely aware of coming across as a grieving widower who's obsessed with his dead girl-friend, which of course is exactly what I am.

'Rach was,' I pause, 'Rachel was amazing; she was funny and bright and sassy and ambitious. She was beautiful and understated and lit up a room. Everyone who met her adored her. She was easy company, yet gregarious, opinionated but not arrogant, she was exciting yet homely, she was… well, she was everything to me.'

She stares at me, doesn't fill the pause, so I continue.

'She was a chef, a bloody good one too. She was hoping to own her own restaurant one day and I'm in no doubt that she would've.'

'How did she—'

'Motorbike accident,' I cut in quickly. 'Hit by a car. A speeding car driven by a drunk driver. He ran her off the road and…' I take a swig of saki and it burns my throat. '…And, well, that was that.' I swallow back the small lump that's formed in my throat. The one that is always there whenever I talk about her death to anyone, which incidentally isn't that often. I try to avoid talking about it for that very reason. No less on a date with another woman.

'Grief,' she says wistfully, 'is a funny thing.'

'Yes,' I agree, 'yes it is.'

'Both my parents are dead,' she says matter-of-fact. 'I have no living relatives. I am, quite literally, alone in the world.' Florence says this with no self-pity, which I admire her for. She doesn't say how they died and I don't ask. We've talked about death enough already.

'So, have you ever been married?' I lower my head. 'God, I'm sorry, is that too personal? I'm really out of practice with this dating malarkey.'

'Don't be daft, it's a perfectly legitimate question,' she dismisses my comment.

'No… I've never been married, never really wanted to be, never was one of those girls who dreamed of a big white wedding.'

'So what did you dream of, as a little girl I mean?' I ask the question playfully. The death talk has demanded something lighter.

Florence pauses for a moment, obviously considering her answer, and she adjusts her slim legs beneath her, popping some edamame between her lips. 'Happiness,' she says finally.

I suppose it's as good an answer as any.

'Now I'm getting older, I've started to warm to the idea of sharing my life with someone. I suppose I've always been a bit of a commitment-phobe, I've turned down a couple of proposals in my time!'

'I'll bet,' I say, smiling at her. 'A real heartbreaker.'

She laughs. 'Not really,' she says, modestly, 'I suppose I've always been a little afraid of giving myself to one person, seems like such an enormous thing to do. But these days, well, now I feel like I'm ready for the whole commitment thing, companionship, maybe even starting a family, who knows.' She digs into her sushi.

I nod. 'That's what everyone wants isn't it, companionship, to share their life with someone they love?'

'No, Daniel,' she replies, correcting me, 'I don't think everyone does. I think that there are people out there who are incapable of sharing their lives with others, or forming deep bonds with other human beings. Zombie people: the living dead.'

'And I thought I was the professional cynic,' I laugh, half expecting her to come back with the line, 'but your heart's not in it…' I feel that familiar ache in my chest. The one where I begin to enjoy myself for a moment and then realise that Rachel's gone and she's never coming back. As much as I'm enjoying talking to Florence, she isn't Rachel and she never will be.

'Have you ever been to Japan?' I ask, trying to lighten the conversation – and my mood. 'You seem to know a bit about sushi and Japanese culture.'

'No I haven't, sadly. But it's definitely on the bucket list.'

'Ah yes, the bucket list! So, what else is on it?'

She smiles at me a little provocatively I feel, though I could be wrong, like I say, I'm out of practice.

'You, Daniel.'

We both laugh because I know she's bantering with me. But there is something in the way she speaks that vaguely reminds me of Rachel: her directness, her strong spirit, the fact she doesn't come across as needing to be rescued. *A warrior woman.* And yet somehow there's a vulnerability to her as well, just like there was with my girl.

'Have you ever cheated on anyone?' She comes right out with it. The question throws me but I try not to show it. It's probably some kind of test.

I consider lying. 'When I was a lot younger,' I say, honestly. 'But at my age now, I wouldn't dream of it. I don't understand cheating,' which is true, I don't. 'I figure that if you want to cheat in a relationship then you can't really love the person you're with, not truly, not deeply, and you should have the courage to walk away. Integrity is important to me. When I met Rachel, after I met her, I never looked at another woman again, never even noticed them really.'

I think this is the right answer because she holds my gaze intensely with a look that could be mistaken for being almost loving.

Florence replies slowly, 'I believe in monogamy within a relationship. I've made mistakes in the past. I stayed too long, didn't want to hurt people, which of course, inevitably, was exactly what I ended up doing. Which is why,' she explains with florid hand gestures between chopsticks, 'these days I believe in total honesty. People are inherently dishonest in relationships, don't you think? They encumber themselves with all the trappings – romantic notions, flowers, valentines' cards, expensive meals and holidays – but really they don't always *feel* the right things beneath the platitudes. They convince themselves that they're happy and in love because they want to be, they feel that they should be, they project their desires onto the other person, like a mirror, even if that other person isn't really the image they wish to see. So they become disappointed and despondent when that person comes up short, leaving them feeling like they've done something wrong even though they've probably done nothing differently, and then this opens them up to desiring others, running away from themselves and the pain they feel inside… They stay connected to someone they should've disconnected with a long time ago as a result. In a paradoxical way, they put the happiness of others before their own and lie to themselves, hurting everyone, unintentionally or otherwise.' She takes a breath, 'I prefer brutal honesty, me. Once the gleam comes off it's always time to move on. Better to be left with a beautiful memory and accept that some things have a shelf life and aren't meant to last.'

I am, quite literally, stunned into silence by this eloquent but brutal confession.

'No,' I say, eventually, 'please, tell it like it is, Florence, don't hold back.'

She laughs, a flicker of self-consciousness perhaps.

'It's the saki,' she says, 'but actually, *seriously*, I do really believe what I said.'

Deep, I think, *she's deep*. But that's okay. Better than shallow I suppose, and at least she has opinions. Rach had those too. Plenty of them.

'I agree, mostly,' I reply, 'the bit about projecting what you want the other person to be without them really being it… that's quite an astute social observation.'

Florence looks satisfied with my remark.

'I think the initial gleam comes off everything in the end,' I muse. 'Muse' is the right word because I'm still trying to digest what she's just said. 'It's impossible to sustain the honeymoon period forever because life doesn't work that way.'

'But that's just it,' she interrupts, 'life *gets* in the way, which is why I like to keep things simple. No expectations. No meeting of families, no sharing friends: meaningful sex with no strings. No making too many plans or promises I may not be able to keep, just living and enjoying the moment.'

So far, Florence is proving to be nothing if not fascinating.

'That's very, well, New Age,' I say and she shakes her head.

'Not New Age, Daniel,' she replies, mock-crossly, 'just honest. I would rather a man tell me he no longer found me attractive and didn't want to fuck me anymore than pretend to fake a future.'

'I'll bear it in mind,' I say, with what I hope is humour, because I feel as though the conversation could do with some.

'Good,' she says brightly, placing her chopsticks down on the square plate. 'In that case do you want to get a hotel room?'

I stare at her, wondering if I've just heard her correctly.

'Too soon' she asks, 'after Rachel? Or are you not attracted to me?'

I'm not a man who is easily silenced. I sometimes think I've seen and heard it all, horror stories of the most inhumane nature, sleaziness on a level so base as to make you need a shower, and yet I'm so shocked I'm not sure how to answer. She places a shoeless foot on top of mine and takes my hand across the table, placing it underneath her dress. I can feel the smoothness of her thigh against the tips of my fingers and I sense the stirrings of an erection. I don't want an erection right here, right now, sitting cross-legged in a sushi restaurant, but Florence, it seems, has other ideas. She slides my hand further up her thigh until I feel the thin fabric of her underwear, the outline of her. I feel her stickiness between my fingers as she pulls on my hand, guiding my fingers inside her. She maintains eye contact with me for a few moments until I come back to reality and pull my hand away.

I don't do this kind of thing, finger-fuck women in sushi restaurants. Rach and me, we were adventurous sometimes, we made love in a field once following a boozy picnic, and on a beach – on a few beaches actually – but there's something about this encounter that's making me feel out of my depth.

'Well,' she says, 'shall we get the bill?'

CHAPTER THIRTY-SIX

It's a beautiful evening, there's a soft, warm wind left over from a sunny day: 'balmy' I think the word is. I know a place. I know many places, but for some strange reason I've thought of this place. And we're walking there, through the park, together. We're drunk, or at least I definitely am and I'm pretty sure she is too because she's taken her shoes off and keeps running ahead of me, forcing me to catch up with her. It's nice to be with a woman again, a vibrant, fun woman who seems so alive and in love with life. It's making me feel alive too, or maybe that's the saki and beer, but I feel some sort of a release in her company that I haven't felt since Rachel died, a trickle of hope that I might one day be happy again. And I'm getting the feeling that she might be the type of woman who could distract me; she's clearly leading the way, in every sense, even though I suggested this particular hotel that we are heading to, but only at her request that we get one at all.

I keep getting wafts of Florence's perfume as she runs ahead of me, without self-awareness, like a girl half her age. She smells of summer and abandon. And I remember doing this, or something very similar, with Rachel when we first met. I don't recall the exact moment I fell in love with Rachel, although looking back I think I loved her from the very beginning. The clear memory I have was of holding her hand and realising how much it would hurt to ever let it go.

We're arm in arm as we enter the Portobello Gold. I ask for the top room, the one with the private roof terrace, and luckily for us, the woman behind the bar says there has been a cancellation and it's available. We order drinks to the room.

The view from the room's small roof terrace is one of my favourite London views. Don't ask me why, I know there are millions of arguably better spots across the capital but there's something about this particular point that gets me right in the chest and provokes an emotional response. Perhaps it's the distant view across West London of mismatching urban buildings, the rich red of the low sunset bouncing off brickwork, the church spires, and the glorious Victorian homes juxtaposed with imposing tower blocks. Eclectic, non-uniform, all mixed in together, just like the city itself.

Florence likes the roof terrace too, she says it's quaint and quirky with its miniature, Astro-Turfed putting green and creative artisan furniture. She throws her body into mine and I wrap my arms around her small waist as we stare out across Portobello. She's giggling and so am I, caught in the moment, like it's unreal and happening to someone else.

I try and stroke her hair, but she pulls away from me and runs back into the apartment, pulling her dress over her head as she does. It's a clear invitation to follow her, and I do, into the bedroom, watching. She's naked in seconds, discarding her clothes almost with disgust, like she shouldn't have been wearing any in the first place. I undo my shirt and take it off, fall onto the bed with her. We're kissing, her wet lips taste sweet, like cherries, and I feel the stirring of an erection. 'Did you like the view,' I ask between kisses and she says she does, but she prefers this one. And I laugh and reach over her to grab a swig of the Jack and coke I ordered up to the room.

'Me... me...' she says, opening and closing her mouth like a fish. She wants me to transfer the contents of my mouth into hers and I duly oblige, but it reminds me of Rachel because we often did that, shared drinks and chewing gum, shared everything.

She squirms beneath me, though I dare not look down at her and I keep my eyes closed. *I'm scared*, I'm actually scared to look at her, to see her naked body beneath mine because she's not Rachel, she's not my girl and yet if I keep my eyes closed... She's pulling at my belt now, opening it and the buttons of my fly. Her hands feel soft and warm, her body tight and silky smooth; the intimate, light scent of her reaches my nose. I pull away from her a little so she moves in closer, throwing her leg over my side, almost locking me into her. She starts kissing me again but senses my reluctance. The moment is broken and she rolls off me gently onto her back, the breeze coming in from the roof terrace covers us.

I suddenly feel completely sober and with this sobriety comes the feeling that this is all wrong and I don't want to be here. I feel wretched and make to speak but she stops me.

'It's okay Daniel,' she says gently, 'really.'

I swallow back the tears that have formed in the corners of my eyes and hate myself.

'Are you just not ready or is it me?'

I want to look at her but don't. I'm consumed by guilt, guilt that I almost let Rachel go by making love with another woman and guilt for not making love to Florence, naked Florence who is lying next to me on a hotel bed I have paid for. And it's such a strange and alien experience, turning down a beautiful, naked woman, one who actually seems genuinely interested in and turned on by me. It's a first for me and, I suspect, for her too.

I want to tell her that it's not her – *that it's me* – but even in my head it sounds so corny that I inwardly cringe. And the truth is, I'm not entirely sure if it is her or me, or both of us, or everything, or the drink, or the case I'm working on...

'I'm so sorry,' I finally say. I feel drained, exhausted, hit by a sudden and powerful malaise. 'I should go.'

I sit up but she gently touches my arm.

'Don't go Daniel,' she says and the tone of her voice almost undoes me. 'Stay here, lay with me, just lay with me.'

And although I'm overcome by an urgent need to leave, I do as she asks because I can't be that cruel. It's not her fault.

We're both silent for a while and it's not uncomfortable exactly, more resigned. It feels like an age before Florence says, 'tell me about her, tell me about Rachel.'

The sun is rising as I make my way home; it's a beautiful morning, clear and bright, the promise of a new day unfolding. I like this time of the morning, not least because London looks different without the traffic, almost serene.

I switch the radio on; it's playing Fleetwood Mac's 'Go Your Own Way'. I'm desperate to get home, to shower, to wash away some of the guilt and sadness that's sticking to me like sweat. Coffee and a shower, that's what I need. Then I'll be okay…

My phone rings. Immediately I think it's her, but then I realise she doesn't have my work number.

'Are you awake Dan?'

It's Delaney. It irks me, the way he calls me 'Dan' in such an overfamiliar way, even though I know it probably shouldn't. I think about berating him over the phone-record cock-up and for passing the buck to Davis, but I overlook it because there's an urgency in his tone; it's all over those few words, and it's making me edgy.

'Well I am now,' I say, 'why?'

There's a very slight pause before he says, 'Because there's been another one. We've got another body.'

CHAPTER THIRTY-SEVEN

The smell is unholy: putrid, choking, cold and heavy. I'm trying not to gag before I even enter the room. It's difficult to describe just how rancid it is to those who're lucky enough never to have smelt the scent of death, or a decaying corpse. People ask me about dead bodies sometimes, whether I've seen any, what they look and smell like, and even Rach was curious. But it's very difficult to put into words just how vile, how offensive and aggressive the smell is. It varies of course from body to body and in different circumstances: how long they've been dead, the temperature, that sort of thing. But it's a smell you instantly recognise and never ever forget. Gasses and compounds in a decomposing human body that is liquefying from the inside out, emit an odour that is unmistakable, instantly recognizable and yet indescribable. I suppose if you took a full rubbish bin filled with leftovers and left it out in strong sun for a week, then added a gallon of diarrhoea, some rotting fish guts and entrails, and a thousand rotten eggs then you'd get something close – and that's the best death could ever smell like. It *really* is that sickening.

Forensics have sealed the apartment off and the photographers have just turned up. I put my sleeve over my mouth in a futile attempt to prevent myself from inhaling the stench.

It's like a scene from a horror film, like that flick *Seven* that Brad Pitt and Morgan Freeman were in, where Kevin Spacey severs Gwyneth Paltrow's head and puts it in a box at the end. The victim is sitting up in bed, slumped more than sitting really, and her head is hanging forwards, her chin resting on the left side of her chest like a marionette whose strings have been abruptly cut. Her skin is pallid grey and mottled. Blood is noticeable on the sheets, black, dried pools of it stain the floral duvet. Her exposed wrists are cut open vertically. I notice the pill bottle, a few tablets scattered on the bed. There's a book, open, on the small bedside table next to her. The white venetian blinds are open and the sunlight streaming through them illuminates the scene like a film set, highlighting dust particles and Lord only knows what else that's in the air, which incidentally I'm breathing in. Then I see the bear, lying at the end of the bed. It's on its side as though it's been randomly discarded, not strategically placed like it was with Baxter. It's wearing a dress this time, an apron dress in a small floral Liberty print. I want to pick it up but the smell is like a barrier, preventing me.

'Same MO,' Delaney says miserably. He looks puce.

I nod, unable to answer him. I turn my back to him but I can sense the exasperation and regret coming off him in waves. *We weren't able to save this one.* The toggies are moving around in their white suits like giant marshmallows as flashes go off and I ask if Vic Leyton is on her way. Delaney nods. I take a deep breath, largely for motivation, and walk towards the body, crouching down to take a look at her.

'So who found her?'

'Security bloke,' Delaney says, flipping through his notebook, noticeably blinking – the acrid smell even gets in your eyes somehow. 'A Simon Johns, he's downstairs with the DS. He's in a bad way, Dan.'

'Get him up here,' I say sharply. I can't help it. I'm fucking furious, with myself, more than anyone.

Delaney leaves and Vic Leyton arrives almost simultaneously. I can't help but feel glad to see the back of him, rightly or wrongly his presence winds me up. I pick up the bear from the bed.

'Mummy Bear,' I say under my breath as I grapple with the nausea that's rising up from my guts to my solar plexus, and threatening to spill itself out onto the duvet. This is as grim as it gets.

'So, Dan,' Vic says as she enters the crime scene, 'we meet again. And so soon. People will talk.'

CHAPTER THIRTY-EIGHT

'She's been dead about a week I'd say, maybe a day either side. Difficult to determine the exact cause of death. In usual circumstances I'd say it was blood loss as a result of self-inflicted wounds to the ventricular artery, but hazarding a guess, I'm sensing these aren't usual circumstances, so we will have to wait until the post-mortem to be sure.' Vic turns to me, 'It's another one, isn't it Dan?'

She's using my forename again. It hints at the severity of the situation.

'Yes,' I say, 'the bear...'

Vic nods. 'The wounds are deep,' she continues in that clinical, observational way of hers, yet I sense a slight humanity to them that I haven't heard before.

She goes straight up to the body, fearlessly, and I can't help but think that she might be someone worth knowing on a personal level. The smell is overwhelming me now and I know that soon I'll have to leave in case it stays with me forever.

'Female, obviously, late forties or early fifties I'd say. Do we know who she is?'

'We're waiting on ID,' I say, routed to the spot. 'Building security discovered her – the smell...' I explain.

Vic nods. 'Yes, well, Chanel wouldn't want to bottle it. If the heating is on timer it will have helped speed things up a bit... and the sunlight... So, are we dealing with a serial killer?'

'It's a fairy tale, Vic. Goldilocks is acting out a fairy tale... Daddy Bear and now Mummy Bear...'

Vic blinks at me and I actually see a flicker of horror cross her features, '… and Baby Bear,' she finishes. But we both know she doesn't need to.

CHAPTER THIRTY-NINE

He looks exactly how you might expect someone to if they'd just unexpectedly found a ripe, rotting corpse sat up in bed. He's running his hands through his hair and can't seem to decide whether sitting down or getting up and pacing helps. I understand the conundrum. When Rach died I paced. I paced the apartment for days, weeks even, like a man waiting outside a hospital room for his child to be born, or for a life-changing operation to be over. Only there was never any outcome. There was no baby at the end of the pacing, no doctor who appeared and looked at me with gravitas to say, 'she'll be okay.' Death is so final. *Too final.* How do you come to terms with such finality? The brain doesn't factor in the end of something or someone. Only time reconciles this, or so they tell me. But time *doesn't* heal. Time just passes.

And yet I still find myself passing off clichés and platitudes to people, to victims of loss and crime, because who the fuck wants to hear the truth?

I mentally pull myself together. I'm at work. 'Simon, is it?'

He's hovering outside the door of the apartment, beside himself. He's just seen a putrid, rotting corpse. One for the pub I suppose.

'Yeah, I'm sorry you had to see that,' I say, like it's somehow down to me. 'Do you need some water?'

He shakes his head, still pacing the small area. 'They complained about the smell, the stench, you know? The couple below, especially. So I had to go up… I had to have a look.' He's understandably agitated.

We've got an ID on the victim now, Karen Walker, forty-eight, though the poor bitch sure as shit looks a lot older in the (rotting) flesh. She owned the apartment, but hadn't lived there too long by all accounts. Recently divorced. She's known to us, a victim of domestic violence, her old man served a six-month stretch for kicking the living daylights out of her back in the early 2000s. I tell the boys to locate him immediately, but somehow I know this isn't his handiwork. *That gut instinct again.*

'Karen… did you know her?'

His jumper looks like it's shrunk in the wash. Bad material.

'No, no… I didn't… not really, not by name… I'd seen her a few times, coming and going, you know… like I do everyone here. You get to recognise people, you know, their faces. She was friendly enough, always said hello and smiled at me… polite… seemed normal, nice, you know? Normal…' he says again, 'she weren't stuck-up like… well, not like some of them are here. More money than manners most of them. She seemed a bit timid, shy, or at least I got that impression – a bit jumpy you know? Nervous type…'

He's seen death for the first time and he's blathering. It usually goes one of two ways: people either can't shut up or they clam up. And he's definitely the former. He needs a brandy. And yeah, before you think it, they ain't paying him enough.

'Okay, thanks Simon.' I say.

Davis is here now. Simon is continuing to mutter to himself. We'll get fuck-all sense from him tonight and I make a mental note to try again tomorrow, once his initial shock has had a chance to dissipate into something more lucid and he's had a little sleep, if he can get any, poor fucker.

I nod at Davis and go to leave.

'It's been a weird couple of weeks… weird shit happening… first that bird… that girl last week and now this…' Simon mumbles.

I turn back around. 'What girl is that Simon?'

He's shaking his head. 'The girl who lives in the opposite apartment… the one opposite hers – the dead woman's.'

'Okay,' I reply as calmly as possible, 'what about her? What happened?

'She wanted to see the CCTV. She bought me pizza and beer… she… she… Fuck!' He's pulling at his hair again, looking very distressed, embarrassed even.

I'm silent.

'Look,' he says, 'it may be nothing – probably fuck all – but this girl… I think she may have drugged me.'

CHAPTER FORTY

'I need you to run a check on someone called Danni-Jo Nichols, female,' I tell Harding. I give her the address and tell her to get back to me as soon as she can.

'She's not answering the door, Gov… she's not in.' Delaney looks at me.

'We'll come back later,' I say. We need to talk to Danni-Jo, urgently. I'm inclined to kick her door in and worry about the consequences later, but I can't afford a mistake at this point.

Simon Johns tells me his story with a mix of acute embarrassment coupled with an intuitive nag that something is definitely amiss. He needs to get it off his chest. Danni-Jo, he tells me, is a real looker. So the fact she had showed an interest, a sexual interest no less, in a middle-aged, aesthetically challenged no-mark like him naturally set off some alarm bells. He doesn't say this of course, because he doesn't need to. Poor bloke has faced enough humiliation and upset. He's cringing as he tells me what happened, and I can see he's inwardly berating himself for being stupid enough to have allowed his ego – and dick – to fall for what was quite clearly one of the oldest ploys in the book.

He tells me he woke up some hours later from what felt like the deepest sleep of his life, 'almost like a coma' as he puts it. And his penis is hanging out of his trousers, exposed. He says there was a porn film playing on repeat on his screen, but he has no recollection of owning it or ever having seen it before.

He feels the need to express most vehemently that he isn't into schoolgirls and never has been, except for when he was a school-boy himself. I nod. I believe him. He says he can't remember too much – what time of the day it was even, but that it was dark when he came round. He didn't know how long he'd been out for, or much about what had happened before, only that the girl from apartment six, the fit one, had come to see him to ask about CCTV footage. Something about her brother and missing items… he can't quite remember and I watch him struggle with frustration as he attempts to recall more details. They must've eaten pizza because when he woke up there was a half-eaten pepperoni in a box on his desk and a pack of Budweiser, two of which were empty. He assumes he drank them, or they drank one each. Simon tells me he knows it's stupid and that most men would've counted their lucky stars that a girl like that wanted to, well, you know, but he doesn't know what took place and he feels violated and used, like he's been set up, which tells me he's a fairly normal person with normal reactions. He explains that there was nothing missing from the room when he woke up, aside from Danni-Jo of course. But the CCTV footage had all been wiped. I ask him what was on it, if he can remember seeing anything unusual, anything different, or if this Danni-Jo's 'brother' could be spotted on the footage? He shakes his head. He can't remember.

'I feel like such a twat,' Simon says, 'like this bitch has really taken the piss, tried to set me up, make me look like some kind of nonce or something…'

I nod sympathetically. It could've been worse I think: she might've slit your wrists. But I don't say that.

My phone rings and I hold a finger up to Simon to excuse myself. He stops talking, but not pacing or running his fingers through his thinning hair.

It's Harding.

'There is no Danni-Jo, Gov, it's a bogus ID, another one. The apartment actually belongs to someone called Rebecca Harper. She's thirty-one years old, from London, no previous...'

I rub my temples and tell Harding to hold on while I ask Simon if he would recognise this woman, this *femme fatale* who allegedly drugged and violated him. He nods without hesitation and tell me he knows exactly what the bitch looks like and that, in fact, he's got her on CCTV. I tell Harding to get some photo identification of this Miss Harper and that I'll be back at the nick soon before hanging up.

'Can you look back through the footage, past footage, and see if you can get her up on screen?'

Simon nods. 'Yeah, she's in and out all the time you know... although I haven't seen her all week.' He looks at me sheepishly. 'I've got a confession to make,' he says and I brace myself as I nod encouragingly.

'Okay—'

'There was no couple complaining about any smell. The apartment below is vacant, has been for about six months... I went up to her apartment, Danni-Jo's. I wanted to speak to her, have it out with her I suppose. I mean, she could've got me sacked, my reputation would've been in ruins if someone had found me like that. I was mad, you know... freaked out. But when I got up to the top floor... well, that's when I noticed the smell. Fuck me,' he pulls a face, 'it was awful, the closer I got—'

'It's okay,' I tell him.

'I knocked on Danni-Jo's door, rung the bell, even called out her name and said who it was, but there was no answer. It was silent, so I assumed she wasn't in, guessed she was working or something. She told me she worked funny hours, was a student or something... can't remember what she told me she was studying.' He's looking down at his cheap shoes. 'Anyway, I put the smell down to the cat—'

'The cat?'

'Yeah, the dead lady's… Karen's cat. She wasn't supposed to have one. You're not allowed pets in the building. It's an upmarket place, you know. But I knew she had one and turned a blind eye. Sort of felt sorry for the woman somehow. She always seemed a poor old soul, downtrodden, even though she lived in luxury… I thought maybe she'd not changed the litter or something and that was the reason for the hum.'

'Some hum,' I reply.

'I knocked on Karen's door and no one answered so I went back the next day, and the next until the stench really started kicking up and then… well, that's when I sensed, when I *knew*, that something was really wrong. Danni-Jo hadn't answered her door for ages and neither had Karen. Then some estate agent guy came round with some Japanese dude and he said something about the smell on the way out, asking me to get it sorted immediately or else he would complain to the management company. And so I went up there again, you know, with the spare key. She – Karen – had locked herself out of her apartment not so long ago and had to call the emergency locksmiths. I had a spare key she'd given me. So I go up there… and by the time I reach the second landing the smell is pretty fucking bad, like I'm gagging and everything and—'

'Do you have a key to Danni-Jo's apartment?'

Simon shakes his head.

'The estate agent with the Japanese student, do you know which company he was from?'

He rubs his head, thinking hard. 'He left a card, a business card.'

My phone rings. It's Harding again.

'Boss, something of interest's come up…'

'Go on.'

'There's a log on the system – seems like our victim reported a crime a couple of weeks back—'

'Oh?'

'Yeah, apparently she claims... *claimed*, someone had killed her cat... reckoned it was the ex-husband.'

I ask Harding if they've located the ex and she says they're bringing him in now.

'What happened to the cat?' I ask.

She pauses for a second. 'According to the incident log, it was poisoned.'

CHAPTER FORTY- ONE

Her fake references have checked out. One from a reputable UK nanny agency, one from Australia, postmarked and everything. The internet. As good as it is evil. Magenta had muttered something about running a CRB check on her, but clearly hadn't gotten around to it yet, too preoccupied with finding a replacement cash cow by the looks of it. The 'official' references from the 'official' nanny agency and the glowing report from the Aussies seemed to more than suffice for now at least. Plus, by the time that selfish irresponsible bitch ever did get around to it, the job would be complete and she'd be long gone.

'He's so gorgeous,' she says, 'can I pick him up?'

'Of course,' the woman says brightly, smoothing her hands down her expensive trousers. 'Rachel meet George, George meet Rachel.' She hands her the baby, almost offloading him. He feels soft, cool, perfect in her arms, his legs kicking and pulling up in responsive touch, uncoordinated, jerky like an octopus. George smells so good, like a fresh hopeful morning.

Baby Bear.

'Ahh, he likes you,' the woman says turning away, probably thinking about the facial she's got booked later, already finding fault with the treatment and the therapist who'll give it. Nothing will ever be good enough for Magenta. *Magenta.* The name says it all. She holds him in her arms and coos over him naturally. So beautiful, so helpless and reliable, so real and vulnerable. Babies need. It's all they do. Need feeding, need a nappy change, need holding, need cuddles, need love. Need, need, need. But really they're no different to adults. Adults have had to learn that wailing and whining and crying will not bring you these comforts. That no matter how much you cry, no one will come. *No one ever comes.*

'George has an afternoon nap around 3 p.m., but only for an hour or so, then he has to be woken, or else he won't sleep at night... He's not the best sleeper, light, like his father.' She snorts. 'Although he never had difficulty in finding a bed if you know what I mean.'

'Is George's father away on business?'

Magenta raises her perfectly shaped eyebrows.

'You could say that,' she smirks, 'he's away anyway,' she says, adding dryly, 'he likes to keep himself busy.'

Rachel's careful not to press any further.

'I suggest we have a trial week, see how you and George bond, see if you like one another. I'm planning a trip away in a couple of weeks, so if all goes well I can leave George in your capable hands.'

Rachel smiles. Pleased. She senses that Mr Magenta has left his wife in the lurch somewhere along the line and the idea of full-time single motherhood has rapidly lost its glossy sheen. Magenta has money though; this much is obvious by the quality of her home furnishings – and the fact she clearly doesn't work yet can still afford to employ a nanny. *Daily Mail* fodder. She talks about hours, wages, time off, notice periods, George's sleeping and eating patterns, how he can't be without his squidgy giraffe, how the Bugaboo stroller is a bitch to dismantle, how she'll only use organic products on his perfect baby skin and how she must follow the Annabel Karmel recipes for his puree to the letter. George is fascinated by TV apparently, but she'd rather he listened to classical music and she's bought him some Baby Mozart instead. There's a local drop-in group on a Thursday she'd like them to attend; it's £50 a pop but the babies get to sit in a circle and watch a menopausal, childless woman with a sock puppet and a tambourine sing and help them learn through play. He also has sign-language lessons on Tuesday mornings, despite the fact George cannot yet speak. Magenta wants to know if she speaks Spanish, or if she's prepared to learn quickly so that she can speak to George in another language.

Rachel nods and tells her she knows some German, that her father's parents were from Berlin. Magenta looks thrilled and says 'perfect'.

She wonders if perhaps she should kill her instead? Either way, she feels she would be doing her a favour.

'Are you single?' Magenta asks her boldly.

'Yes,' Rachel replies, 'not looking.' This is the correct answer, she knows.

'No plans to marry, have babies, travel?'

'None.' She thinks about Daniel again.

George is still wriggling in her arms; he's a beautiful baby. She feels his strong life force, his chubby, milky-skinned face observing her as he exerts his strength. Babies are much more robust than they look; people treat them as if they might easily break, like china dolls. But she knows differently…

'He smiled!' Magenta jumps up, 'Gosh, he rarely smiles!'

Rachel refrains from making a caustic remark like, *no shit, with a cunt of a selfish mother like you*, or something. She smiles back at him, then at Magenta.

'I think he likes you.'

'Perfect,' she says.

Magenta smiles brightly. 'Okay Rachel, when can you start?'

CHAPTER FORTY-TWO

I'm back at the station and Ken Woods collars me for an update. He's looking pensive as I sit opposite him; it's a familiar look yet it still unsettles me. He's getting pressure from the top, I can tell. It's a domino effect in this game: his boss leans on him for results, he leans on me, and I lean on the team. Tic-tac-toe.

'We've got a serial killer on our hands, Dan,' he says, like I haven't deduced this very fact for myself already. 'The same MO by all accounts… Verralis is doing his nut. Says we can't afford any bad press and that he wants this tied up fast.' Verralis is the boss's boss. The Chief Commander. A man so beholden to the hard work of others to maintain his good reputation that he's forgotten what it's like on the ground.

'Any news on this missing Joanne Harper?' Ken shuffles some papers on his desk and looks at me over the rim of his glasses.

'It's Rebecca Harper, Sir,' I correct him, 'and no positive ID yet. The security guard who found Karen, he's provided us with CCTV footage, so we'll go through it and then put an APB out on her, bring her in. I suspect she's not gone far. The estate agent says she told him she was putting some stuff into storage while she was away on business.'

'Good, well, find the lock-up place and see what that turns up. Bloody hell – if this is our woman she could be sunning herself in the Costa del Sol by now.'

I shake my head. 'My intuition tells me she isn't.'

Woods snorts. 'It's not that I don't trust your hunches, Dan, it's just that… well, we can't afford not to cover our backsides.'

I feel annoyed. Deflated. Clearly this isn't about the victims; it's about not looking bad in the press; it's about how we're perceived in the eyes of those who matter, or who Woods' believes matter.

He sighs. 'Anyway, your intuition—'

'Yes, Sir. My intuition tells me she hasn't finished yet.'

'Finished? Finished what, murdering people? Yeah, well it's our job to make sure she has, that she bloody well does finish.'

'She hasn't completed the story yet.'

Woods looks at me like I've just fallen from the sky, an expression that shouldn't but does give me a tiny slither of pleasure.

'Care to elaborate, Riley?'

'Goldilocks,' I explain. 'Goldilocks and the three bears: Baxter was Daddy Bear, Karen Walker was Mummy Bear and so—'

'Jesus Christ, Riley.' Woods is staring at me with a grave expression that might make me want to laugh were the situation not so dire. For such a serious man he has a rather comic face, rubbery like a Spitting Image puppet, almost a caricature. He gets up from his chair, an indication of the seriousness of the matter. Woods' desk is like a shield to him; away from it he appears far less threatening and important, something I think even he is aware of.

'The press will go berserk.'

I tip my head sideways. *No doubt.* 'Once the results of the post-mortem and forensics come back, I'll release the news to the public – and Rebecca's photo once we get it. It's in our benefit. Someone will know where she is or will have seen her. Someone will come forward. And if she's nothing to hide she'll come forward herself.'

'We need to act quickly, Riley.'

'The team have alerted local schools and nurseries – it's the best we can do right now.'

Woods rubs his forehead. 'You think she's acting out the fantasy of a nursery rhyme?'

'Technically it's a fairy tale,' I correct him.

'Nursery rhyme, fairy tale, it's all the bloody same Riley,' he barks. It's worse than his bite though.

'Goldilocks and the three bears… Daddy Bear, Mummy Bear and—'

'Yes… yes… I know how the story goes,' he snaps, 'it's the ending I'm worried about.'

'She runs off into the woods, Sir,' I say, facetiously, 'the bears chase her away.'

He affords me a humoured look. He's alright really. Woods pretends he wants an easy life. But he chose the wrong profession for that and he knows it. He thrives off the drama, the pressure, without it he wouldn't feel alive. *He's misrepresenting himself.* That said, Woods feels like he's done his time on the ground – and to be fair, he has – and now he just wants to see out the rest of his career on a high, on the back of the hard work of others. He's earned that right really, just as I may do one day. But try as I might, I cannot imagine myself as a Woods character; part of an all-boys club, back-slapping each other over rounds of golf, even if I've earned the stripes. In that respect he's a TV cliché. And I promised myself, and Rach, that I'd never become one of those.

'So, is that it, Sir?' I'm keen to get on. Work to do.

'No, no it isn't,' he replies, but his tone is slightly softer which intrigues me. 'Sit down will you, Dan?'

I do as he says, sensing I have little option.

Wood inhales deeply. 'There's been a complaint.'

I blink at him. 'A complaint?'

'Yes… about you.'

'Me?'

'I've had Craig Mathers' father on the phone. Says you've been harassing his wife.'

I visibly recoil. 'That's a lie, Sir. I've… I've not been anywhere near Mathers' mother.'

He's silent for a moment. 'I didn't say Mathers' mother, I said his wife.'

I don't follow.

'You were seen Dan, parked outside their address. They wrote down your bloody reg number for God's sake. Mathers' parents divorced while he was inside. He's remarried and the new wife saw you watching the house while she was out walking the dog, put the willies up her.'

I inwardly smile. The Mathers' marriage broke down. *I'm glad.* I hope the whole thing destroyed their lives like it has done mine, and of course, Rachel's.

'I see.'

'Why were you there, Dan?'

He meets my eyes again but stays silent. He's using my own trick on me to get me to talk.

'I need closure, Sir. I need to look him in the eyes.'

Woods raises his eyebrows. 'And you think that'll give you closure do you? Wasn't the trial enough?'

'I wanted, *I want*, to be straight with you, Sir. I need to see him.'

I see Ken Woods almost change before my eyes then, his expression visibly softens. 'Dan, do you really think it's a good idea? Turning up on Mathers' doorstep? You know it could be classed as harassment or intimidation.'

'I don't intend to harass him Sir. I just want to talk to him.'

'And what if he doesn't? Want to talk to you I mean? What then?'

'I'm under no illusion, Sir. If he won't see me he won't see me. There's nothing I can do about that.'

Woods shakes his head.

'I know you Dan Riley, you're not the type of man who takes no for an answer, which is why you're one of the best bloody coppers I've got.'

This is the closest thing to a compliment I've ever heard from Woods and it blindsides me momentarily.

'I appreciate that Sir, really. But this is something I have to do.'

'Dan', he uses my Christian name again, 'it's common knowledge, as clear as the credit-card bill my wife runs up each month, that you loved that girl and you've suffered greatly since her passing. People see it; they sense it, they feel it, it's, it's…'

'It's what?' I ask. I thought I had done a good job of hiding my pain and I feel a bit put out. Have people been pitying me, whispering behind my back. 'Look, there's the one who lost his girlfriend in the motorbike accident and can't get over it, poor bastard'? I've maintained my professionalism; I stayed in the job; I returned to work just three weeks after Rachel's death, and I've got results since. They've fuck all to complain about.

'It's inked on you like a tattoo,' Woods says, somewhat expressively, for him anyway. 'Not a day goes by when you don't talk about her to someone… the very fact that you've managed to get the results you have, the very fact you've delivered, it's the only reason I haven't signed you off because whatever therapy you've been having hasn't worked.'

I sit there, stunned. I let his words hang above us, try to absorb them. Pretend he's not saying them and they're not right. *Is he right?* I think of my dad and what he would undoubtedly say. *Does it matter if he is son, unrepentant, remember?*

'So I've gotten the results and my pain can be overlooked,' I say, 'as a fair trade-off. I guess if I hadn't had the results then my pain would count for fuck all and I'd be on leave, Sir?'

Woods has the grace to wince. 'You should know by now I don't make the rules.'

'And what if you did, *Sir*?' I attempt to keep the sneer from my voice but fail.

Woods gets up again. He comes round to my side of the desk and places his hands on it, in front of me. 'Then I would say you're the best copper I've got, maybe have ever had, on my team, and that I understand your pain, or want to, like it's my own because whatever you might think of me, Daniel Riley, I'm nobody's fool, and I haven't got to where I have just to play fucking golf with a bunch of old conservative, smug, self-satisfied bastards.'

Bloody hell, he can add mind reader to his list of skills then.

He's in my face now, and I imagine him as a younger DI, like me, and how intimidating yet paradoxically human he might've come across in interview. I see his absolute brilliance in that brief moment, possibly for the first time.

'Don't go there again, Dan. Stay away. It won't bring her back.'

I go to speak.

'I'm arranging for you to have more therapy, at the Met's expense, of course, this guy's supposed to be the best, he'll help you, specialises in grief apparently.'

I bite my tongue.

'We'll get you on a programme as soon as this case is dealt with… but you find this Goldilocks first. We've got a serial killer at large acting out some fairy-tale nightmare and we both know how bad that is for business.'

Bad for business. Yeah, and pretty shit for the families too.

'Go and have breakfast,' he says, already looking down at his paperwork, the emotion all but disappeared from his voice.

'Yes Sir,' I say, the facetiousness evident in my voice. 'Can I bring you up some porridge?'

CHAPTER FORTY-THREE

'The body: Karen Walker. We know who she is; we know the killer's MO. We know we're looking for Rebecca Harper, or Danni-Jo, or both if they turn out to be different people.'

The team look tired but elated as they sit behind their messy desks. It's been a long night yet we're getting close, we all know it and it brings an urgency to proceedings. You can literally feel the energy coming off them in waves, the gear up for the final push. I glance around the incident room; it's full of ready-meal plastic wrappers and Costa coffee cups. It smells of fast food, stale sweat and hard graft.

'If I'm right about the Goldilocks theory then Baby Bear is next,' I say calmly. I see the looks on the team's faces. 'We need to act quickly. Rebecca Harper is a very dangerous and clever woman; she's sly, devious and likes to change her identity. We need to find her.'

'We're interviewing everyone in the building, Karen's employers and family, and the ex-husband is downstairs now in room three.' Delaney informs me efficiently.

'Good,' I say, 'send Davis down there, I—'

'I want to take this one...' he interrupts me, quickly adding, 'if that's okay with you, boss?'

I glance at Davis. She's looking down at some notes, oblivious, or acting as if she is. I see what's gone on here. Delaney feels left out, that I've been giving Davis preferential treatment and he feels undermined and undervalued. Or perhaps he's worried she'll take some of the glory that he seems to have already awarded himself. Or perhaps I've got it all wrong. I've heard titters that it's been said I've got the hots for little Davis, which is absolute childish nonsense. She's a reliable, hard-working and efficient copper, no more no less. Although admittedly I prefer her company to Delaney's, she's easy-going, plus she smells nicer. They wouldn't say the same if she was man of course and I feel a bit sorry for her because of it. But I won't let power struggles disguised as playground rumours effect my decisions or judgements and Delaney had better know it.

'I need you on the storage unit,' I tell Delaney, 'I think Davis ought to talk to the husband, seeing as though he has such respect for women.' I say this tongue-in-cheek of course. I don't look to see his response, but I can pretty much imagine it. 'Good going gang,' I finish up, 'talk to everyone, as many people as you can, but it's Harper we need to get to, and quickly.'

'The estate agents knew her as Danni-Jo,' Harding says, 'but can't shed any light as to her whereabouts, said she told them she was going away on business for a while and to lease her apartment on a short-let basis. They've provided us with her details, her phone number, but it's already been disconnected.'

I roll my eyes. *Another dead end.*

'We did get a description of her though boss: blonde, striking, around 5ft 5in, early thirties, well-dressed, slim. She fits the bill. They've agreed to meet us at the property – they've squared it with the tenant. We need to have a look around, search the place. Forensics found unknown DNA in Karen's apartment and if we're lucky we'll get some from her apartment and a potential match. She could even already be on the system.'

'Well then,' I say, looking at Harding, 'what are you doing sitting here – check it!'

*

Before I leave, I take the opportunity to call Fiona Li but first, on a complete whim, I decide to send Florence a text message. It says just one word: '*Sorry.*' I hope it's enough.

CHAPTER FORTY-FOUR

PC Burns, a friendly-faced middle-aged woman who strikes me as a solid, hard-working copper is briefing me on the house call she and PC Choudrhi made after Karen put in a complaint. She's referring back to her notes with precision.

'Karen seemed distressed', she tells me, 'when we arrived at her apartment she appeared nervous – and she also appeared a little paranoid. She was convinced that her ex-husband had poisoned her cat, Esmerelda, after the vet had claimed it was likely she had ingested poison and needed to be put down. Karen's ex-husband, Richard Marks, is known to us. Delightful bloke who liked to give her a good battering on the not-so-odd occasion, apparently.'

'Yeah, so I hear,' I say flatly.

'Yes, well Karen looked much older than forty-eight,' Burns says sadly, 'that's what abuse does to you… I've seen it so many times.'

It almost fractures my heart to hear about Karen's miserable, wretched life, of all the adversity she had faced and struggled so fiercely to overcome, only to be met with such a grizzly, horrific end. No fucking justice to any of it. Anger rushes like blood to the surface of my skin, making it prickle.

PC Choudrhi strikes me as the still-waters type so I ask him a few questions. Silent types, in my experience, sometimes have unbelievable observational skills. While others are busy engaging, their brains are operating on another level, watching and absorbing the minutiae of life around them. I turn to him.

'What impression did you get from the suspect?'

'I didn't like her,' he says, no window dressing. 'There was something disingenuous about her.'

I like this word, *disingenuous*.

'Disingenuous, how?'

He shrugs almost subconsciously, pausing as he thinks. 'She seemed… she chose her words carefully, at least in my opinion, placing ideas and thoughts into the conversation.'

'Like what exactly?'

He pauses again, I can see he's struggling to explain and I understand, I understand better than most. 'It's not really what she said… not even what she didn't say… It's just, I don't know, intuition,' he explains. 'Sorry Sir,' he apologises, 'not much help I realise.'

But I smile and nod.

'She was a dark blonde,' Burns says, 'slim, around 5ft 5in or 5ft 6in maybe, late twenties or early thirties, said she was a student…' She flicks through her note pad, scanning the pages, 'performing arts… ULC I've written here.'

Burns tells me that the blonde had a key to Karen's apartment, she'd been given it after she'd locked herself out a few weeks' prior – she had seemed like a caring, concerned neighbour. She told Burns they were friends, explained that she occasionally stopped by for a cup of tea or a glass of wine. Burns talks about the apartment, how beautiful and tasteful it was and how Danni-Jo had said her father had left it to her in his will. She was chatty and helpful, expressing sympathy for her neighbour, and said that she was glad to have established a relationship with her.

'She was very pretty,' Burns says, almost as an afterthought.

Suddenly I get a chill. One of those icy numbers that makes you shudder a little involuntarily, like someone's just walked over your grave.

CHAPTER FORTY-FIVE

George is a delightful child. He's smiley and even-tempered. He doesn't cry much, except for when he's hungry or needs his nappy changing, and he sleeps like a dream – for hours on end without waking – and even then, when he wakes, he's usually in a good mood, making contented gurgling noises and cooing.

She watches him in his cot as he stirs himself awake, pulling his knees up to his chest and grabbing hold of his tiny toes. His face is a library of expressions as though he's testing out every muscle. She dresses him beautifully; he has a wardrobe stuffed with exquisite designer outfits, stripy Petit Bateau rompers and matching Ralph Lauren two-pieces, corduroy shorts and miniature shirts, dungarees and tiny leather jackets, soft pram shoes and Converse chucks, and Gucci loafers for special occasions. Nothing but the best and finest for George.

He's taken to her like most men do – easily, though perhaps, even she admits, that this is more to do with George's sunny disposition than anything else. He loves being cuddled and held, tickled and attended to, yet he's also quite happy being left on his little mat to play independently, kicking his legs and rolling over onto his belly, something he's only just started to do, she's noticed. Watching George is her new favourite pastime. Every day there's something new to marvel at: a noise, a movement, a facial expression, a milestone. His selfish bitch of a mother couldn't seem to care less. She goes out to 'work' so she says, but secretly Rachel believes she's off shopping, drinking, at the gym, socialising with friends and attending to her myriad beauty needs. She doesn't seem the slightest bit interested in little George and his progress; she's too busy preening, getting herself in shape so she can snare herself another rich business man to rinse dry and pretend to love while she impresses the neighbours.

There's something so fickle about babies she thinks as she picks up his warm, strong little body and pulls him into her, as long as they're getting what they want they're happy. 'Shall we have breakfast, George?' she asks him, examining his fluffy head, his tiny ears and perfectly shaped nose, a real button of a nose. 'Some pureed pear perhaps, you like that don't you? Not too tart.' George gurgles and coos, making little high-pitched sounds of what she thinks are appreciation, as if he's really trying to talk to her. 'Then we'll go for a walk in Langley Park, see the swans and the ducks, the duckies, yeah, duckie wuks… quack, quack… We can go on the swings and the slide too, hmm? Yes, good boy,' she sings to him in babyspeak as she places him back on the mat and begins the process of preparing breakfast, peeling, coring and pureeing the soft pears with care and warming his formula, enjoying the responsibility of her new role. This motherhood business has really given her a new sense of purpose. So much so that she thinks she may even want to do it herself one day, one day soon in fact. Having someone so small and helpless dependent upon you for everything: sustenance, love, cuddles, cleanliness, stimulation. It's a powerful, omnipotent feeling that she likes. She doesn't understand why so many women bitch and moan about how difficult it is, how emotionally taxing, draining, exhausting, compromising… They must be just weak and selfish, the lot of them. She has an image then, of George's mother bending over his tiny graveside, the grief-stricken mother in black, bereft and inconsolable yet somewhere within her a tiny slither of relief lingers. *She has her life back.*

She thinks about Daniel then. Not so much the man himself but what he'd had the potential to represent to her and the outside world. A hard-working, loving husband and father, solidity, a unit; something she has never been part of or fully understood. All her points of reference have been garnered from listening to others, or from TV, films and books. She tries to really feel these feelings, conjure them up inside of herself, but she simply has no benchmark to go by, just a beautiful fantasy of a reality she isn't familiar with. *Daniel*. She'd tried to excite and intrigue him, but it had failed. That he'd snubbed her open invitation to have sex with her had threatened her very existence at a deep core level, although she had ensured he would not know this. Instead, she'd asked him about Rachel, the woman he so obviously deeply loved and missed, a woman who had been cruelly taken from him suddenly and unexpectedly, leaving him broken, damaged and unable to recover. How beautifully he had spoken of Rachel and his love for her, of their love for each other. And with each word she came closer to the truth that no one, no one ever had or would feel the same things about her. She thought of all the times she had given herself to men; hundreds, possibly thousands of times, the feelings she had experienced in those moments, of being desired and special, however fleeting and ephemeral, however transient, they had existed, she had *felt* them, even with the paying clients. She didn't mind the rough ones, in fact, she had always felt more at ease with the ones who wanted to debase her, hurt her physically and degrade her, there was comfort in familiarity. Because after the degradation came the love, just like it had with her father. She could still feel him now, bearing down upon her tiny frame, the weight of his protruding stomach on her small pelvis… His power, crushing her, weighing her down. She still felt the sharp pain of him inside her sometimes, and with other men, the well-endowed ones, the pain seamlessly blending into pleasure. Afterwards he would hold her close to him, stroke her hair and arms until she fell asleep against his stomach, cradled in is arms. *Daddy Bear*. But Daniel had been different somehow, *was different*. Or perhaps she felt differently with him, a kinship, an understanding of what it was to be broken and bleeding inside. Whatever it was, lying there on that bed together in that quirky little hotel room above the restaurant had made her feel human, hopeful, that perhaps there could be redemption for her after all, at least once all of this was over.

She wondered, as she maneuvered George into his high chair, his legs kicking in all directions, if she would ever have a child of her own. The doctors had told her that it was highly unlikely, that the damage to her insides would prevent it. But there were other ways, IVF, adoption, even surrogacy. *There is more than one way to skin a cat.* The saying makes her think of Esmerelda and in turn, Kizzy. She wonders if they've found her yet. She'd be starting to smell bad by now.

She began to feed George his pear, scooping little blobs of puree into his open mouth like a baby bird in a nest. He liked his food, did George. In fact, George seemed to like just about everything really.

'There's a good Baby Bear,' she said as he swallowed greedily.

CHAPTER FORTY-SIX

I put the lights on as we make our way down to Rebecca Harper's apartment block. And I feel every justification in doing so because as far as emergencies go this is pretty high up there. As much as I don't want to conceive of the idea that there's a human being on the planet that would want to harm a baby, I know that there's a very real possibility, even probability, that this is Harper's intention, or worse, that she's already completed her twisted fairy tale.

My phone rings as I tear through West End streets thick with traffic and tourism, bypassing them all in a flurry of blurred colour like a watercolour painting. There's an urgency inside me now, a shift in adrenaline, because I know we're getting closer and the situation is critical. I imagine Rebecca Harper with a child in her arms, I see her in my mind, pretty, blonde, pushing a pram, or holding a young child's hand. Slipping unnoticed through society, another young mum out and about with her child; her dark intentions never suspected… It's as dark as a thought can get really.

It's Harding. 'Rebecca Harper, boss, it turns out that she was in a young offender's institute for quite a while when she was a kid… then transferred to Greene Parks, the psychiatric unit for minors. She spent eight years there, boss, for allegedly killing her own mother – *when she was nine years old*.'

I close my eyes and draw breath. We're dealing with a psychopath. I'd suspected this but it makes the impact no less disturbing. She's a child killer – in every sense. I ask myself how a nine-year-old child comes to kill their own mother.

'Okay. You've been on to them, Greene Parks?'

'Yes boss, we've requested the file. She was under the care of a Dr Elizabeth Magnesson. Apparently Magnesson continued to see Harper and counsel her up until quite recently, two years ago in fact.'

'Call Greene Parks and tell them we're coming down to see Magnesson as soon as we're finished at the apartment. Make sure she's available. This is urgent, Harding. Don't be fobbed off. Any photo ID yet?'

'No Boss, but it's imminent.'

I nod, but of course she can't see this. 'Well done Harding,' I say before I hang up.

CHAPTER FORTY-SEVEN

I don't much like estate agents. I remember the estate agent who showed me and Rach around our apartment for the first time, some jumped-up little upstart in a Burton suit with a Gucci belt (that was probably snide) called Miles. His affability betrayed his insincerity with such transparency that it made us both feel a bit queasy. The cheap suit coupled with the pseudo-expensive belt summed up the disparity he was clearly grappling within himself: what he really was and what he hoped to become.

Lana Jones, however, appears efficient and helpful. And terribly posh.

'Such a dreadful business.' Her blonde bob wobbles as she shakes her head in something resembling concern, 'the woman opposite…'

I nod, and ask her if she can let us into the apartment. She duly obliges. I can see she's dying to ask questions, to know more about the 'terrible business' at number seven. It's human nature of course. There's police tape covering Karen's front door and she looks at it, visibly shudders.

'Gives me the heebie-jeebies thinking of that poor woman left in there… It was definitely murder then, Detective, not suicide? I read it the paper… same thing happened to that man didn't it? Nigel someone, in the hotel room – at Le Reymond, beautiful hotel that, the suites are something else – have you been? So you're looking for the girl… the one who lived here, Danni-Jo? Do you think she has something to do with it, that she could be the killer?' Her eyes light up.

I'm half expecting her to jump up and down and start clapping her hands together like a seal. I haven't seen the papers yet, but I hope Touchy has done me proud. We didn't have any ID on Danni-Jo, or Rebecca Harper or whoever the hell she really is, so I told Touchy to use the CCTV footage from the hotel, maybe jog a few memories that way. It was the best I could give her. All I could give her.

'Chills my blood really, to think I've come face-to-face with a serial killer, well, a potential one anyway, such a pretty girl too, well, *woman* I suppose, but thinking back there was something quite childlike about her really.' She pauses, as though this recollection has only just struck her. 'But to think... well, you'd never have thought by looking at her that she was a psychopath, I mean, she *slit their wrists open...*' Lana visibly shudders again.

I'm tempted to tell her that psychopaths tend not to advertise their psychopathic tendencies, but it's not my job to educate her. You'd think, by her accent, that her private school might've done that.

'We'd appreciate it if you could let us have a look around the apartment, Miss Jones,' Davis gives her a thin smile and she rolls her eyes apologetically as though she realises she has forgotten herself.

'God, yes of course, of course.'

I ask her what they had talked about, she and Danni-Jo, and to give me her overall impression of her. This request seems to make her day.

'She seemed very pleasant all in all, quite chatty and friendly, but it was a while back now you understand, so forgive me if I can't recall the conversation verbatim, I talk to a lot of people day in, day out, you know, the job... must be the same for you... All the boys in the office were quite taken with her though, that much I *do* remember, couldn't keep their tongues inside their heads when she walked in... like dogs on heat.' She laughs and I nod mandatorily – nothing of note then. 'Of course I remember her not just because she was rather pretty but also because she bought this place clean outright. Cash buyer. It's not highly unusual, given that we're Winterton's and we deal with a certain calibre of clientele, but still.'

She's adjusting the lapel on her sharp and expensive yet ill-fitting suit, and I can't help imagining that she attends slimming classes and doesn't include the pricey wine she drinks every night on her intake sheet. *Sins for the seven glasses of wine*!

'So you definitely think it was her then, this Danni-Jo, the same girl?' She has one of those shrill voices that cut through you like nails on a blackboard.

'Did she elaborate on her personal situation; a boyfriend, family, work, where the money came from to purchase the apartment?'

'Hmm, inheritance I believe, at least I think that's what she said. Actually, I've brought along the file. It contains her photo ID and the name of the solicitors she used for the sale. I'm sure they'll be able to help you fi…'

I almost snatch the file from her, which causes her to look at me in momentary alarm.

She just said photo *ID*.

Davis, who has already started rifling through drawers and cupboards, clocks my urgency and comes over. I spread the papers out over the white leather couch, deeds and letterheaded paper, searches and land-registry administration and… there's a photocopy of a passport, yes… I pick it up and look at it and then I go dizzy.

CHAPTER FORTY-EIGHT

'Well she was up her own arse wasn't she? *Our clientele…*' Davis mimics Lana Jones' clipped voice as she pulls out of the underground car park with a screech. 'Can't stand estate agents, all the bloody same, right up themselves.' She takes a double glance at me. 'You okay, Boss? You looked a bit unwell back there, a bit pale.'

I manage a nod. My throat is tight like a vice. My heart is in overdrive, banging against my chest cavity, breathing is becoming a problem.

'Well, up her arse or not, thanks to her we know what the bitch looks like now,' Davis says, elated, 'and now we'll have her.'

I literally can't speak, not even a rasp. My brain feels as if it's been lobotomised and won't connect to my mouth. I think I'm going into shock. The picture, the passport picture… the girl – the woman – in the picture, it wasn't Danni-Jo, at least not as I know her. *It was Florence.* Florence Williams. The woman I recently spent the night with. The woman whose forehead I kissed, whose intimate scent still hangs heavy in my nostrils.

Florence is Goldilocks. And this unexpected revelation has floored me to the point that I've mentally flatlined; a similar feeling to when Bob Jenkins told me Rachel was dead. This seriously compromises my position. In fact it compromises the whole fucking case. A court scene plays itself out in my mind, her barristers, Rebecca Harper's briefs, taking me apart on the stand. 'You wanted to have sex with her didn't you DI Riley, and when she turned you down you set about instigating a campaign of hate against her…'

I tell myself not to panic, panic solves nothing, but my guts are frantically unravelling like old rope. This is a nightmare, an unreal and diabolical coincidence that I'm struggling to process. And the questions that keep putting their heads above the parapet are *why* and *how?*

Our 'relationship' plays back like grainy CCTV footage in my mind. The first 'date' in the pub when I'd forgotten I was supposed to be meeting Touchy… The night at the sushi restaurant, the flash of her underwear, her hand as she guided mine up her thigh, her soft wetness… The walk in Hyde Park afterwards, listening to the birds singing as we stumbled along slightly intoxicated, Florence running on ahead… the dress and biker boots that she was wearing, and the flower I picked and gave to her. It doesn't seem real. None of it.

Did she know who I was?
Is this some kind of sick and twisted game?
Has she been playing me all along?

But the thing that's eating me up most is that I didn't sense anything. No alarm bells, no red flags, no niggly feelings that something was amiss. No tug on that infamous intuition of mine that I rely so heavily upon. And I feel embarrassed; she's duped me completely, pulled the wool over my eyes in spectacular fashion. I think about that night again, at the hotel, her naked skin against mine, and how close I had come to making love to her.

I say 'Thank God' aloud as I signal to Davis to pull over, and then promptly throw up out of the car door.

CHAPTER FORTY-NINE

Greene Parks gives me the shits. It's the kind of place that looks as if it could be welcoming on the outside, with its jaunty Victorian charm and smooth stone façade, hanging baskets full of petunias and a bright red door. But it's the metaphorical equivalent of covering up piss with perfume. And here it seems, the top notes of *eau de* urine have won out.

A nurse greets me and Davis with an affable smile that belies the nightmarish sadness I'm sure she experiences on a daily basis. I find it odd, really, because despite my job I've never got *used* to seeing, and hearing of, the atrocities human beings encounter and cause one another. They can still shock me. However, Nurse Arlington, as she introduces herself as, appears to have become desensitised to her surroundings.

Never become hardened Danny, Rach used to say, don't let the job rob you of that soft sod I know you are inside.

But although Greene Parks looks like it could be a hotel from the outside, there's no room for ambiguity inside. It's a hospital; a mental hospital, an *asylum*. There is an expanse of grey that seems to take over your pupils and all your peripheral vision, people walking around in white suits like astronauts. The atmosphere is punctuated by shrill noises and cries, the sounds of anguish and despair. It's the kind of place that would soon make sane people mad. Yeah, it's basically *One Flew Over a Cuckoo's Nest*. That was Nicholson's defining moment wasn't it? He even outshone his performance in *The Shining* in that film, and he's pretty fucking brilliant in *The Shining*. Shit, who was the lead actress who played his wife in it? I can see her, I know her name… fuck… all toothy and awkward, played the terrorised victim brilliantly.

Nurse Arlington strikes me as a hard bitch beneath the smile, robotic, almost sub-human. Or perhaps she's just found a way to cope working in a place like this, a place for mentally disturbed children and young adults. Sadness literally drips off the ugly, faded floral curtains that somehow seem incongruous, a failed attempt at brightening up hell. I have to wonder what Arlington's calling is? I'm pretty sure Lidl pay better.

'Doctor Magnesson is expecting you', she says in an accent I can't place. Eastern European maybe? Doesn't really matter, but it sounds as hard as she looks and I think about how the little hat and dress she's wearing have always represented comfort, comedy, even sexuality in our culture, yet probably mean something very different to the lost souls that exist like ghosts among these grey walls.

Davis looks as pissed off and uncomfortable as me, which reaffirms that she's completely sound of mind. We're led down the cold, grey corridor. The doors to the cells are on the left, and faces appear at them as we walk down it to a soundtrack of banging doors and the clatter and rattle of keys. The air is punctuated by the occasional shout and cry. A young girl, a teenager, fifteen tops I'd guess, with greasy black hair and a grey tracksuit that seems to blend into the walls waves at us, and I smile and wave back.

'Don't be alarmed. New people. New faces. They always react like this,' Arlington says, like they're dogs in kennels. I sense she feels contempt for the poor wretches she looks after and I dislike her for it. Smiles seems scarce here. The young mentally ill and criminally insane. How does that happen? I think of her, of Florence, of Rebecca Harper, and wonder how you can be so fucked up at nine years old that you end up here? Am I naïve? Probably. But children aren't born evil, are they? Neglect, abandonment, abuse… It's rare that you don't see at least one of these as prefixes to the deterioration of a child's mental well-being. Statistics prove that many people who are victims of abuse go on to become abusers themselves. I don't think it's right; I don't think it's an excuse. But I do think it explains a lot.

'Doctor Magnesson is very busy, I'm sure you'll understand, but she has agreed to fit you in. Your colleague explained the urgency.'

I think Nurse Arlington is expecting a thank you so I deliberately withhold it. I've not really taken to her. I'm struggling to hold it together as it is.

'This is her office,' she stops abruptly and knocks on the grey door. I half expect her to say, 'the doctor will see you now,' but she turns abruptly on her spongy heels without so much as a goodbye and as she does it comes to me… *Shelley Duvall.*

CHAPTER FIFTY

Elizabeth Magnesson, in stark contrast to Nurse Arlington, has a kind, open face as round as the moon and almost as pale. Somewhere, I would say, in her mid-fifties; her hair is an unruly mass of wobbling black curls peppered with grey and she wears glasses perched at the end of her thin nose. She is oddly attractive in a quirky, bohemian sort of way and I imagine she was probably quite striking in her prime.

Her office is stark; unadorned grey walls and a desk with two mismatching chairs opposite. There's a cabinet, a wastepaper basket and a low wooden table in the middle of the room. The potted palm plant in the corner is an attempt to make it appear marginally less uninviting, but the accent is heavily on marginal. It's grim, the interior equivalent of despair. 'You're here to talk to me about Becca, yes, Becca Harper?' Her accent is faint but detectable. My money's on Scandinavian.

Becca.

'Yes. I'm DI Riley, Dan Riley, and this is DS Davis. We're investigating the suspected murders of Nigel Baxter and Karen Walker and believe you may be able to assist us.'

She nods officially at us. 'I can certainly try, Detective Riley. Please, take a seat, both of you.'

I politely decline. I'm concerned that if I sit down I may never get back up again.

'She is in some kind of trouble I take it, Becca?'

I clear my throat a little too loudly. I feel queasy, still reeling from shock I think. Florence is Danni-Jo and Danni-Jo is Rebecca and Rebecca is Goldilocks. And Goldilocks has savagely murdered two people. And I've been to bed with her. I've been intimate with a cold-blooded killer and the reality of this has only just started to trickle through the firewall I've attempted to erect in my head in a bid not to accept the truth. I remind myself that I'm here to do a job, *my job*, and that I need to hold it together now more than ever.

'Some water, Detective?' She says, perhaps sensing my turmoil. She pours a little into a paper cup from the jug on her desk and I accept it gratefully.

'We need to speak to Rebecca Harper in conjunction with the murder of two people. Murders which were both made to look like suicide. We think she may be responsible for these murders, Dr Magnesson, and that she may be acting out some kind of fairy-tale fantasy, namely the story of the three bears… are you familiar with it?'

'Yes, yes of course I am.' She appears mildly affronted but if she's surprised or shocked by this suggestion she certainly doesn't show it.

'We were hoping you could give us some information on Miss Harper. We believe she spent some time here at Greene Parks as a child, and that you were her therapist, is that correct?'

'No. I was her doctor. Still am, officially. And as such, you'll appreciate that I have an obligation towards my client, Detective – client confidentiality. But I am also aware that the law requires me to share information in the event of a situation such as this.'

I'm relieved to hear it. 'Lives are at stake here Dr Magnesson. We believe Rebecca Harper is very dangerous and that she may be on the lookout for, or may have already targeted, her third victim; a victim we strongly believe could be a child, *a minor.*'

'Baby Bear you mean?'

'Yes. You don't seem surprised Doctor. Was this a fantasy she discussed with you, the story of the three bears?'

Magnesson exhales as she removes her glasses and places them on the desk. 'We discussed many, many things in the time she spent here during our sessions, you understand. I ended up knowing Becca quite well in the end, or perhaps not knowing her at all. I never knew which for sure. I'm saddened to hear of this situation, but surprised?' She shakes her head, curls wobbling.

'And why is that?' I can feel the bile rising up through my stomach to my mouth again and will it back down.

'Please,' she says, 'I really do think it is best if you sit down.'

CHAPTER FIFTY-ONE

'Rebecca Harper first came to Greene Parks over two decades ago, twenty-four years ago to be precise. She was nine or perhaps ten at the time she arrived here, I forget which, transferred from a young offender's institute as it was clear that she was suffering with mental-health issues and needed specific care. She should never have been put into mainstream care to begin with in my opinion; she arrived in a terrible condition. She was assigned to me, my first ever case after qualifying as a psychiatrist actually, perhaps this is why I have such a…' Dr Magnesson is searching for the right words. I suspect she is going to say 'fondness' though wisely she stops short of it.

But I understand her feelings better than she knows.

'To this day Detective, after twenty-four years at this hospital, of all the patients I have seen who have been under my care, Becca remains one of the most difficult, and frankly fascinating cases I have ever worked with.'

'You say this like it's some kind of accolade Doctor.'

She smiles, wistfully. 'Well, from a professional point of view, Becca was a rarity.'

'Oh, and why is that?' I sip the water and quickly place it on the desk. My hands are shaking.

'She was a child psychopath, though many of my contemporaries prefer to give the condition other, more palatable labels, especially when it comes to minors, but this does not prevent it from being what it is. *What she is* – in my professional opinion, of course. But she scored extremely highly on the Levenson Scale, which was relatively new at the time.

'The Levenson Scale?'

'Yes, the psychopathy test invented by Michel Levenson. It's a series of yes or no questions. This of course is not to be confused with the Leveson Inquiry, which is quite a different thing altogether.' She smiles, seemingly self-satisfied with such a topical political joke.

'Rebecca Davis was incarcerated here because she killed her mother, is that correct?' Davis asks.

'Yes. Supposedly. Although the inquest recorded the death as accidental. There was no evidence, just a confession from Becca.'

'Do you believe she was responsible?'

'It does not matter what I believe really, Detective Riley. Importantly *she* believed she was responsible, though it is just as likely that her mother took her own life.'

'If that was the case then why on earth would Rebecca claim to have killed her own mother? Have herself incarcerated as a result?'

Dr Magnesson pauses and meets my eyes directly. 'I should explain a little more about the case. It's complex, really not as straightforward as you may think – and not very pleasant.'

'I think nothing, Dr Magnesson, that's why I'm here, so that you can tell me. Why would a child confess to murdering their own mother if this was not true?'

She exhales again. 'All of us possess psychopathic traits, Detective Riley, in the right measure they can be highly beneficial to navigating through life and achieving success, no doubt in your line of work too.' She gently raises an eyebrow. 'Becca was textbook really, completely lacking in empathy, charming and persuasive, extremely likeable in fact. However, she was a highly manipulative fantasist, grandiose, fearless, completely unfazed by her own destructive behavior and the effect it had on others. It is probable that she killed her mother, but also equally as probable that she enjoyed the attention she received for saying that she had. Her story would change to suit her; in one version she would cast herself as the victim, in another she was the unrepentant perpetrator.'

'You said Rebecca was just nine years old when she arrived here. That's so young,' Davis says, unable to hide the sadness in her voice, 'do you think she was born a psychopath?'

Dr Magnesson opens her hands. 'Ahh, the great debate. Some experts believe this is possible, yes, others, no, and many more are undecided. It is not an exact science.'

'So where do you fit in Doctor?'

Magnesson ponders the question carefully. 'Each case is individual but with Becca, her brain patterns were different, the structures of her prefrontal cortex,' she points above her eyes, running her finger horizontally above them, 'this part here is responsible for your emotions, rage, anger, happiness, joy, pain, the ability to feel empathy, love, sexual pleasure, fear; it regulates them all, releases chemicals in response… This part of Becca's brain, after tests, showed impaired responses and unusual patterns. I remember once she took part in an experiment where we showed her various images, monitoring her responses and blink reflexes. The images ranged from the very cute and cuddly, kittens and babies, fields full of flowers, beautiful scenery and the like, to dismembered bodies, the charred remains of children who'd perished in fires, grizzly murder scenes, quite sickening stuff, not least for a child to see. The results were striking. Becca's reflexes and responses were almost identical to all of the images she'd been shown – meaning that she could distinguish no emotional difference between seeing a headless corpse and a cute puppy; she was neither moved nor repulsed, unfazed by both. It was unusual to see this in someone so young.'

'You didn't answer the question, Doctor.'

'The difference between a psychopath becoming the CEO of a successful company and going on to become a cold-blooded murderer I think is a fairly straightforward one...'

'It is? How?'

'Trauma,' she says, 'abuse. The psychopathic killers I have encountered throughout my career have all suffered abuse or early childhood trauma of some sort without exception. So to answer your question, yes and no. In my opinion I believe Becca was born with distinguishable differences in her prefrontal cortex and brain patterns, so perhaps genetics played a part, but it was the abuse and trauma she suffered as a young child that triggered these characteristics and turned her into what she was and *is*.'

'Which is?'

'A psychopath, Detective, like I've said.'

I don't want to get into the nature or nurture debate with Dr Magnesson; I suspect she has twenty-four more years of experience to draw upon than me.

'Rebecca seems to have assumed many identities in her time Dr Magnesson. Used aliases and disguises.'

'Yes, this is not so surprising. Becca claimed, when she was in my charge, to have more than one personality. Though she was certainly not schizophrenic, not in the traditional sense. She genuinely believed she was more than one person with a completely separate, unique set of emotions, thoughts, and opinions. In medical terms we call this "splitting", whereby a severely traumatised individual who has internalised their defective feelings creates different personas as a coping mechanism. Essentially, those afflicted discard their true selves in favour of a more... palatable personality, a mask if you will, though one which, I should point out, is very real indeed. You see, mostly, their authentic selves, feelings and emotions have betrayed them, gone unmet or been ridiculed, ignored or disparaged somehow, therefore they rid themselves of those feelings altogether by becoming someone else. To feel something would make them human, force them to face their deep, emotional wounds, and this would be far too painful, perhaps even induce suicide, which I have seen in some cases with psychotic patients who have attempted to heal their core wounds.' She looks depleted as she says this, 'Rebecca Harper was deeply disturbed, perhaps the most disturbed child of her age that I had ever treated in my career. She was also exhibiting bipolar and anti-social behaviour when she arrived.'

Top of everyone's birthday party list then.

'She was not a well little girl, Detective. But she was still a little girl.'

'A little girl who killed her mother.' Davis adds.

Dr Magnesson stands then. She's small and curvy. I wonder if she has children of her own. 'That's as may be. But in Becca's mind she truly believed that what she was doing was an act of mercy *not* murder, her mother's death was a mercy killing in her mind, or so she had us believe.'

'And did you, *believe her* I mean?'

She exhales again. 'Becca was, even back then, a highly manipulative individual, intelligent, very plausible, showing all the marked traits of such individuals afflicted with psychopathy. She fooled many people in authority, I think,' Magnesson adds, 'even me, at times. It's a complicated, complex disorder... I shall be honest Detective, I was never sure whether Becca herself believed that what she had done was indeed an act of mercy, or if she simply tried to make us believe this in a bid to control and manipulate her surroundings. One thing I am convinced of however, was that she did suffer abuse at the hands of her parents, and most certainly her father. A fantasist she may be, but my experience, my intuition told me from the beginning that she was not lying about the abuse.'

Ahh, the old intuition thing again.

'How did she do it?' Davis asks, which was going to be my next question. 'How did she kill her mother?'

'She said her mother fell down the stairs, only it didn't kill her outright so she put a pillow over her face to complete the job, though this was not documented in the inquest. There was no record of asphyxiation anywhere in the post-mortem.'

'And she attempted to cover it up by making it look like her mother had committed suicide?'

Nobody's fool then. Even at nine.

'That would take a calculated mind, wouldn't it Dr Magnesson, to deliberately try to cover up one's crimes?'

She peers at me over the rim of her glasses, which are perched back on her nose again. 'The police thought this initially, yes. But actually I believe Becca *wanted* to be found out. In doing what she did, Becca told me that by removing her own mother she hoped she too would be removed from her diabolical situation – an act of desperation, of self-preservation. She told me that her father was a brutal deviant of the very worst kind; that he brought prostitutes back to the home and would tie them up and abuse them while Becca and her mother were present. During regression therapy she recounted early memories of hearing these women's screams of terror and pain. Sometimes, she said, he would make her and her mother watch as he raped them or force his wife to join in with the abuse. She claims he beat them both regularly and viciously but was careful to ensure most of their bruises were hidden and unseen – the worst being the psychological ones of course. Another time she recalled an occasion when she ate some sweets before dinnertime, a common childhood misdemeanour. As punishment she claimed that her father burnt her tongue so badly with an iron that it swelled to three times its size and she was unable to talk or eat for well over a week. Her mother gave up trying to protect her in the end and became so desensitised to the abuse that eventually she was like the walking dead, a zombie.

Often during our conversations Becca referred to her mother as the 'ghost'. So adept, she said, was her father at conditioning and controlling their environment that in the end Becca told me that she and her mother sometimes fought over who could take the bigger beating. It actually became a competition between them who could withstand the most punishment. When she arrived here at the hospital her cortisol level was off the Richter scale. The girl was in constant fight-or-flight mode and did not appear to understand any other way of existing, which certainly fits with the abuse she described.'

'Didn't anyone notice what was going on? The school, a relative, a neighbour – *anyone*? Why weren't the authorities alerted? Surely someone must have suspected they were being so mistreated. Was the father ever brought before police, was there any investigation?'

'There was no record ever of any reported or even suspected abuse, Detective, but this is not to say it never took place. I'm sure you know well in your position, just how clever and manipulative these people can be, psychopaths and abusers, and I am truly of the opinion that Becca's father was probably one himself. They will go to great lengths to ensure they slip under the radar undetected. And it's usually completely plausible. Psychopaths are by their very nature incredibly believable. In fact, their believability is one of the greatest symptoms of psychopathy itself.' She pauses.

'Assuming it's all true of course.'

Magnesson looks at me intensely. 'He denied any wrongdoing of course, the father. On the occasions we spoke to him to give feedback on his daughter he told us that he truly believed that Rebecca had been born evil. He told us that he and his wife had noticed she had exhibited 'unusual' behavior practically from birth and that on numerous occasions he suspected she had harmed or maimed various pets in the neighbourhood. He told us a story of a rabbit they bought her for her seventh birthday.

How Becca had adored it and became inseparable from it, until one day she'd attempted to put it back in its cage and the animal had scratched her. The next day the rabbit was discovered dead with its neck broken and an eye missing. Becca had told her parents that she mustn't have shut the cage properly and that a fox had attacked and killed it, and then she casually asked what was for dinner.

'However, Becca's stories were highly contrastable; she explained how her father began sexually abusing her at five years old and that eventually she learned to look forward to the abuse, and the love and affection he would show her after it had taken place. It was this brief window, this five minutes of favour that she longed for. The abuse itself was just an unpleasant prelude to reaching that moment of comfort.'

Five years old.

Davis and I exchange looks.

'To be frank Detective, I wanted to help Rebecca Harper more than I've ever wanted to help another child in my entire career. But she was so damaged it was like trying to glue together a pane of glass that has shattered into a million tiny shards. I – *we* – did try of course: psychotherapy, drugs, CBT, regression, electric-shock therapy, hours upon hours of treatment both conventional and unconventional. But the drugs didn't work.'

They just make you worse…

'Not really anyway; they kept her in a calm, almost vegetative state sometimes, but they did not undo the damage. There were times when I felt we had made progress; she was, *is* a highly intelligent girl, well, woman now, but all empathy had been killed off within her, essentially rendering her little more than an emotionally-barren shell. During puberty she became suicidal, suffered from eating disorders and self-harmed.'

I think of her body; I've seen it, I didn't look closely, not closely enough.

'I was under no illusions about Becca's prognosis,' she continues, 'but I always hoped I could help her reach a level where she might go on to lead a relatively normal life, one where she would not continue to carry so much trauma. Where she could learn to manage her condition, to control it, if not to cure it. Which brings us back round to your original question. If one is born a psychopath, it can no more be cured than you or I can change our eye or hair colour. A colleague of mine once described it like this: a psychopath is a cat among mice. You can teach the cat to act like the mouse, and the cat may learn how to act like the mouse and live among them, but it will always be a cat.'

It's obvious that Dr Magnesson is a woman who cares very much about her patients, that she takes her responsibilities seriously *and* personally. It's admirable. I think of the night in the Japanese restaurant, of the woman I'd sat with and ended up holding in my arms; the pretty, almost beautiful, witty, intelligent woman who had even fleetingly reminded me a little of my Rachel, and I can't reconcile her with the person Magnesson is describing now. I'm consumed by guilt and regret and anger all at once, like I've eaten every one of my least-favourite foods at the same time and I'm about to throw them all up.

Davis' phone goes and she gets up, excuses herself from the room.

'Do you think Rebecca Harper is capable of murdering a child, Dr Magnesson?' I ask.

She pours herself some water from the jug and takes a sip, audibly swallowing as she pulls her lips back over her teeth. 'I think, Detective, that Becca is purging herself and her past with these killings; the man represents her father, the woman, her mother and the child...' she pauses, 'the child is the equivalent, in her mind, of killing off herself, her false self – perhaps allowing her to become whole again, in her mind, of course. So, to answer your question Detective,' she says gravely, 'yes, regrettably I do.'

CHAPTER FIFTY-TWO

According to forensics, the prints found in Karen's apartment match prints found in Rebecca Harper's, so it's pretty safe to assume that they belong to the same person. Of course, this proves nothing other than the fact that Rebecca has been in Karen's apartment, which she'd already admitted to and that doesn't make her a criminal.

All we've got is supposition; circumstantial evidence, nothing concrete. It's enough to bring her in though, which is all I care about right now. I don't want the death of a child on my conscience. Hell, I don't want anyone's.

'Asphyxiation,' I glance at Davis, who has just hung up from speaking to Vic Leyton and is relaying Vic's findings. 'Like her own mother… and forensics have found DNA, Boss,' she's animated now, excited, 'on the bear. Same DNA found in Rebecca's apartment.'

I say a silent prayer.

'Even better, Boss… she bought it from a shop in Piccadilly. The assistant has ID'd her. She came in last week, had the paisley dress specially made and everything. Oh and they've found her lock-up… some storage place in Queensway. Harding and Baylis are on their way there now.'

'Good,' I say, 'tell them to get forensics down there too.' I'm wondering what they will find there. Her computer perhaps; her computer with our brief email exchanges on it.

Davis is visibly buoyant.

'Don't count your chickens before they've hatched, Davis. We don't know where she is, remember?'

I don't want to kill her buzz but it pays not to get too excited when you get a break like this, I know from bitter experience.

We're silent for a while. It starts to rain a little and the sound of the wipers punctuates it.

'That's some pretty messed-up life she's had there...' Davis says, finally speaking, like she's been thinking the same thing as me – only it's really not the same because she hasn't slept with this potential killer.

I can all but nod again. My brain aches, like it's been infected by a deadly disease and is slowly turning black. I know that if I go back to the station now then I'll have to come clean with Woods; I'll have to explain the morbid coincidence that somehow I have come to know the suspect personally. His first concern will be how much jeopardy this puts the whole case in, but *my* first concern and the only thing that matters right now is that Rebecca Harper doesn't get to kill again. And I've got an idea.

CHAPTER FIFTY-THREE

I call Fiona Li.

'Touchy?' It's gone straight to voicemail. Bollocks. I leave a message asking her, well, telling her really, that whatever happens she is not to publish a picture of the suspect she knows as Danni-Jo. I say it twice, accentuating the 'do not' part. I hope she gets the message, in every sense.

I drop Davis off at the station and tell her to follow Harding and Willis down to the storage place, let me know what they find. Then I tell her to hold off the press interview we had planned and to field any calls and wait until I'm back.

'But I thought you wanted her picture released? I thought you wanted to go public? And I had my bloody hair done especially, cost me a fortune as well.'

'Hold off until I say so. Oh, and Davis...' she turns back and I smile, nodding at her head, 'you was robbed.'

I pull up outside my, *our*, flat and switch the engine off. Instinctively my head falls into my hands, heavy like a bowling ball. I think about Janet Baxter in her practical shoes and sensible cardigan, about the moment I'd told her that her husband had been murdered, watching as the grief somehow crept over her face like poison ivy. And the image of a five-year-old girl flashes up inside my mind, a pretty little blonde girl being repeatedly abused, being forced to watch her own mother being beaten and gang-raped by a succession of strange men, of her father making her do unspeakable things. Images of slit-open, bloody wrists run through me like still frames, and I see her holding a child – a baby – in her arms triumphantly. There's blood running down her arms as she hold him up like a trophy.

Speaking with Dr Magnesson, I realised that Rebecca Harper is even more dangerous than I could have imagined. Perhaps now I have some idea why and how she came to be what she is. And it's giving me an ache in my chest you know, one of those deep, nagging hollow kind of aches that leave you short of breath. My mind slips off like mercury in all directions, a conflicting junction of sadness and pity for all involved. And yet I cannot, *I must not*, feel the pull of empathy. I must think of the victims, I must remember what Magnesson said about psychopaths and their hypnotic powers of persuasion, their manipulative guises. And yet part of me feels that she, Rebecca Harper, is nothing more than a victim herself.

I pick up my phone and look at it. It's a gamble I realise, one that could cost me the whole investigation, perhaps even my career. And I take deep lungfuls of breath.

'Hey, it's Daniel,' I write, 'I can't stop thinking about you. Can we meet tonight?'

CHAPTER FIFTY-FOUR

The park is busy, full of women with prams and pushchairs, myriad kids in tow. High-pitched shrieks of childish delight punctuate the temperate spring afternoon as the play park fills up with little people, their mothers attempting to have conversations with each other that are inevitably broken as they attend to their overexcited offspring.

'This is George's special day… yes it is,' she coos at him, picking him up from his state-of-the-art pushchair and securing him into the baby swing.

'Weeeeeeeee!' she laughs as she beings to push him gently, her heart filling with something close to joy as his little face lights up. He laughs, a cute, gurgling, infectious giggle. Today is going to be his best day ever and if he could, he'd remember it as such. She will forever hold it dear in her heart and memory, treasuring his final smiles and chuckles. His eyes widen as she pushes him back and forth, and feeds him ice cream that his mother would disapprove of. After his stint on the swings she takes him down to a grassy area by the pond where he can see the ducks and swans.

'Look Baby Bear, duckie ducks…' she points at the birds on the water as George makes excited, appreciative noises from his pushchair. He really does love the ducks. They watch them together as they glide effortlessly across the still water like little floating boats, but she knows that beneath the surface their tiny webbed feet are paddling furiously like motors. The ducks are deceptive; they make it look easy, effortless, and she suddenly has the urge to throw a stone at one of them, to watch the animal's distress, ruffle its feathers, cause ripples in the water. She reaches into her tote bag for the bread she had brought with her and begins to tear it up roughly before handing some to George. He puts it straight into his own mouth and she laughs.

'No, no Baby Bear… the bread is for the ducks.' She throws some into the water and watches as the birds do a 180-degree turn and propel themselves towards it, racing each other in a bid to get to the bread first; it's survival of the fittest. There's a mother with her ducklings, though they are notably older, not fluffy but feathered now, and she bypasses her offspring to feed herself first. 'Selfish Mummy Duck, 'she says and it makes her think of her own mother and George's simultaneously.

A woman appears alongside her with two preschool-age children.

'Don't get too close to the edge now, Spencer…' her voice is clipped and stern. 'Spencer are you listening to me? Let Camilla see the ducks… Spencer! Camilla wants to see the ducks too! Hold her hand… that's it, hold your sister's hand.'

The woman briefly glances at her with the faint acknowledgement of a smile, a silent code of recognition between mothers that she's observed, like they're all secretly thinking the same things.

'Beautiful day,' she remarks to the woman.

'Lovely isn't it,' the woman agrees, sizing her up, presumably to determine whether she is deemed worthy enough of her conversation. But she's not worried; she has the right pram and George is impeccably dressed in Petit Bateau's finest, Breton stripes and brand-new Converse boots, and he's clutching his squidgy Sophie giraffe, a giraffe that seems to be a benchmark among mothers in the clique, a rubber toy that is akin to a VIP pass to an exclusive club. George begins to uncharacteristically grumble.

'He wants the bread for himself.' She rolls her eyes, smiles.

'You're not supposed to feed them, you do realise,' the woman says bossily.

'Children or the ducks?'

The woman glances at her, unsure of how to take the remark. 'There's a sign,' she points to it, a wooden placard down at the water's edge that clearly requests, in peeling red paint, that patrons refrain from feeding the birds. 'Recently some hideous teenagers injured one of the swans you know, threw sticks and stones at the poor thing and tried to feed it crisps and chocolate…'

'That's horrible,' she says. 'Do you know if they prefer salt-and-vinegar flavour…? Think I have some Pom-Bears in my baby bag.'

The woman doesn't appear to have heard her. 'Little sods… their parents should be ashamed.'

'Yes, they should be locked up, the parents.'

Sensing a kindred spirit, the woman moves closer now.

'Spenny and Camilla adore animals. We have two dogs, a cat and some chickens in our garden. They're so at one with nature and animals, they love the flora and fauna… I've brought them up vegan… They tried chicken once but never again, neither of them enjoyed it. You live around here?'

'Yes, in Beckenham.'

'Ah lovely. We used to live there, moved to Langley Park this year.'

'Moving house with two little ones and all those animals – bet that was a joy. How old are they, Spencer and Camilla?'

'Three and a half, they're twins. And yours?'

'He's almost ten months.'

'Gosh, believe me it goes so fast, like a whirlwind. Not sure how I've gotten through it all really, Pinot and Dominos mainly… the two 'o's mainly.' She laughs loudly, like gunshot across the pond. 'Yours is at the age when they're still so dependent, my two are just beginning to find their feet. I can't even go to the bathroom alone for a few minutes now.' She guffaws, a horrible horsey laugh that makes 'Rachel' want to spit in her face.

'It's tough, yes,' she says, 'but *so* rewarding.' These are the things she's overheard mothers saying, words and phrases they seem to share with each other, lying to each other and themselves.

'I'm still bloody recovering from the birth three and half years later... Fifteen hours of sheer hell, but I still managed to have them naturally, only a little gas and air. Spenny was the most difficult because they thought he was breach at first, they were going to attempt to turn him but I got a second opinion, which turned out to be correct. He was the right way round after all... so glad my husband insisted in the end. Had them in The Portland, the private place up near St John's Wood.'

'I was just five hours with him, not even gas and air. Chose a water birth. He came into the world listening to Mozart. I had him at home.' *Ha! Take that!* She senses the woman is one of those middle-class, pompous, competitive baby mothers who is always trying to best other mothers with her birth stories and children's milestones. That should royally piss on her fireworks.

'That's unusual for your first, a home birth,' the woman looks put out.

'Easy pregnancy,' she shoots back, 'midwife and doula were present, no complications.'

George is still grumbling and he throws his giraffe onto the floor and begins to cry. The woman stoops to pick it up and leans over to give it to him.

'There we go little man, here's your... Oh, it's George!' she says, taking a step back and looking at her. 'This is George, isn't it?' The woman looks confused. 'Magenta's boy... are you?' she looks at her with a puzzled expression, 'are you Mags' new nanny?'

She feels her sphincter muscles contract. The stupid woman has only gone and recognised George, only knows that silly cunt of a mother of his. They must be friends.

'No,' she says calmly, 'this is Milo isn't it say hello Milo.'

The woman is staring at her blankly. 'But, but this is George… I'm Mags's friend, Lavinia, we come here all the time together… I didn't see his face until now, but…' she points, 'that's George.'

She can see that Lavinia's mind has gone into overdrive.

'You must have that wrong,' she says coolly, 'maybe he looks like George, whoever George is, but I assure you this is Milo, MY Milo.'

The woman is closer now, fearlessly inspecting the pushchair and looking at George in the way posh and privileged people are want to do.

'You have the same pushchair and pram toys… George has a *Guess How Much I Love You?* buggy book and a Sophie the Giraffe toy. Look, that's definitely George. I recognise him, that's definitely Mags's George. I see them here in the park all the time. Who are you?' Concern suddenly flashes across her face.

'Sorry, you're mistaken. Like I said, this is my son, Milo. We don't know any Georges and I don't know anyone called Mags or Magenta.' George is still grumbling and she hands him some bread, instantly silencing him.

The woman steps forward defiantly and she feels a rush of adrenaline flush through her body. Lavinia starts to speak but suddenly Rachel gasps, 'Watch out!' and points behind her, to where Lavinia's two children are standing dangerously close to the water's edge. 'I think you should be more concerned about your own children than mine,' she says before grabbing the pushchair and steering it away.

'Camilla! Spencer! Away from the edge now!' The children scramble obediently back up the small bank towards their mother. 'Hold on a moment,' Lavinia barks, following Rachel and placing a hand on her shoulder to stop her from trying to leave.

She looks down at the hand on her shoulder and then back up at the woman. 'Put your fucking hand on me again and I'll chop it off and feed it to those fucking swans,' she hisses, 'do you understand me, you jumped-up, sour-faced old cunt?'

The woman springs backwards, visibly shocked.

Rachel walks away at a steady pace and, once she's sure that she's not being followed, she glances back over her shoulder back.

Lavinia is already on the phone.

CHAPTER FIFTY-FIVE

Talk about bad fucking luck. Why did she have to bump into someone who knew George and that silly bitch mother of his? She assumes the woman, Lavinia, has gotten straight on her phone to Magenta and is now asking all sorts of questions. Perhaps she can talk her way out of it; perhaps she can say that Lavinia must've got it all muddled up, or explain that she'd said she was his mother just to fit in, play for pity. *Fuck, fuck, fuck.* But Magenta is not the particularly understanding or empathetic type. It's no good; this has fucked everything up. She'll have to bring her plans forward, do it this afternoon, a little sooner than planned and then she'll be out of there. Magenta is in Bath, visiting family she says, but she's lying. She's seen the weekend spa confirmation that she'd left on the kitchen table some days ago. Selfish bitch is off pampering herself with a couple of peri-menopausal friends, no doubt on the lookout for some rich dick to suck while they're at it. Sluts and whores dressed in respectable designer clothes, that's all they are. No more than prostitutes who think just because they drive four-by-fours and shop in Waitrose, they're superior to a council-estate whore who shops in Primark or Lidl and sucks off men for a six-pack. Well, Magenta would soon suffer the consequences of her neglect and self-serving behavior. Soon she'd be joining a very different club altogether, one no parent ever wants to join. She'll take George home now, feed him and then bath him, cuddle him to sleep one last time. Her beautiful, precious Baby Bear. She remembers Magenta's words during her interview for the job, 'He sleeps like an angel, Rachel' – and it makes her smile.

The sound of her mobile pinging makes her heart sink as she approaches the house. That stuck-up snitch at the park… grabbing it she opens the text message, only it's not from Magenta at all. It's from Daniel. *Dan, Dan the disappearing man.* Her heart begins to race. He can't stop thinking about her. He wants to see her, tonight. And she swiftly feels her spirits returning as though the angels themselves are looking down upon her.

Of course he does. They always do.

CHAPTER FIFTY-SIX

Fed, bathed, changed and full of 'milkies', George is asleep in his cot. He looks so beautiful, so peaceful as she studies his face, like a porcelain doll, so perfect. His eyes are closed, like someone has drawn them on his face with a pen in the shape of ticks.

'Oh Baby Bear,' she whispers to him, gently stroking his soft skin, feeling the gentle pulse in his temples, the skin still thin around them. She gazes at him lovingly as she holds the nursing pillow in her hands. She wants to watch him slip away beneath her, to feel his final breath, to say goodbye to Baby Bear forever as he joins Mummy and Daddy for all eternity. And then all will be well. But at the last moment she decides against it. *Not yet.*

She leaves George sleeping in his exquisite nursery and goes into the master bedroom to try on dresses from Magenta's wardrobe. Magenta's style is not to her taste, but there are some items, dresses, that she probably owned before she'd had George that appear to be her size. She places them on the bed to inspect them. Demure yet appealing is the look she's going for. A hint of sexuality combined with coy respectability. She won't sleep with him tonight even if he begs her to. She will show Daniel what a lady she really is. The kind of lady he could marry and spend his life with. A lady he could run away with and start a new life where no one knows them. She thinks of the cottage again, of the miniature climbing roses around the wooden door and the window boxes she'll painstakingly plant – ones the neighbours will secretly envy and admire in equal measure. She feels a flutter of excitement, of hope once again.

She can't decide between the black shift dress from Jigsaw or the slightly more fitted plum-coloured one from Whistles. It's a soft crepe material that feels fluid against her body and is the marginally sexier of the two, she decides, though because of its knee-length and high neck it's still what most would consider demure. Yes, the plum dress screams architect's wife. She's arranged to meet him at Limonia, a lovely, vibrant Greek restaurant in Primrose Hill. She'd been there once before with a group of colleagues she'd briefly worked with many years ago when she'd come out of hospital. The occasion has escaped her but she remembers they had been nice people, the evening a pleasant one, and the food delicious. The night stood out in her memory for the simple fact that it had been so normal, uneventful even. She had enjoyed her temporary colleagues' company and, more importantly to her, they had appeared to enjoy hers.

After showering, she dresses herself and styles her platinum blonde wig before securing it to her head. She wants to be blonde tonight. As blonde as when she was born. *Reborn.* She peruses the selection of perfumes on Magenta's baroque-style dressing table: Dior, Dolce & Gabbana, Chloé, Yves Saint Laurent, Chanel, Jo Malone… *Yes, the Jo Malone*, Lime Basil & Mandarin, her new favourite which reminds her of Daddy Bear. She places the small Tiffany diamond earrings he had gifted her in her ears. She checks on George one last time, kissing his forehead and placing the tiny bear inside his cot next to him. It is wearing a little nappy and has a tiny dummy in its mouth, made especially for her sleeping George. She hopes he likes it.

'Goodnight my beautiful Baby Bear. Sleep tight,' she says, as she turns off the light.

CHAPTER FIFTY-SEVEN

I can't crumble. I can't afford emotion. So I tell myself to feel nothing at all. I tell myself that I'm a copper. A good guy. I owe it to everyone to hold myself together, so I will. I turn into a robot. For now, at least.

As far as evidence goes, hard evidence I mean, I've got nothing, well, not enough anyway. Rebecca's lock-up has thrown up nothing of note. Not a fucking damn thing, can you believe it? So her prints are all over Karen's apartment, but even a rookie brief could clear that one up in court, she was her friend and neighbour after all, she had a key, said she was in and out all the time, her DNA presence makes sense. We've got the CCTV from La Reymond but that's sketchy at best. The security bloke at the apartments, yeah, we have his statement and a positive ID and a not-so-positive one from the brass who saw her and Nigel Baxter going into suite 106 on the night of his murder. I've got Dr Magnesson's testimony, the background and a profile on Goldilocks' miserable past, which certainly makes her capable and could even be classed as motive, but it's all circumstantial, there's nothing of real concrete substance, no hard forensics. It all points to Rebecca Harper of course: the fake IDs, the alleged murder of her own mother, the suspect CCTV footage, wigs and bears and tote bags and numerous fake identities... It's enough for the CPS to proceed, but to successfully prosecute, prove beyond all reasonable doubt? In this kind of case you need watertight evidence, forensics and irrefutable DNA. No one's going to put someone away for a double – I'm hoping not triple – murder without it. *I know* there's not enough physical yet, that a half-decent barrister couldn't easily discredit without breaking a sweat. I need a confession. *Fuck, I need a drink.*

I shower and change. She's agreed to meet at a Greek place up near Camden. I'm not familiar with the restaurant. It's not one me and Rach ever went to and I'm thankful about that at least.

I put in a call to Delaney and ask for a trace on 'Florence's' number. I tell him to make it an urgent priority.

I think about calling Davis and organizing back-up. I know that's what I *should* do. The thing about this job is that you can't afford any 'if onlys', you have to think in advance, to plan for every eventuality. And I can't afford to fuck this one up, not least because what I'm doing is at best unorthodox and at worse could pretty much guarantee my very early retirement. I pick up my phone at least twice before I *do* eventually call Davis. I tell her and Baylis to be outside the restaurant by 7 p.m. and wait for my instructions. I've made the reservation for 8 p.m. I tell Davis to have an unmarked vehicle covering any exits, that I've had a tip off our Goldilocks is going to be inside the restaurant. She asks questions but I keep things on a need-to-know basis, largely for her own good, in case there's an enquiry, you know? 'Just be there' I say before hanging up.

As I shower I try not to think about the fact that Rebecca Harper could, right this very moment be murdering a child – a baby – and that maybe I could've prevented it. I'm gambling with my own conscience, which is not an experience I would recommend to anyone, even those I don't care much for. I know that if I'm too late then it'll be game over and I'll take the guilt to my grave with me – and if she gets off, then I can add failure to win justice for Janet Baxter, her family and Karen to the list too. Yet my intuition tells me that this way, the way I've decided to play it, I am more likely to get a confession from her. I sense that sending a swat team to kick her door in and arrest her will cause Rebecca Harper to clam up like a shell and we'll get nothing from her. She trusts me. Something… don't ask me why, I hardly know the woman, fuck, I *don't* know the woman at all as it transpires, and yet I feel that she feels she knows me. *We had a beautiful moment, fleeting in time.*

And it's this hunch, to use a word I don't particularly like, that I think will lead me to the pearl inside that closed shell. Whatever the outcome, and I hope to hell it's the latter because regardless, Woods is going to have me by the proverbials for this one.

I spritz myself with the Tom Ford cologne that Rach loved. 'Good enough to eat' she used to say whenever I wore it, which was a massive compliment coming from a chef. I wear a white linen shirt and dark indigo Diesel jeans, my best pair, with a pair of Superdry black Chelsea boots, casual-trendy, or trendy-casual, I'm never sure which it is. I style my hair with some sweet-smelling putty stuff I've had in the cabinet since The Spice Girls were at number one. It's getting a little long on top and I've noticed a few more greys recently, but Rachel always liked it a little on the longer side, 'I'll make a hippie of you yet!'

I stare at myself in the bathroom mirror and I'm hit by a wave of sadness. Grief and fear strike me simultaneously like an out-of-control truck. Rachel, Nigel and Janet Baxter, Karen Walker… and worse still, *Rebecca Harper.* I try to will it back and remind myself of my duty, but it's there, grief and sadness for her too. I sluice with some minty mouthwash and tell myself to save these emotions, save them for when this is over; it's almost over now and I need to show up for myself more than ever. I can't afford sentiment, but I still feel it inside, I feel like I'm losing my nerve; it's not a strong as it once was, not as strong as it was when Rachel was alive.

I check my watch, it's almost 7 p.m. Davis should be at the restaurant now and I need to get going. 'Wish me luck,' I whisper to myself in the mirror, but really I'm talking to her – the ghost of Rach is all around me. I switch off the light.

CHAPTER FIFTY-EIGHT

Camden is around three miles from Islington and should take no more than twenty minutes in the car, but there's been a burst water main and there's a tailback that's almost as long as the distance I need to cover. I don't want to put the lights on but eventually I acquiesce and feel relief as the stationary vehicles begin to make a path for me. I can't afford to lose a minute. I'm almost pulling up at Limonia when Fiona Li calls.

'Dan?'

Her tone immediately sends me crashing into full alert.

'Tell me you haven't,' I say tentatively.

'I got the message too late, Dan, I'm sorry. The boss told me to run with it with or without the press conference. It was out of my hands, there wouldn't have been anything I could do to stop it…'

'When? How long ago?'

'Evening edition. About 5 p.m.'

I close my eyes tightly and force back the panic that's threatening to plough through me like a runaway train.

'Fucking shit!' I thump the dash. 'Don't you check your messages, Touchy?'

There's a pause on the line.

'Look Dan, I'm so sorry… if this fucks things up for you, the investigation—'

I hear the emotion in her voice and feel like a total shitbag.

'It's not your fault,' I say wearily, 'it's mine.' And it is, you know, *it really is*. 'Do you know if the *Evening Standard* has run it, *The Metro*?'

'Well…'

Her reticence speaks volumes.

'Oh Jesus.' I'm starting to wish I had never taken the call.

'What does this mean, Dan?' she asks in a low, cautious voice.

'It means, Touchy, that I'm fucked.'

CHAPTER FIFTY-NINE

She looks so beautiful as she comes towards me. This is my first thought, swiftly followed by an indescribable sadness at what I'm about to do. I should feel good about this, but I don't, and the inner conflict makes me feel uncomfortable. *Losing your nerve, Detective Riley?* She's smiling, and greets me with a hug, squeezes my torso.

'I'm so happy to see you, Daniel,' she says emotively into my ear, 'I thought I would never hear from you again, after, well… you know…'

My response comes from somewhere genuine inside of me. 'I had to,' I say. The conversation with Dr Magnesson is playing over in my mind on loop, her Scandinavian-sounding 's' hissing through my brain like white noise, *was she born a psychopath or did circumstance make her that way?* I look into her eyes, they're a bluish-grey colour and I wonder which of the two it is. And I try not to feel anything, I try to remember that she has already killed two innocent people, that she may have even murdered a child, and that this makes her the very worst of her kind.

'Shall we order a drink?' I ask as I think about putting cuffs around her delicate wrists.

'Yes, we should,' she grins, 'the retsina here is lovely.'

'You look lovely.' The words come from somewhere inside me.

She looks up at me, eyes shining. 'Thank you, and so do you. But then you're a very handsome man, Daniel Riley.'

I laugh off the compliment, once again reminding myself of what I'm dealing with; she's a cold-blooded killer, a manipulator in the extreme, a human being void of empathy, a monster really, yet I struggle to reconcile this with the pretty, vivacious and smiling woman sitting opposite me. And I think of the time in the hotel room, how she'd felt in my arms, how she'd made me feel. I want to be angry with her. I want to hate her, to feel disgust and contempt for who she is and what she's done and for the kindness she showed me that night. For the words she said that had given me such comfort at the time. *Consummate liars who can fool the most seasoned professionals....*

We order the retsina and some dolmades and olives. 'Those big green ones,' she says to the waiter, 'the ones that taste of sunshine.'

She props her elbows on the table, tucks her platinum hair behind her ears. I suspect she may be wearing a wig.

'Do you like the new blonde?' she asks, catching me staring, obviously. 'They have more fun, allegedly,' she laughs that pretty laugh of hers, like bells tinkling, 'and gentlemen prefer them. And you *are* a gentleman, Daniel,' she says.

The retsina arrives and the waiter pours us both a glass with such dramatic showmanship that I find it borderline irritating.

'What shall we toast to?' Her eyes are like diamonds and I feel a terrible stab in my solar plexus. I actually feel guilty for what I'm about to do, I feel empathy for a ruthless, cold-blooded killer and I have to remind myself of what she is once more.

'Whatever you like,' I manage to say.

'How about new beginnings?'

I nod, touch her glass with my own, but I can't bring myself to repeat the words.

'So, tell me, what made you decide to contact me again? I really thought that after... well...' She looks down a little coyly. 'I must apologise, I realise it was too soon...' she says and I put my hand up to stop her.

'Please, no need.' I remember her skin against mine, her soft body wrapped around me, how it fit so well with my own, just like Rach's. And I try not to think about the connection I'd felt. 'Everything happens for a reason, Danny.' That's what Rachel used to say. *So why this, then Rach? Tell me the reason for this!*

'Life is to be lived in the moment isn't it, don't you think, Daniel?'

'Yes, I think it probably is.' I don't know why I say the word 'probably' because now, after everything, I believe these words more than ever.

'I think I'm having the lamb cutlets' she says, changing the subject as she scans the menu. 'They're delicious. I highly recommend them.'

I don't want to eat, I can't, but I order anyway, glancing outside the window. I spot Davis' unmarked car a short distance away.

'So, tell me about your week Florence?' I lean in closer, my elbows propped to match hers. She looks delighted by my interest and meets my gaze full on. And I'm searching her eyes for something, *anything*, that will bring my emotions in line with the fact that she's evil personified. But her eyes are bright and vibrant, and I see no malice in them.

'Aside from tonight you mean? Well, actually I've got a new job.'

'Oh?'

'Yes, as a nanny, looking after a beautiful little baby boy called George. But it was only temporary.'

I swallow. *A baby boy. George. Only temporary. Was.*

'Doesn't that interfere with your studies?'

She wrinkles her nose and I try not to like the way her face looks as she does this. 'I'm tired of acting… I'm not even sure if it's for me anymore.'

I feign surprise. 'So… how old is George? And why was it only temporary?' My heart is thumping against my ribs. *Has she killed him? Has she killed him already? Is there a dead baby somewhere right now, lying lifelessly in his cot?*

'He's almost ten months,' she says and her eyes come alive as she speaks of him, 'beautiful happy little thing he is, full of… life. I fell in love with him on sight.' Her smile dissipates suddenly. 'But he's not a well little boy, I've tried telling his mother, telling her something is very wrong, but she… well, she couldn't give a fuck, you know, she's always off pampering herself or at the gym, lunching with friends. I smell alcohol on her breath almost constantly.'

My guts twist like a pretzel. 'What's wrong with him, the baby?'

She shakes her head as she pops an olive into her mouth.

'Like I said, I've tried talking to his mother but she doesn't want to listen. Stupid, selfish bitch,' she hisses into her drink, her whole demeanour changing. 'I mean, if I had a child, a baby, I would treasure it, you know, spend every waking moment with it, make sure no harm came to it like a proper mother should. People like her, like that selfish bitch of a mother of his, they shouldn't be allowed to have kids. They should take them away before it's too late.'

I hear the emotion building in her voice as the lamb cutlets arrive. She's momentarily distracted by them.

'Too late for what?' I ask, gently.

'I'm sorry,' she says, as though coming back to herself, 'do you want children, Daniel?' She stabs a lamb cutlet with a fork, tearing at the pink flesh. 'Do you see them in your future?'

I push my own cutlet around my plate like a makeshift paper boat on a pond. Davis will be wondering just what the fuck is going on right about now. I don't know why I'm stalling, why I'm gambling and taking such a huge risk. I'm thinking, hoping, that it's fairly safe to assume that had 'Florence' seen her own mugshot in the evening paper then she wouldn't be sitting opposite me right now. *Just arrest her Dan*, the inner voice inside me is shouting, *what the fuck are you waiting for?*

'Yes, I do. I've always wanted to be a father.'

'Did your girlfriend want them, Rachel, did she want children?'

I go to speak, but a realisation renders me speechless for a split second and it's swiftly followed by a lightning-bolt icy chill. *You're a very handsome man, Daniel Riley.* I'm certain I have never told her my surname.

'Yes,' I say, 'actually she was almost three months pregnant when she died.'

She stops eating then, replaces her knife and fork onto the plate gently and fixes my eyes. 'Oh Daniel, I'm so sorry.' Her head is cocked to one side as she's speaking and it sounds so genuine, so heartfelt, that for the briefest moment I almost forget who I'm talking to. She holds my gaze. 'Will you excuse me for a moment? I really need to use the bathroom. I'm sorry...' she says as she rises from the table, 'ladies stuff.'

I come back to myself and immediately my eyes flick towards the exit. The bathrooms are to the side of the restaurant. It's busy, full of couples, young families and groups enjoying their evening meals. The atmosphere is buzzy, punctuated by chatter and the loud clatter of cutlery, waiters coming and going with hissing, steaming plates full of fresh meat and fish. My intention was never to arrest her in full view of the public. I hadn't planned for a scene. Just a last supper I suppose.

'Of course, no problem.' I smile in a bid to disguise the panic that's swelling inside of me, rising like the fresh bread on the table. I top up her glass, watching as she picks up her handbag, the Kate Spade tote.

'You'll still be here when I get back, won't you, Daniel? You won't disappear on me again?'

I watch her as she makes her way to the bathroom without glancing back at me. Once she's out of sight I pull my phone from my pocket and immediately it buzzes in my hand.

'Boss? Boss, what the fuck's going on?'

'Listen to me carefully, Davis,' my voice is low, almost inaudible, 'I need you on full alert for the suspect. She may attempt to make a run for it.'

I can almost see the confusion on Davis' face as she listens to my instructions.

'The suspect… are you *with* her now, Boss?'

I beckon a waiter over.

'She's just gone to the bathroom. I think she may have rumbled me. Keep that exit covered, you hear me, Davis, keep it covered.'

'Yes Boss… And Boss, something's just come in from Delaney. Apparently a call was made from a member of the public regarding an incident in a park in Beckenham today. I think it could be related. She claims there was a woman impersonating a baby's mother and that when challenged the woman became hostile and aggressive. We have a Christian name for the mother – Magenta – but no ID as yet boss."

My guts feel knotted up like an army assault-course net.

'Locate an address for the mother and get a team down there immediately,' I say. The waiter is hovering nearby, trying to catch my eye. 'Was the baby's name George?'

'Yes Boss, it is… how do you know that?'

'There's every reason to believe that baby might be in danger. Do it now Davis.'

'The team's on it, Boss.'

'Good. But you stay put Davis, you hear me. Don't move from where you are. Do you have good visibility of the entrance to the restaurant?'

'Yes Boss, perfect.'

'Keep it that way. Suspect is wearing a purple shift dress and a platinum-blonde wig. Intervene anyone fitting this description who attempts to leave the restaurant. Oh and Davis, do not call for back-up here unless I give you the nod. I'm bringing her in myself.' I hang up. She's been in the bathroom a few minutes; it feels like hours.

'Can I get you anything, Sir?' The waiter looks at me obligingly.

'Sorry,' I say, replacing my phone into my pocket.

He nods at me and I suspect he's thinking what a self-important, middle-class wanker I am so I show him my badge – at least then I have an excuse.

'I may need to leave the restaurant quickly,' I explain, 'police business.'

He nods again, unsurprised. This is London after all. I guess he's probably seen stranger goings on. 'I understand, Sir.'

'Look, can you tell me if there are any windows in the ladies, any exits or means of…'

But then I see her coming back from the bathroom. She's walking towards me, but she is no longer smiling.

'Doesn't matter where you are in the world, there's always a queue for the ladies,' she rolls her eyes, 'it was three people deep. I mean, a restaurant as big as this and only two cubicles, seriously!' She seats herself.

'Listen,' I say quickly, 'how about we get out of here, finish this off somewhere else, somewhere… more private?'

She tilts her head to the side and gives me this almost amused look before replying, 'You know Detective Riley, I thought you'd never ask.'

CHAPTER SIXTY

I read her rights and formally arrest her on the suspicion of the murder of Nigel Baxter and Karen Walker. She sits, motionless, as I say the words to her quietly across the dinner table. I ask her if she wishes to say anything and explain that anything she does say may be taken down and used in evidence against her.

'Can I finish my drink?' she asks and I tell her that she can't, that we have to leave right now. She tells me she won't make a scene but her eyes have changed, like the light has slipped from them. 'Are you going to handcuff me? Because if you are, this isn't quite the scenario I imagined.'

'Rebecca, can you tell me where George is? Has he come to any harm?' I ask, leading her from the restaurant.

'Will you hold my hand, Daniel, please?' she asks as we make our way past the unsuspecting diners, 'act like we're a real couple.'

I ignore her request and yet the maddening – *the truly fucking nuts thing* – is that actually, I really want to.

Davis cuffs her but I can't watch as she takes her away. I can feel Rebecca's eyes on me like lasers as I walk towards my car. And I should feel elated, you know, I should feel triumphant. I should feel *something*. In that moment I realise that something inside me has changed, that I'm no longer the man I once was. The truth is, I think I haven't been that man since Rachel died. And I feel lost, my sense of purpose and identity shattered. That rush I've always felt when an arrest has been made in a big case like this one is missing this time. I used to think it made a difference, that *I* made a difference, changing outcomes and controlling situations, preventing the bad guys from doing bad things and putting away the ones that did. It used to give me a buzz. Protect and serve and all of that. I suppose it gave me a sense of power, made me feel good about myself. But I don't feel good. Not this time. Two people are dead and maybe a third: *a baby*. And the woman in custody that I knew as Florence, young and beautiful, with a vibrant smile that had made me feel hopeful again, however briefly, is Goldilocks, a pathological liar, a dangerous psychopath, damaged by a childhood so abusive and sickening that I struggle not to feel empathy for her in spite of her heinous crimes.

Worse still, I sense that Rebecca Harper knows I feel this way too, somehow she seems to have an inherent, almost primeval instinct that allows her to tap right into my psyche, giving her access all areas to parts of me that others have failed to reach in double the time, if at all. The fact that her ability appears to be driven by a force of evil makes it no less impressive, and I can't help thinking what she might've been if she had put such gifts to the greater good, into bettering herself and her life.

I make the drive back to the nick, my mind occupied by thoughts of dead babies and girlfriends and just how the fuck I'm going to explain all of this to Woods. I turn the radio on as a distraction. Pink Floyd are playing. 'Dark Side of the Moon' is one of my all-time favourite albums. We used to fall asleep together to it, me and my girl, our warm bodies spooning.

Suddenly I hear Rachel's voice like she's right here, alongside me in the passenger seat, saying, 'you do know that there is no dark side of the moon, Danny, that actually it's all just a myth.'

CHAPTER SIXTY-ONE

She's in interview room three. The clock's ticking. The member of the public who called in to voice her suspicions about baby George and the woman in the park fitting Rebecca's description couldn't give a surname for the mother, only a Christian name, Magenta, and said that she's local to the south-eastern suburb of Beckenham. I figure there can't be too many Magentas in Beckenham, so I'm hoping an address won't be too long in coming.

'I want everyone on that address,' I tell Delaney, 'and when we get it send an enforcement team down there pronto. I want that baby found safe and alive, Martin, do you hear me?'

'Yes, I hear you Dan.'

His use of my name irks me once again.

Davis follows me out. She's hovering, tentative. There's something she wants to say. 'How did you know where she was, Boss? How did you know she'd be waiting in the restaurant?'

I carry on walking. 'Intuition, Davis,' I say without looking back at her, 'intuition.'

CHAPTER SIXTY-TWO

Her eyes light up as I enter the room, like she's spotted an old friend she hasn't seen in a while. She smiles with that air of confidence I found so very attractive when we first met. Now, however, it comes across a little cocksure and irritating. I set up the tape recorder, go through the protocol guff with her, name, date of birth, tell her to speak clearly for the recorder, words I've said hundreds of times before, yet this time I seem to trip over them. A duty solicitor sits a little way back from the table, a small, rat-faced diminutive man who looks like he has a moustache made of dog shit under his nose. Some jumped-up, privileged Tory boy with a suit that looks almost as cheap as his integrity. I half expect him to say 'no comment' when I ask him if we can get him anything to drink. He looks like he says the phrase in his sleep. I say my name and the solicitor's for the benefit of the tape and ask her to confirm her own.

She speaks into the recorder: 'Florence Williams'.

The solicitor casts me a shifty glance.

'But that's not your real name, is it Rebecca? Your birth name is Rebecca Jane Harper, that's correct isn't it?'

She looks at me intently. 'Yes, but call me Florence.'

'Can you confirm for the tape that your name is Rebecca Jane Harper and that your date of birth is 21 June 1987?'

'I've never liked the name Rebecca, never felt it suited me.'

'Is that why you use aliases? Danni-Jo, Florence...?'

'Florence was my grandmother's name.'

'You told me your parents named you after the place you were conceived.'

The solicitor glances at me.

I continue, 'Do you know the difference between the truth and a lie, Rebecca?'

She looks at me, a half smile on her face. She's sitting forward in the seat now, swaying slightly as if she's a little drunk.

'I could ask you the same question, Daniel. Tell me, how's life in the world of architecture?' She giggles. Now I'm convinced she's drunk. I try and remember how much retsina she drank at the restaurant, probably not even a glass.

'Do you know why you're here, Rebecca?'

She nods. 'To finish the story.'

'And what story is that?'

She doesn't answer.

'The story of *Goldilocks and the Three Bears*?'

Silence.

'Where is George, Rebecca?' I keep my voice level but firm. I need to play this very carefully.

'Who?'

She's still wearing the plum dress, but she's not as perfectly groomed as she was a few hours ago. The wig looks as if it could do with a brush. Her bare legs are crossed and she's sitting at the table as though we're still in the restaurant, discussing our respective working weeks over olives and taramasalata.

'The baby, Rebecca, the little boy you had in your charge, the one you told me about tonight: George. Where is he? Has he come to any harm?'

More silence.

'Tell me where he is. Where is Baby Bear?'

She lifts her head up when I say this. Her solicitor whispers something in her ear and I feel like reaching across the table and strangling him with his shitty tie.

'You used the name Goldilocks when you were searching for prospective men online to murder. Why did you choose that name? Were you acting out a fantasy fairy tale Rebecca, the story of the three bears?' I think of Nigel Baxter then, his body in the bath in that beautiful hotel room and I try to imagine the rage and hatred and anger that must've been inside her and driven her to do what she did.

'You were working as an escort weren't you Rebecca? Meeting rich older men, sugar daddys who afforded you a lavish lifestyle in return for sex. But that's not the only reason you went looking for that particular type of man was it? Nigel Baxter was Daddy Bear wasn't he? Did Nigel represent your father? Was Nigel the father who abused you? Is that why you poisoned him and then slit his wrists.'

She visibly shrinks at the mention of her father. I slide the crime-scene photographs across the table and they naturally fan out like a pack of cards.

'You did this, didn't you, Rebecca? You drugged Mr Baxter in suite 106 of La Reymond Hotel on April 12 of this year while he was in the bath, while you were both in the bath, drinking champagne, and then you slit open his wrists and watched him bleed to death, didn't you?'

She tilts her head to one side. Her eyes lower to look at the ghoulish images of Baxter's bloated and bloody corpse, close-ups of his injuries, his open, congealing wounds and his large fleshy form slumped over the tub.

I show her a picture of the teddy bear left at the scene. 'You had this made especially for Mr Baxter, for Daddy Bear. That's right isn't it, Rebecca?' I lean forward across the table towards her. 'That's right, isn't it? You had sex with Mr Baxter and then fed him chocolates laced with enough arsenic to shut down his organs as he sipped champagne with you in the bath. Then you took a razor to his wrists and sliced them open.'

Her eyelids appear a little heavy as she looks up at me.

'You're wearing the earrings he gave to you now, aren't you, the Tiffany diamond studs?'

She's expressionless.

'Then you methodically cleaned up in a bid to erase any DNA – and you did a good job, I have to say – before disguising yourself and making an exit.'

She gently touches the prints on the table, running her fingers along the outline of the deceased nostalgically, like she's looking through old holiday snaps.

'Karen Walker, Kizzy, your neighbour. The woman who lived opposite you in your Mayfair apartment. Tell me about Kizzy, Rebecca. You liked her didn't you? She liked you too. You were friends…'

One of her legs is swinging manically over the other as she watches me silently.

'You poisoned Kizzy's cat didn't you? After she had entrusted you with a key to her apartment. And then you invited Kizzy for dinner, cooked her pasta, a special recipe that included large amounts of sleeping pills, that's right isn't it? Then when she returned to her apartment to sleep, you let yourself in and slit open her wrists, just like you did Nigel Baxter's. Then you staged the scene to look like a suicide once again.'

Rebecca is looking at me but I see nothing behind her eyes, it's as if she's disappeared somewhere within herself.

'Karen, Kizzy… she was Mummy Bear wasn't she? You told a police officer that she'd been like a mother to you. Why, if that was the case, would you want to hurt her?'

Nothing.

'And George. Is he your next victim? A tiny, defenseless baby… Why would you want to harm a baby, Rebecca? The woman I met – she would never do that – the woman I met was beautiful and kind, she had a good heart, she's a *good* woman… Tell me Rebecca – please tell me where he is.'

Complimenting her seems to have evoked a reaction and she turns away from me, lowers her head. I know there's something there, a human part of her that's still alive, barely breathing but still alive, that wouldn't hurt a child. And I need to get to it, quickly. Time is running out.

I change tactic. 'Why did you come, to the restaurant? You knew who I was, didn't you? You knew I was a policeman. When did you find out? If you knew that I would arrest you, why did you come? Why didn't you run? You want this to be over don't you; I know you do. I do too, Rebecca and it *can* be over if you talk to me, tell me where George is…'

The rat-faced solicitor looks confused. 'Excuse me Detective, sorry, but do you two know each other?' He's pointing at us simultaneously as though he's interrupting a private conversation. 'Hang on… Detective Riley, if you are familiar with my client on a personal level then this is highly unorthodox and I must insist that another officer conduct the interview immediately. You have arrested my client on the suspicion of two counts of murder in the first degree and I—'

She turns to the solicitor. 'I want you to leave,' she says sternly, 'I want to talk to Daniel alone.'

I suspect that Woods is watching all of this and is probably on the verge of a heart attack. I'm expecting him to knock on the door any minute and terminate the interview, but I have to get a confession from her, I have to find out where George is.

'Ms Harper, I would strongly advise you not to do this,' the solicitor addresses her gravely. 'It is in your best interest to have a solicitor present, given the nature of the accusations against you I must insist that you—'

'I want you to leave,' she says again.

'Ms Harper, look… Detective,' he turns to me, 'it is clear that my client is not in any fit mental state to make any rational decisions—'

'Just get out!' she screams and he visibly flinches, takes a step back from her in shock.

'As you wish, Ms Harper,' he mutters, gathering his briefcase and papers hastily, 'it's your funeral.'

CHAPTER SIXTY-THREE

'Alone at last, Detective Riley,' she says once the solicitor has made a hasty retreat.

I sit down, adopt a less formal stance and lean in towards her from across the table. 'How long have you known, about my identity I mean?'

She smiles.

'We didn't get to finish our dinner together Daniel… shame, the lamb cutlets really were tasty. I think they use a special marinade you know, an ancient Greek recipe…'

I get up from the seat and the scraping sound startles her, momentarily shattering her cocksure façade that's as brittle as glass.

'Why, Rebecca. Please, tell me why?' I place my hands flat on the table. The photographs are still strewn across it, gruesome images of her victims staring up at us. I point a finger at one of them. 'Just tell me you haven't done this to that child… tell me he's safe. You can do that, *I know you can*,' I say, imploring her, 'you can redeem yourself, just tell me where he is and let us go and make sure he's okay. He's just a baby, a tiny, helpless baby.' I hear the emotion in my own voice, unable to disguise my desperation.

I touch the tips of her fingers with my own and she runs her index finger gently over the top of mine for a second before pulling her hand away.

'I know about your childhood; Dr Magnesson told me about the abuse, what happened to you and your mother – what you did to protect her. Talk to me and perhaps we can do some kind of deal? I can talk to the right people, have you sent to a secure hospital, somewhere they can help you. Do you know what they do to baby killers in prison? Do you? I don't want that for you, Rebecca. I know you've suffered enough.'

I hear the click in her throat as she swallows. Her face seems to be getting paler by the second and suddenly she bends double as though in pain. I ask her if she's okay.

She sucks in breath through her teeth. 'Cramps,' she explains, grimacing, 'time of the month.'

'Do you need some pills, some paracetamol? I can arrange for a doctor to come down and administer some.'

She smiles through her obvious discomfort. 'That's your trouble isn't it, Daniel? You care too much. It's been both your success and downfall in life hasn't it?'

'Yes,' I say, 'I do care. I care about George. And I care about you too.' Worse still, *I actually mean it.*

She sucks in another breath before straightening herself up. 'Don't listen to that bitch Magnesson, she knows nothing.' Her face changes and I catch a fleeting glimpse of the malice within her. 'Silly cunt thought she had all the answers. But the truth was she never even had the right questions.'

'And what *are* the right questions? Jesus, Rebecca… what are?'

'No hospitals,' she says quietly after a moment, 'please.'

'I can help you,' I say, 'let me help you, let me help you help yourself. Tell us where George is.'

She appears to be somewhere else, lost in thought. 'Do you know what it's like, being in one of those places as a child? Greene Parks was nothing more than a concentration camp, a torture chamber masquerading as a hospital. It was no better than the home I had come from, just in a different sort of way. They abused me too; studied me, experimented on me like a laboratory rat. I wasn't treated as a human being, I was a subject.'

'You were just a child.'

'I was never a child,' she hisses, 'I was sucking my father's cock at five years old.'

I grimace inwardly. I look at the photographs on the table to remind myself of what she is, what she's capable of.

'Is that why you killed Nigel Baxter and Karen Walker, Rebecca? Was it retribution for your own suffering, for what your father did to you?'

She snorts at me like I'm an imbecile who hasn't got a clue.

'You mother suffered too didn't she, years and years of horrendous abuse, is that why you killed her, put her out of her misery, stopped her suffering for good?'

'Oh Daniel, you really don't know anything do you?' She throws me a pitiful glance. 'I didn't kill my mother,' she says, 'my father did, well as good as. Mother, she tried to take her own life so many times over the years I lost count in the end. Pills, alcohol, slit her wrists twice… She threw herself down the stairs in the end. We had this big house with a large Victorian staircase. First time she just knocked herself out so she tried again and broke her ankle, didn't make a very good job of it. The third attempt she almost succeeded.' Rebecca seems to drift off somewhere else for a moment. 'She broke both her legs, one an open fracture, and her back. She was still breathing when I found her but I knew it was bad, I knew that she would suffer more, that she was already suffering and wanted to die. I figured that it would only be a matter of time before my father actually murdered her, or that she would once again try to kill herself. I just couldn't bear to watch her in so much agony. The physical pain was torture enough, but it was the emotional and psychological anguish that was the worst to witness. She couldn't even get killing herself right, she was just so… so defeated by him, by the years of abuse, and so I sat with her for a while, at the bottom of the stairs, watching as she slipped in and out of consciousness, high on a cocktail of prescription drugs that basically allowed her to function as a human being, jabbering nonsense, wailing. And then I kissed her and put a pillow underneath her head and one over her face, held it there, and sang nursery rhymes to her, just like the ones she used to sing to me when I was a child. She didn't kick or scream, she couldn't I suppose because of the injuries, but I don't think she would've done anyway. She welcomed her death. If she could've thanked me I know she would've.'

My heart is knocking against my ribs but I stay silent, let her finish. 'My father, he panicked, thought that he would be exposed, that it would all come out in the open, the things he had done, the years of physical, emotional and,' she pauses slightly, 'sexual abuse, and so he threw me under the bus, concocted a story to the police, told them that I was evil, a devil child, mentally defective, sick, and that I had killed her. He said I needed psychiatric help and so he, *they*, had me incarcerated.'

'Why didn't you tell the truth? Why didn't you confide in someone sooner, a neighbour, a teacher, a friend's parents?'

'Friends? I had no friends,' her tone is dismissive, she seems as cold to her own suffering as she is to that of others. 'Do you understand fear, Daniel? Real fear I mean?'

'Yes,' I pause, I think I do.' And my memory flashes back to the night they came to tell me that Rachel was dead, thought of the icy fear that had penetrated through my flesh and bones like fire.

'Fear is the most debilitating of all the emotions. It paralyses you, governs your every waking moment and thought. It conditions you. And I lived in fear. Lived with it every moment from the day I was born. I was trained to be so terrified of my father that I learned to accept it, to accept all the abuse. Fear became my normality. In the end I found that I couldn't live without it, couldn't function. I told Magnesson about the abuse, but by then I had been written off as a psychopath. A danger to myself and others apparently; damaged goods, beyond repair. It was easier, in a way, to say I was responsible for my mother's death. It kept me away from my father, kept me from his evil, deviant, depraved ways. But it brought a new set of fears.'

'What happened to your father?' She blinks at me. Her skin is pallid, almost as white as her hair. 'The checks we made say he died of natural causes.'

She laughs then and throws her head back. It gives me the chills. I take another sip of water and refresh her glass, even though she hasn't touched a drop of it.

'Nothing my father ever did was natural.'

'You continued to live with him though, that's right isn't it? Right up until his death? Why? Why, if your father was the monster you say he was, did you go back to live with him after you left Greene Parks? Was it some kind of misplaced loyalty? Were you still scared of him?'

'Yes,' she says. I notice beads of sweat have formed on her skin, small shiny beads, glistening. 'I was always scared of him, right up to the end.'

'What did he die of?'

'He was a strong and fit man, my father, in the "rudest health" as he used to say. Would've lived to a ripe old age no doubt... those bastards always do. Only the good die young don't they, Daniel? Like Rachel—'

I try not to show any emotion at the use of her name.

'So why didn't he live to a ripe old age?'

'I poisoned him,' she says with a look of triumph, her eyes narrowing. 'But I did it s-l-o-w-l-y... gradually, very gradually, day by day by day... I watched him deteriorate over a long period of time. Tiny, miniscule amounts of thallium administered every day in his food and drink. I was patient, I waited. And over time, well, thallium builds in your system, it's a toxin – and it was just enough to make him sick, slowly but surely, to debilitate him and keep him in constant poor health. After a while he began losing his hair, that really pissed him off.' She's smiling now and I can see Florence has all but disappeared. 'He was so vain, my father, and his hair, it was thick, you know, took after his mother's side. The Harpers were all very proud of their crowning glory and the fact the men in the family never went bald. But I made sure he broke the mould.'

'Did he seek medical attention?'

'Oh yes,' Rebecca says, she appears to be enjoying the conversation now. 'They were miffed. He became something of an enigma to the GP. They ran all sorts of tests on him, especially when his teeth started falling out. Said it was a vitamin deficiency of some kind. They misdiagnosed him many times.' She seems pleased by this, like it was a great achievement. 'He was on all kinds of medication. He needed me to care for him when he got really sick in the end. And I did. I nursed him. Fed him, washed and dressed him, administered his medicine – and some of my own. He was completely dependent on me in his final months.'

'You wanted him to suffer?'

She smirks, a look that appears to change her whole face. And I think of what Dr Magnesson said about multiple personalities, how psychopaths can literally morph into someone unrecognisable in front of your eyes.

'I never wanted that man's suffering to end. I was sad when it did. Funny, I remember the doctors and nurses at the hospital showing me sympathy as I was crying over him on his deathbed, how they put their arms around me and comforted me. But I wasn't grieving for his death. I was crying because his suffering was almost over.'

I exhale.

'So you got your revenge in the end… you murdered the man who abused you, a man who should've been protecting you. Many people, Rebecca, even a judge, might go some way to understanding your actions given the nature of your father's crimes against you.

But why go on to murder Nigel Baxter and Karen Walker? Was your father's death not enough for you?'

She laughs again, a manic horrible sound, and her eyes roll in the back of her head making her look deranged. 'You said it yourself Daniel – sometimes there is no why.'

CHAPTER SIXTY-FOUR

It's gone midnight. She's been in the interview room for almost two hours. I feel like I'm close to a confession now and I can only hope that Woods senses this too and doesn't call a halt to proceedings. I just need a little more time: the one thing I'm running out of. And yet I can hear Dr Magnesson's words echoing around my brain, 'psychopaths and serial killers rarely, if ever, confess to their crimes because the truth is they don't see them as such.'

'Where is George?' I ask her again. 'The baby, Rebecca, where is he? What have you done with him? It's been, what?' I look at my watch and then at her.

Her face has a yellow tinge to it. Perhaps it's just the light, but her eyes appear sunken in their sockets like she's aged ten years in two hours, her pupils are as small as pinpricks and an oily sheen of sweat covers her cheeks and forehead. Her arms are folded protectively across her waist.

'What is your first childhood memory, Daniel?' Her voice is raspy and shallow. She's tired. Tired is good. Tired is usually the prelude to a confession. It's often a battle of wills, the interview process, a process of gradually wearing someone down until they're exhausted and backed so far into a corner the only way out is to cough it all up. But Rebecca Harper is a woman who has spent her entire life in a corner, conditioned to unspeakable torture. But she knows the game is up, that it's over, or at least the part where she gets to kill people is. Only she's still the one in control, and she knows it. She may be looking at a life stretch behind the door but she still holds the key to the little boy's whereabouts and safety; she still has the upper hand.

'Choking on a sweet at school,' I say, 'I almost died.'

She looks intrigued.

'My cousin gave me a boiled sweet, one of those big old-fashioned humbug ones. I put it in my mouth and somehow swallowed it whole. It got lodged inside my oesophagus and I began choking, coughing and spluttering, you know, I couldn't breathe and I remember the panic I felt – pure icy-cold terror.'

'What happened?' Her eyes glint a little, interested in the outcome.

'A quick-thinking teacher slapped me hard on the back a few times until it flew out of my mouth... I'll never forget it.'

'How old were you?'

'I don't know, four years old maybe.'

She smiles. 'You could've died, Daniel. Death by humbug – I might never have known you...' Her voice trails off, like she's suddenly lost her train of thought.

'Guess it wasn't my time.'

'Time...' she says, 'the bad news is that it flies.'

'And what's the good news?' I ask.

'That you're the pilot.'

Touché. Well, I'm flying right now alright, by the seat of my pants – and with no working parachute. 'Why did you kill Nigel Baxter and Karen Walker, Rebecca? Baxter was besotted by you, he paid you for sex, bought you gifts, he never harmed you, or abused you did he? And Karen, she trusted you, thought of you as a friend, said you were like "the daughter she never had". So why kill them, either of them?'

She's silent for what feels like a very long time. 'Nigel was a sad, pathetic spineless man, a pervert who betrayed his wife and got his kicks from prostitutes and watching other people fucking each other.'

'Hardly warrants poisoning him and slitting his wrists does it? Betraying your wife and indulging in a kinky perversion with other consenting adults? At worst it's unsavoury, disloyal.'

'Kizzy was a pathetic wretch,' she says, 'destined for a life of misery, much like myself really. No matter how much she tried, no matter what she did to try and improve herself or her situation, she would've continually lurched from one disaster to the next.'

'Even if this was so, it doesn't give you the right to play God, to decide who gets to live or die, Rebecca.' I'm careful to keep my tone even, as void of emotion as possible.

'Some of us are destined for a life of pain Daniel,' she says poignantly, as though I am included in this statement.

I'm worried she might be right, that she senses this within me, that she thinks of me as a kindred spirit in this respect, but I don't let it show. And I'm getting worried, like, seriously concerned, about her well-being. She's shaking almost uncontrollably now, sweating profusely and her skin has changed from yellow to a deathly grey colour and I suggest that I call a doctor again. Then it hits me, hits me like a sucker punch in the guts. *She went to the bathroom in the restaurant…* she could've taken something.

'Oh Jesus, Jesus, Rebecca,' I say the words over again as I rush over to her, seizing her by the shoulders. 'What have you taken? What have you done?'

She starts to vomit, as though on cue, violently spilling the contents of her stomach out onto the table and over the photographs, retching and convulsing in spasms as her slight body tries desperately to rid itself of whatever toxic substance she's put in it. She attempts to stand but I crouch down on my knees and hold her in the chair, tell her not to move, explain that help is on its way. She feels floppy within my grip, spittle leaving a long thin trail from one corner of her mouth and her head is wobbling on her neck, like it could be knocked off with a gentle push. I feel a rush of horror as I press the panic button, immediately alerting the two officers outside. I shout at them to get an ambulance and call for emergency medical assistance. I'm screaming at them like they can't hear me, the shock on their faces lingering for a nano-second longer than I can afford.

'Hurry up,' I shout. I can feel her slipping in and out of consciousness in my arms and so I pick her up, hold her across my lap and tell her to stay with me.

'My first memory…' she struggles to speak, so I put the plastic cup of water to her lips and tell her to drink it, my heart is knocking violently against my ribs, my hands shaking almost as violently as her own. It spills out onto her dress, leaving dark stains.

Davis rushes into the interview room, she's clutching a piece of paper and she's about to tell me something, the words struggling to escape her lips. I expect Woods to follow but he doesn't. A mask of horror fixes itself across her face as she looks at the scene.

'Jesus Christ, Boss. What the fuck's happened…? Listen, I've got something—' she holds the piece of paper up like trophy.

'Not now, Davis!' my voice is even louder than I expect, more of a scream really. 'I think she's ingested poison… She needs help – we need help, now!'

And I know she's thinking what I'm thinking, that if Rebecca Davis dies then so does baby George – and my career with them both.

'Rebecca,' I say, grabbing her chin between my thumb and forefinger, 'what have you taken? Tell me… what have you swallowed?'

'… Mummy,' she says, her eyes are half closed, the stench of vomit hits me and I swallow back the bile that is rising through my gullet. 'Read me the story again… the story of the three bears, the one where Goldilocks breaks into the cottage and eats their porridge… It's my favourite… one last time Mummy, read it to me one last time…'

And in that moment it all makes some kind of sense, her memory of her mother reading her a bedtime story as a child before her life became a waking nightmare. *It's the only happy memory she owns.*

Davis hesitates for a second and I'm not sure why. She hands me the note and tries to speak, 'Get out!' I bark at her, causing a flash of terror to flicker across her features. 'For fuck's sake be quick.' And she turns and runs.

Rebecca's organs are shutting down. I think she's swallowed arsenic. I'm furious with Davis for the interruption, probably at Woods' request. Hell, I'm furious full stop. I pick up the note. It had better be bloody important is all I can think, we've got a suspect potentially dying on us and… I open the note and read Davis' unruly scrawl.

'Baby George found safe and well. He's in St Thomas's being checked over but looks as though he'll be okay. His mother is with him now.'

I re-read it. I can't be sure but I think I might be crying because my face feels wet with relief, maybe it's the water. 'Rebecca… Rebecca…' I shake her like a rag doll and she vomits again, violently, involuntarily, spewing her guts over herself and into my lap, it's hard to keep a grip on her, she's like mercury in my fingers, her body almost folding beneath itself, slipping from my grasp. I'm about to tell her that we've had news that George has been found, that the game is over and he's safe but I stop myself. She's trying to speak, to tell me something and I think I know what.

'The baby… George,' Rebecca's voice is barely audible, crackly and laboured like that of an asthmatic old woman, 'the address is in my handbag, King's Hall Road, Beckenham. That's where you'll find him.'

I nod and reach for it, screwing up the note in my fist and letting it drop to the floor.

'Thank you,' I say to her, 'thank you.'

CHAPTER SIXTY-FIVE

Rebecca had gone by the time the ambulance arrived. They did their best to revive her, but I knew it was too late. The dose was 'lethal enough to kill a horse' Vic Leyton told me after the post-mortem. She'd left no room for error. She died in my arms in the incident room, an agonizing, undignified death, covered in her own vomit, wailing in spasmodic pain as the arsenic gradually attacked her from the inside out, obliterating her internal organs, shutting them down one by one. 'Don't die,' I'd whispered in her ear, 'don't you dare fucking die.' I knew that her death would be seen as the easy way out, that this way she doesn't pay for her crimes and there will be no justice for Nigel Baxter and Karen Walker, for their families and loved ones. Her suicide will be seen as a cowardly act, a calculated, selfish means of escaping justice, but in truth I don't think it really was. It was a means of escaping herself. Because the sad truth is, really, Rebecca Harper died a long time ago. She never confessed outright to the murders of Nigel Baxter and Karen Walker, just like Magnesson said she wouldn't, but her oblique answers were as good as. Magnesson was wrong about her being her capable of killing a child though. When it came down to it, she'd been unable to go through with it, she just couldn't do it, it was a step too far, even for a cold-blooded killer.

'This is where the story ends, Daniel,' she'd said as she lay dying in my arms. *The final chapter*. I'd brushed the hair from her face, her platinum wig slipping from her scalp as I did. I took it off her head, revealing her real hair underneath, shoulder-length and mousey brown. It felt soft to touch. 'No more Goldilocks,' I'd said aloud as her breathing became short and labored, an unnatural sound emanating from her throat, the sound of impending death. I didn't tell her about the note that Davis had passed to me informing me that they had found George safe and well. I wanted her to die thinking that she'd done the right thing, as mad as that sounds – and I'll admit, it does. Her crimes were abhorrent, evil really, and yet I still felt empathy for her. I couldn't help it.

Once the paramedics had taken her body away I sat in the interview room for a few moments, alone, tried to gather my composure. After a few minutes Davis entered the room. She didn't say a word but her expression spoke volumes.

'It's okay,' I say, standing, 'tell him I'm on my way up.'

CHAPTER SIXTY-SIX

Woods is shouting so loudly that I can't entirely make out what he's saying.

'The IPCC is going to be all over us now… *and the press*, Jesus fucking Christ Riley, what a complete and utter cock-up! Do you realise what they'll do to you if they get wind that you were actually fucking the suspect, screwing a serial killer for God's sakes? They'll bury you, Riley, bury you – and me with you no doubt!'

His pacing is getting shorter, like he's about to start walking in circles. This is the angriest I've ever seen him, maybe it's the angriest he's ever been in his life. He looks and sounds like a different man.

'Who exactly knows about this…? Who knows that you and the suspect were in a relationship?' He runs his fingers through his thinning hair manically. I don't know why people do that, run their fingers through their hair when they're under duress. I can't see how it could make you think any clearer.

'No one, Sir,' I say, 'though I think, well, I think Lucy Davis may have got an inkling… But we weren't in a relationship, not as such… We weren't fuc— I wasn't sleeping with her.'

He shoots me a look of disbelief.

'Look, we met online, one of those dating websites, you know, matches you up with potential singles in your area. We started messaging, met up for coffee briefly. I took her out for a meal, we walked in the park…' I shake my head like it's not my own. 'The shock, when I saw her photograph in the estate agent's file…'

I can hear the emotion in my voice, like it belongs to someone else, like I can't really believe it myself. 'I was just looking for, oh I don't know. I liked her, Sir…' I say quietly, 'I had no idea, not even the slightest suspicion. Not even for a second, right up until I saw her photograph.'

Woods stops pacing. 'Sit down, Dan,' he says, his voice levelling off.

I do as he says and pull up a chair.

He's running his fingers through his hair again and I feel like a naughty schoolboy: embarrassed and awkward.

'So you met online. She gave you a false ID?'

'Well, she obviously didn't announce herself as a serial killer.' I'm being facetious but I can't help it. 'She told me her name was Florence Williams and that she was studying to be an actress—'

'You didn't check her out, run her name through the system?'

'I had no reason to disbelieve her. Jesus, and I thought I was the cynic.'

Woods sighs. 'So it was pure coincidence, just a horrible, dreadful piece of bad luck?'

'It's my middle name Sir.' I'm being facetious again, I can't frigging help it. Woods brings it out in me. 'If they're not being killed by someone else, they're the ones doing the killing.' I think he gets the irony, the regret in my words disguised by lame humour.

'You should've come straight to me the moment you discovered you were sleeping with the enemy, why didn't you Riley?'

'Well, I wasn't sleeping with the enemy. We didn't… I didn't… Jesus, I couldn't,' and I feel it then, I feel my soul emptying out, my humanity rushing to the surface. All those feelings; pride, confusion, sadness, happiness, hate, the complexity of everything I feel coming at me at once, a horrible paradox, a fruit salad of fuckery. 'I couldn't sleep with her because of Rachel…' the words leave me of their own accord, 'betraying her, I felt I would be betraying her. Rachel's memory stopped me. I couldn't do it… however, whoever, she turned out to be.'

Woods looks at me then, a strange kind of expression that I don't want to indulge. *Is it empathy? Or worse, pity?*

'Or perhaps it was a different reason, Riley.' He bangs his fist on the table, startling me. 'Perhaps it was that you knew a good woman from a bad and your instincts, those instincts that have made you the man – the copper you are now – standing in front of me, they stopped you…'

There's this moment, this moment between us, where suddenly I see him as a human being, I see his humanity and his anger as vulnerability, and he's given it to me, he's put it out there first somehow. He's telling me to come back to myself. And I see how much he believes in me and respects me, his faith in me and how much it takes for him to see that in someone. Actually, what I see is that he likes me. He doesn't understand me maybe, but he likes me. Above all else, he is on my side. And if someone is on your side it's worth a lot. It is golden.

'The boy, the baby was missing. I knew I could get her to come to me. The photo was published in the press that night. I told Davis to hold off on the conference but it was too late… I knew, I thought there was the chance she would abscond—'

'But for Dan's big dick, eh?'

I want to laugh. The whole thing is laughable really, absurd. I have this strange feeling, like he wants to hold me for a second. It's in that moment that I realise he's going to bury it. *He's going to bury it and I'm not sure I want saving.*

'You knew the suspect intimately and told no one… you arranged to meet her without proper back-up, and then the mad bitch goes and swallows poison and dies in our custody!'

He doesn't give me time to respond. 'Procedure,' he says, 'you know it as well as I do. You put yourself at risk, the whole operation, you withheld information from the team, you took unorthodox measures—'

I nod. I'm tired. 'I got the result we wanted,' I say, quietly, 'George was found safe and she as good as confessed to both murders.'

Woods smiles like I've just told him a secret he already knew.

I continue to explain that I knew she would come to meet me. This way, the way I played it, pretty much guaranteed an arrest. I tell him how I used our relationship as a means to capture Rebecca Harper and that while it was a gamble, I felt it was one I had to take. As I'm telling him all of this, I can hear how ridiculous it all sounds, how unbelievable.

I watch Woods, the strange, funny man he is.

'This was found among the stuff in her lock-up,' he says, placing a folder onto the desk and nodding at it. 'She knew who you were, Dan.'

I look down at the table. Scared to open the folder, but I do, tentatively. I pick it up. Look at it. It's a scrapbook filled with newspaper and internet cuttings of Rachel's death and the trial. There's a picture of me, taken when I had given a short statement to the press after Mathers' sentencing. There's one of me and Rachel too, an inset photo of us together at a friend's fortieth birthday party – my arm around her – and one of Rach on her bike, in her leathers, holding her helmet underneath her arm, smiling.

'She knew for a while.'

CHAPTER SIXTY-SEVEN

So I became part of Rebecca's story. A story which she had pre-written and already knew the ending of. She'd been in control the whole time, played me like a guitar. Only Woods wasn't completely on the money. She hadn't known *all* along. My mind keeps drifting back to the night of her arrest in the Greek restaurant, when she'd used my full name. I never recalled telling her it, but she already knew. I google the words 'Rachel' 'motorcycle accident' and 'death'. My girl makes the top three: '*Policeman's fiancé, 35, killed in motorcycle crash.*' It's under Touchy's byline. I blink at the screen.

Rebecca wanted to be caught; and she'd wanted me to catch her once she discovered who I really was. *But why?* It's a question that will remain unanswered now, a question she took to the grave with her. Was it like Magnesson said, that Rebecca had completely separate personalities and was literally two different people who she could compartmentalise?

Perhaps she wanted the kind of love that Rachel and I had, and she hoped I would give it to her? I don't know. Perhaps she had fantasised about leading a normal life, like the one she thought I had, and perhaps she knew she would never get it, but it felt good to pretend. Perhaps she knew deep down that neither of us could ever truly have the lives we both wanted, and she felt a connection with me because of this. I don't know, but these questions will haunt me for the rest of my life.

Sometimes there is no why.

*

I've been given six weeks paid 'leave' due to personal circum-stances, which Woods tells me is enough time for him to 'clean up the bloody mess I've left behind', and smooth things over with the IPCC. He told me to take a holiday and as part of the deal I must undertake some counselling. I've done neither yet, but I am thinking of going to LA, maybe stop off in Cambria, go to where I scattered my girl's ashes one last time.

I pay Janet Baxter a visit and explain that we caught the woman who killed Nigel. I owe her an explanation; I owe her a full stop. I tell her about Rebecca Harper and give her a little background, and then I finally reveal that this woman had taken her own life and died in police custody, that there will be an inquiry, but that I'm truly sorry there will be no trial as a result. I put my hand on hers as I explain, and it feels warm to touch.

I don't tell her that I had come to know Rebecca or how. Woods has told me to keep this quiet, he said that no one needs to know. He and I are the only two privy to this information. Davis has been silenced. But she's a good copper is Lucy Davis, loyal to a tee. Woods is going to do a cover-up job. I'd like to think it's a decision he made to save my bacon – and reputation – but in reality I think it's more likely to save his annual golf membership and his face. Still, it's an unprecedented move on his part. I don't know if I'm grateful or not.

Janet Baxter is relieved when I tell her about baby George and how close he came to meeting the same grizzly end as her Nigel. Even now, with no one to put behind bars for the crime against her husband, she's shows nothing but compassion. Without malice, she says she's glad that Rebecca Harper is dead. 'Perhaps now we can all try and move on.'

I feel a sadness from Janet Baxter that I recognise in myself, a sort of *fait accompli*, a weary resignation to her situation – and a life without the man she loves. 'He was a silly old fool,' she says, 'but he was my silly old fool.'

And I have to fight back tears as she says it. She thanks me profusely for 'all your tireless hard work' and tells me she knew I would never let her down, she'd always had faith in me to get to the bottom of this and find her husband's killer. I can barely look in her watery eyes. Before I leave I hug Janet and she reciprocates. She smells of freshly washed clothes, of the expensive stuff. 'Life goes on,' she says, 'that's what's so sad.'

'Things will get better, Janet.' I reply. It's the last lie I hope I'll ever have to tell her.

After I leave Janet's place I drive up to the cemetery near Wandsworth where Karen Walker is now resting and I lay flowers on her small headstone. It takes me almost an hour to find it. Just three people turned up for her send-off – myself one of them – and I think of all the people out there, faceless, nameless people like Karen with no family, their tragic lives unwitnessed, their passing unmissed. There's a picture, a photograph of her cat, Esmerelda, next to a bunch of dead flowers. I think about throwing them away but I don't. Whoever left them there, I hope they'll never forget her, just as I won't.

CHAPTER SIXTY-EIGHT

I'm listening to a little-known Liverpool band, Shack, in the car as I park up a little way from Craig Mathers' family home. The album is called 'HMS Fable' and it's a melancholic masterpiece of haunting guitar tunes and acoustic melodies. It reflects my mood perfectly. Rachel loved it, even if she always said it was 'a touch on the maudlin side, Danny, you miserable sod.'

I know, after everything, that I shouldn't be here and I'm gambling with myself once again. But I needed to come one final time. It's getting late now, and the sun has all but disappeared, leaving a blood-red sky full of promise for tomorrow. Dusk is my favourite time of day, even if it does signify the end of something. I used to tell Rach that I found sunsets beautiful, but also sad somehow. I never wanted the day to end when I was with her.

There's always tomorrow, Danny.

Only there wasn't.

Almost an hour passes before I see him; the music has long since stopped playing. I watch him in silence as he parks up with his girlfriend, a young, pretty girl with long brown hair and cute smile. They're holding hands and laughing and I think I can hear their voices in the distance, but maybe that's my imagination. She goes back to the car at one point, she's forgotten something, and he throws his head back in mock exasperation. Just a young, happy couple with their whole lives ahead of them. They disappear behind the front door and I wait, stare at it for a little while and prepare to drive away. But then it opens again. They're walking in my direction and I feel the first flutters of panic swell within me; I can't be seen. I promised Woods I'd keep away. *I promised myself.* As they get closer I can see that the girl is pregnant; she has a small rounded belly protruding from her light summer jacket. Her arm is linked through his as they begin to stroll and she rests her head on his shoulder. I try to slide down into my seat but I'm paralyzed and can only stare and watch them, smiling, laughing, touching. Happy.

So happy and so young. In love and pregnant.

They pass me by on the opposite side of the street and I watch in my rear-view mirror as they disappear from view. It takes me a few moments to gather my composure; the violent ache in my chest feels like an open wound debilitating me and my hand subconsciously covers it as though it's real. I suppose it is really.

The knock on the window startles me, sending a jolt of electricity straight through my aorta. I turn to see him at the window, Craig Mathers, the man who killed Rachel and our child and destroyed my life. Instinctively I've already opened it. His face appears much younger up close – clean-shaven, handsome even. A young, handsome man out for an evening stroll with his pregnant girlfriend. We make eye contact but the torrent of adrenaline flooding through my system renders me silent, my throat constricts.

'I'm sorry,' he says, his eyes directly on mine. 'Please, I'm truly, truly sorry.'

And then he walks away.

EPILOGUE

During my visit to the States I took a run out to Cambria to say one final goodbye. The tiny town looked different from the last time I was there, during the scarecrow festival, when they decorate the entire place with crazy straw people. The scarecrows are gone now and it looked much like any other small town you might pass through on Route 66. I throw flowers into the sea from the cliffs of Moonstone Beach where I scattered her ashes. They disappear into the abyss below me, swallowed up by the dancing waves: *forever dancing*.

On my return, I clear out Rachel's things from our apartment. I box up all her shoes that have been sitting in the spare room in neat pairs, her 'going out' stilettos and summer sandals, flip-flops, trainers and, of course, the biker boots she used to wear with feminine floral dresses. It was always my favourite look on her, the paradox of salty but sweet, tough but pretty – it's how I see her when I close my eyes. I put the boots to one side, along with a big silver cocktail ring I bought her in Camden and a few other mementos of hers that I cannot bring myself to give to charity. I know I should have done this a long time ago, my grief counsellor advised it, but the truth is I wasn't ready to. I'm not sure I'm ready to now either, but I know I must.

I flick through some old photos, snapshots of our life together, holidays and trips we took, days out on the beach, a friend's wedding where we're all suited and booted, a selfie she took of us in a hotel room, our heads touching as we peep out beneath the white sheets of a king-sized bed. There aren't that many really, I wish now I had taken more, so many more… I place them all in a large envelope and put them in the box.

Finally, I go through the condolence cards, a vast wad of them; expressions of sympathy and sadness from everyone whose lives she had touched. I flick through them until I come to the one with the butterfly on the front, it's wings are a little faded through sun and time. It's from Touchy and it has Chinese writing on the front.

I reach for my phone.

'Fiona?'

'Hey, Dan!' She sounds pleased to hear from me. 'How's tricks?'

'Believe it or not, Touchy, I'm on holiday, due back in work next week.'

'You? On holiday? I don't believe it… you live for that nick Dan, have you missed it?'

'Not in the slightest,' I lie. I don't think she believes me.

'I was just looking through some of Rachel's old things,' I tell her, 'boxing up a few bits, having a spring clean, you know.'

Touchy tells me that's a good thing. Her voice is soft and kind.

'I came across your card,' I say, 'the one you sent after Rachel's death, the one with the butterfly on it.'

'Yes, I remember.'

I tell Touchy that it was my favourite card and I ask her what the writing on the front means.

She pauses for a moment, thinking, I presume, before she says, '*Wàn shì kāi tóu nán* – All things are difficult before they are easy.'

I smile and invite her out for a drink.

LETTER FROM ANNA-LOU

Dearest Reader,

I am so grateful and humbled that you chose *Black Heart* as the latest addition to your reading list. This novel was a natural shift in direction for me as a writer, which has been a little nerve-wracking to say the least, so I hope it will be well-received and that you enjoyed reading it as much as I have really loved writing it. Dan Riley's character literally came out of me compulsively and I could not write him quickly enough.

If you want to keep up-to-date on my new releases, or view my past ones, just click the link below to sign up for my special newsletter. You'll need to give your email but I will never share it with anyone and only contact you when I have a new release, promise.

www.bookouture.com/anna-lou-weatherley

Your comments, feedback and reviews mean everything to me, so I'd be thrilled to know what you thought of *Black Heart* and if it was everything you hoped it might be. So, if you enjoyed *Black Heart* it would mean a lot to me if you would take the time to leave a review and let me, and other readers know why. I'm always recommending books to friends and family and vice versa, so if it encourages others to read one of my novels and enjoy the ride then I cannot thank you enough.

Detective Dan Riley will be back very soon with yet another dark, unusual and challenging case that sees him pushed to his psychological limits. Will he manage to break the case before it breaks him, and will he turn a corner in his grief for Rachel and find love again? You'll just have to wait and see…

Much love,
Anna-Lou x

ACKNOWLEDGEMENTS

I have many people to thank who have helped me one way or another throughout the duration of writing this book, so in no particular order I want to say a heartfelt, enormous thank you and give a virtual hug to the wonderful Claire Bord at Bookouture for her unwavering faith, belief and support of me as a writer from the very beginning. Without your encouragement and advice, plus all your helpful comments, this book, and in fact all of my books, would not have been written. You have been such a solid support for me and have spurred me on in my darkest moments. I really cannot thank you enough and feel privileged to work with you. Also, thanks to Oliver Rhodes at Bookoture and the super, effervescent and warm Kim Nash for all your continued support and hard work on my behalf, it's always so much fun seeing you and working with you. Thanks also to my lovely agent, Madeline Milburn, and also to Hayley Steed for all your continued support, advice and much appreciated help.

My friends and family never quite know just how much inspiration and support they give me when I'm writing – and when I'm not, which isn't often. Mum, thank you for always being there for me, helping with the boys, inspiring me daily throughout my life, and being such a fun, positive, encouraging, loving mummy who always smiles and looks super glam in the face of adversity – put your lipstick on and smile! You are my inspiration in every aspect of my life and I love you so much. Similarly, my sister, Lisa, an incredible, kind, loving and understanding woman who I look up to and adore, thanks for being such a great sister and best friend (and fashion finder!). And to my friends, namely Kelly for all the late-night chats, for a holiday to remember, for her friendship, words of wisdom, kindness, understanding and laughs, plus my lovely LM for being such a true, real friend who is and always will be close to my heart – I love you lots! Andie (always) and my dearest Rabbit, Susie. Also my Scouse bird, Michelle, a truly altruistic, inspirational woman and to Qefs too, my surrogate sister. Some friends are like stars, just because you can't always see them doesn't meant they aren't there. Also to my best girl, Sue, for the kindness, literal belly laughs (and other noises), crazy days (and nights) out and for all the fun and sing-alongs. You're always a breath of fresh air. Also to my pole princesses: Kelly, Kate, Laura and Julia. Teaching you has brought me so much happiness and it makes me proud to see how much you have all achieved.

My precious boys, Louie and Felix, it's been a difficult couple of years for us but you remain my driving force, my reason, my hearts outside of my body – love you both more than words, always. You're both amazing and watching you grow is my biggest privilege and achievement so far. We are family.

Lastly, I want to thank Paul for all his support, help and for the fact that this book wouldn't have been written without him – or perhaps only by hand! For the belief, encouragement – and proofreading. For the inspiration, for the travels and adventures, for the music, the mayhem, the planes, trains and automobiles, the memories we've built and the ones we will go onto build, for all the feels, the salty sweet, the highs and the lows – but always, just always, for the love. I keep my promises. So Sinno, babe, this one is yours.